BLOOD ON THE BAYOU

Books by Douglas J. Wood

FICTION

Presidential Intentions

Presidential Declarations

Presidential Conclusions

Dark Data: Control, Alt, Delete

Dragon on the Far Side of the Moon

NON-FICTION

Please Be Ad-Vised

101 Things I Want to Say

Asshole Attorney

BLOOD ON THE BAYOU

DOUGLAS J. WOOD

PLUM BAY PUBLISHING, LLC
New York, New York
Morristown, New Jersey

For permission requests, contact the publisher at the website below
Plum Bay Publishing, LLC
www.plumbaypublishing.com

Library of Congress Control Number: 2021920313
Hardcover ISBN: 978-1-7348848-5-2
Paperback ISBN: 978-1-7348848-6-9
eBook ISBN: 978-1-7348848-7-6

Printed in the United States of America
Cover and interior design: Barbara Aronica-Buck
Editors: Jeremy Townsend and Kate Petrella

"I believe that the only way to reform people is to kill 'em."

—Carl Panzram, serial killer

PROLOGUE

The man lay in the decaying gutter of a New Orleans French Quarter alley. Blood oozed from the slit in his throat, mixing with the puddles from the hot September night drizzle, and blending into the rancid stench of vomit and sewage. His killer stood over him, smiling. He tried to ask why, why him? Bourbon Street was alive with miscreants of all types who deserved to die more than he did.

But his killer just nodded, pleased with a job well done.

The man felt his life ebbing away. Darkness fell upon him, and just then he heard the whisper in his ear, the reason for his death . . .

By the time the body was discovered, the morning aromas unique to the French Quarter had overtaken the stench of the night. Freshly baked beignets and hot brewing coffee laced with chicory in the New Orleans way, masked, for a while, the smell of a body decaying in a pool of blood and filth. The Bayou Slasher was long gone from the scene, having crossed another off the list.

CHAPTER ONE

Raleigh Broussard, captain of the New Orleans 8th District Police—the French Quarter—greeted every weekday morning with his usual routine. Up at 5:30 a.m. to an ever-annoying alarm, he dressed in shorts and took his morning run. He was a large man, a former linebacker, and being Black he knew he presented an imposing figure as he clocked his two-mile run around his Exchange Place neighborhood. His neighbors left him alone, and that's how he preferred it. Although he missed his wife, dead now for five years, and cherished breakfasts with his daughter, who had followed in his footsteps and was attending LSU, he still preferred his solitude.

He also cherished his cigars and bourbon, two habits he'd succumbed to as a collegiate and professional athlete. His NFL career was cut short by a blown knee after just three seasons with the New Orleans Saints, but his pension was the gift that kept on giving, affording him his expensive townhouse and his premium cigars and whisky.

On a normal weekday, Broussard would finish his run, shower, grab a coffee and head to work, but today was Labor Day. He decided to splurge on a big breakfast, and relax with the newspaper. He generally found the news boring, unless it concerned his beloved Saints.

As he picked up the paper from the front stoop, however, the front page story above the fold caught his attention.

Another body was found in the French Quarter, throat slit. Most days, he'd read such reports as just another crime in a city riddled with violence, particularly in the heat and stifling humidity of summer. But summer was nearly over, and the weather would soon cool. Because the latest body had been found only hours before the paper was printed, the report was void of much detail except for one fact that made Broussard's stomach turn. The victim held a crude wooden cross in his hand and had "XXX" carved in his forehead. The reporter wrote that it was the mark of the so-called Bayou Slasher, New Orleans's name for its latest serial killer.

The report abruptly brought Broussard back to what he most wanted to avoid—a ruined holiday—knowing that he'd get a call to go to his office and begin an investigation of yet another in what had become a series of killings paralyzing New Orleans. Horace Guidry, the city's Superintendent of Police, had been demanding Broussard find the killer and put an end to the random bloodletting.

Guidry's direct pressure on Broussard was leapfrogging the chain of command by ignoring Chief of Police Lewis Gersh, to whom Broussard technically reported, but Guidry didn't care. This was a case where reputations could be made or broken, and he was not about to let someone else make the calls between him and the man in charge of the district where the murders were taking place. Neither Broussard nor Gersh liked it, but there was nothing they could do. No one liked to get in Guidry's way.

Guidry insisted on being called "Commissioner," not his official title of Superintendent. Commissioner was a moniker great cities like New York gave their top cop. Guidry thought that was the least he deserved.

As if on cue, Broussard's cell phone rang and "Superintendent" appeared on the caller ID. He had no respect for Guidry any more than Guidry did for him. If Guidry could, he'd fire Broussard, but every mayor of New Orleans Broussard worked for liked him and had no intention of letting him go. Indeed, the current mayor was inclined to promote him. If the mayor could fire anyone, it would be Guidry, but because the superintendent was a political appointee who knew where the bodies were buried, firing him was impossible.

"Raleigh, I assume you've read the paper," began Guidry. "This is the third murder tied to this religious zealot. I could dismiss the damned press labeling him a serial killer after two murders, but now we have a third. And his latest is the son of a councilman. It doesn't get worse than that."

Sure it does, thought Broussard. He'd seen enough murders in the past fifteen years that were far worse than the killing of a councilman's son. New Orleans had the dubious honor of being in the nation's top two or three cities in homicides every year. Atrocities happened every day.

"Listen, Raleigh, I know we don't get along."

No shit, thought Broussard. *You're just an overweight politician who acts like an old southern plantation owner overseeing his slaves while he enjoys a cold cup of iced tea from the porch of his mansion.*

"But as smartass a man as you are, Raleigh, you're a captain and in charge of finding this homicidal maniac. These killings have to stop. And it's your job to do it. So either get it done or I'll take over the investigation myself or get someone who can."

Broussard would have enjoyed watching a political hack with little practical police experience conduct an investigation. He may have been a beat cop once, but Guidry long ago lost the edge. Broussard knew he would never get his hands dirty in a real investigation. Guidry preferred the cheap seats. Cops-turned-politicians like him want to take credit but never accept blame or do the hard work. Broussard regarded Guidry's threats as nothing more than empty air.

"Every one of them with the same MO," Guidry continued. "A slit throat, Xs on their foreheads, and a wooden cross in their hand. All white. And I'm sure we'll once again find no DNA or other evidence. The scene will be as clean as the others. Same with finding any witnesses. They won't exist."

Broussard sighed. "Yes, Super . . . uh, Commissioner, it looks like another murder possibly linked to one killer, but we can never assume anything." He immediately regretted that observation.

"Not assume? What the fuck is the matter with you?"

screamed Guidry. "You can't be serious. Throat cut, Xs, cross, alley, no DNA, no witnesses. You don't see a pattern?"

"Common elements in crimes of passion are typical, Commissioner. And we can't rule out copycats. This has been all over the press with someone leaking what little evidence we have. That doesn't help."

Broussard was convinced that Guidry was the source of the leaks. Guidry manipulated the press his entire career by trading favors for positive ink. Even when Broussard tried everything he could to keep Guidry out of the loop or away from evidence, he somehow found what he wanted. Someday, Broussard would often remind himself, he needed to do an internal investigation to find Guidry's mole in the office.

Broussard also knew that the murders were not crimes of passion committed in an emotional moment where someone's control is lost. These murders were planned. They were too similar to rule out a common killer. While he didn't want to admit it to Guidry or anyone else just yet, Broussard knew he was dealing with a serial killer. One very committed to plying his horrors in New Orleans.

"Commissioner, we also can't be sure if there is or is not DNA or witnesses associated with this crime scene," continued Broussard. "It's just too early to tell if this latest killing is related to the others. I admit there are similarities and perhaps a relationship, but I don't want to rush to any conclusions until I get the evidence. I'm on my way to the office now."

"Good. Keep me posted."

"Want to join me?" Broussard asked, not trying try to hide the sarcasm in his voice, anticipating the answer he always received.

"I'll pass, Raleigh. Just do your damn job."

CHAPTER TWO

The morning briefing at the 8th District began as it usually did with daily announcements of scheduled events in New Orleans on the police department's watch list. There would of course be the usual cleanup after a holiday weekend. That meant processing more arrests from the days before. But not much more.

The officers on duty that day began with a briefing from Lt. Mike Dickenson, Broussard's second in command. Although the morning meeting was normally conducted by the watch or shift commander, norms had changed since New Orleans lost officers to early retirement, many fearing a decline in community support. That left the police department short of personnel. Duties were reassigned, and Dickenson was given the morning briefing by Broussard. The captain assured Dickenson that he'd find a new watch commander, a promise now eight months old. Dickenson harbored some resentment for what was essentially a demotion, but he'd been with Broussard for fifteen years, right from the academy. So, he followed orders.

Broussard and Dickenson were partners on the streets for years before each advanced in rank. When Broussard made captain and took over the division, he made Dickenson his right-hand man. Just as they did on the streets,

Dickenson played the "bad cop," and Broussard the "good cop." While they'd switch roles occasionally when Broussard lost his temper with suspects or inexperienced officers under his command, Dickenson was usually the tough guy. As a result, he didn't have many fans among the officers. Dickenson was also Broussard's filter before issues were referred to internal affairs for investigations into officer negligence or corruption, neither of which was lacking in New Orleans. It was a thankless job, but Dickenson was loyal to Broussard, so he didn't complain.

The briefing room was small. Only twenty feet wide and long, it was a sorry place that desperately needed to be painted. The overhead fluorescent lights, too many of which didn't work or often flickered, only made it more uninviting. And no one suggested the place be spruced up or the lightbulbs replaced with ones that worked. Such luxuries were not part of the budget. At least that's what Dickenson told those gathered. In truth, he liked it shabby. Kept everyone humble.

As always, those on call were seated in rows of gray folding chairs split down the middle with an aisle, chairs on each side. A podium bearing the seal of the City of New Orleans sat in the front of the room. To one side stood the American flag; to the other, the flag of Louisiana. Two pictures hung on the wall behind the podium: one of the mayor and the other of the superintendent of police. The ever-present coffee machine was in the back. The walls had old posters of tourist spots in the city, most of them faded and in need of new frames. But that also wasn't in the budget. So, the room remained dingy and dark.

Dickenson's main job each morning was to make official announcements, most of which meant nothing more than assigning officers to cover the more sensitive areas of the city. While unruly crowds and demonstrations are common in cities like New Orleans, they had become increasingly violent in recent years as poverty deepened after the hurricanes and floods. The growing schism within communities that divided the populace over how the police did their jobs had gotten worse. It all made police administration more difficult.

Dickenson's other job was to administer discipline when Broussard thought it was necessary. Dickenson was happy to get his hands dirty and keep Broussard's clean.

As Dickenson was about to finish the morning call, Broussard walked in and the officers rose.

"Be seated," ordered Broussard. "How many times do I have to say we can dispense with formalities?" He said that whenever his officers rose as he entered a room. But despite his protestations, they always rose out of respect. The support among his officers was unquestioned. Every officer had Broussard's back—because Broussard had theirs. And with a superintendent like Guidry, Broussard's support was deeply appreciated by the people he led and protected.

Dickenson stepped aside and Broussard took the

podium. "You all know," he began, "that we had another murder in the Quarter last night that looks like the others we've seen with the cut throat, three Xs in the forehead, and a cross in the victim's hand. This now makes three, so the commissioner . . ."

A number of officers, hands over their mouths as if to cover a cough, mumbled, "superintendent." While childish, it was a habit among them to call out the right title as a show of disrespect for Guidry, someone they considered an incompetent fool. Broussard generally enjoyed it, but not today.

"Please, let's dispense with humor today. There is nothing to be laughing about."

The officers lowered their hands. Some looked down at their feet.

Broussard continued, "The commissioner has declared that we have a serial killer in the city. While I would not have gone public with that just yet, he's probably right. So we need to ratchet up our surveillance in the Quarter beginning tonight. It will mean extra work and comp time for those of you who put in the hours."

Tightened city budgets could not afford overtime pay for the police. Instead, they received additional time off. It was not popular among the officers, and Broussard tried his best to apportion the additional duty fairly among the force.

"Mike will assign two officer teams for patrols. Any questions?"

There were none. There never were.

"OK, then," Broussard concluded. And as he always said at the end of these morning meetings, he added, "Watch your backs and don't come back a dead hero." It had become his trademark closing and was considered by some, including the mayor, to be an inappropriate caution that translated to less committed officers in dangerous situations. But the officers knew better.

As Broussard moved from the podium to the door, the officers began to rise. "Dammit. Sit the fuck down!" He didn't miss the smiles on their faces as they disobeyed his order yet again and stayed standing.

"OK," began Dickenson retaking the podium. "Here are the assignments . . ."

CHAPTER THREE

"So who's driving today?" asked Detective Rebecca Simone.

"I couldn't care less," responded Officer Joseph Bundy. "You usually bitch about my driving, so I'm fine with you taking the wheel."

Simone and Bundy were not officially partners in the traditional sense. Simone, a detective with the homicide division of the New Orleans police department, was assigned to the 8th District in the French Quarter to assist in murder investigations. Police Superintendent Guidry decided it would be more efficient if homicide detectives were embedded in the various districts in the city to work the neighborhoods together with the local cops. Broussard didn't like it, because it meant that most of the grunt work on murder investigations would be done by his officers. On the other hand, he knew they'd learn to be better cops as a result of discipline homicide detectives brought to their jobs. Sloppy was not an option.

"I don't mind your driving, Joe. I just think you drive like a woman," Simone smiled.

"Very funny, Becca. You know I could report you to HR for a comment like that."

"Oh yeah? Are you sure you have the balls to do that?" Simone asked, laughing. Such playful banter was common between the two. It was simply the way most cops spoke to one another to help lighten what was otherwise a difficult job.

Simone, a seven-year veteran of the police force after a six-year stint in the U.S. Army, was thirty-six years old and single. With two combat deployments in the Middle East, she was as seasoned an officer as Broussard could want. That's why she remained one of his favorites. Her hometown was in Georgia, but she had fallen in love with a fellow serviceman in Iraq, and followed him to Louisiana. The relationship ended amicably when he decided to reenlist, something she had no interest in doing. So, she stayed—more out of inertia than any love of New Orleans. But over the years, the city grew on her.

Simone preferred to remain single and live with her dog, Sully, a sixty-five-pound Catahoula Leopard, the official dog of Louisiana with a heritage that dates back to the mid-1700s when French settlers brought Beauceron dogs to Louisiana. Simone had studied the folklore regarding the breed before adopting Sully. She read that the settlers crossbred their dogs with swamp hunting wolves owned by Native Americans and created a short-haired working dog that could grow to a hundred pounds or more of pure muscle. Bred to be hunting dogs, Catahoulas are known for loyalty and protective instincts. Needless to say, any visitor knew better than to get on the bad side of Sully. He and Simone made a formidable duo. Her colleagues suspected that tight relationship was why Simone seemed to have such a sparse dating life. It certainly wasn't lack of looks.

Simone kept trim with a dedicated exercise regime. She worked out almost every day at a local gym. She also dressed down at work so most officers didn't have a reason to focus on her beauty. In fact, when out of the work environment and dressed in the part of someone with a social life, her fellow officers would barely recognize her, particularly since she so rarely socialized with her colleagues.

As she and Bundy passed the front desk to begin their assigned rounds, the desk sergeant said Broussard wanted to see them before they left.

"You can go right in," said Donna Castagna, Broussard's assistant and gatekeeper. If you wanted to see Broussard, you had to get through Castagna first. She guarded him like a lioness with her cub.

"Captain, you asked to see us?" began Bundy.

"Yes, sit down," ordered Broussard.

"Thank you, sir," responded Bundy as he and Simone sat in chairs in front of Broussard's desk, which was strewn with papers and an ashtray half filled with cigar butts. Broussard's love of cigars left his office smelling of the rancid, burned plant, but he didn't give a damn. He was either smoking a cigar or chewing on one all day. Anyone who didn't like it learned quickly that objecting was a mistake. He had one special box of Padrons that he saved for days when his team solved a crime and he wanted to enjoy a reward. It was an expensive reward at more than $25 a stick. But it was his victory smoke when he was on the Saints, and he kept up the tradition. Otherwise, he smoked cheap ones he picked up at a local roller on Bourbon Street.

Only Castagna dared to suggest he not light up when dignitaries arrived after she made sure the office was cleaned up and given a massive dose of air freshener. The running joke in the station was that if you smelled lilacs, the mayor must be visiting. Years earlier, the officers in the precinct presented Broussard with a high-end air filter. It remained in its box in the corner. Most thought it was Broussard's way of saying, "Thanks but no thanks." Today, he was not smoking a Padron. There was nothing to celebrate.

"Becca, Joe, I want you to devote one hundred percent of your time to the investigation of the Bayou Slasher murders in the Quarter. Dickenson will reassign your other cases."

Becca and Joe looked at each other briefly in surprise. They had other well-developed cases, and being reassigned to a single murder investigation was unusual.

"Why us, Captain?" asked Simone. "You know I'm working on other important cases, and it's not as if our work can be easily picked up. So, you're basically saying that Bundy and I are going to have to do double duty, breaking in new officers on our old cases and chasing down the Bayou Slasher, a case we haven't been involved with." It also meant their work would now be second-guessed by the same officers assigned. That was probably what pissed

Simone off the most. She hated being second-guessed. As far as she was concerned, no one was better at her job than she.

"I realize that, and I suppose you'd like me to tell you that I chose the two of you because you're the best." Broussard loved to rib his officers. It was his way of motivating them. His version of tough love.

"No, sir, of course not, sir," interjected Bundy.

Simone flinched and turned to look at Broussard, ready to play his game. "What? We're not the best? C'mon Captain, admit it. You know we're the best." She smiled.

"Tell you what, Becca," Broussard responded, "I'll admit you are the best at what I've got. But that is a pretty low bar."

Simone's wry smile and shaking head did not go unnoticed by Bundy. He was young and had a lot to learn. He could tax Simone's patience, but she was his mentor and his partner. So, Simone needed to have his back. But he was also a complete toady when he spoke to Broussard. He took whatever Broussard said as serious, even when the captain was obviously joking. Bundy seemed incapable of seeing humor even if it was plain as day. Simone chalked it up to Bundy's lack of experience in real standoffs like the ones she experienced in Iraq, where questioning superiors was expected and humorous banter common. In her eyes, Bundy was just a good old Cajun boy who simply followed orders, no questions asked. That suited Simone fine. She liked giving orders and having them followed.

Broussard could see that Bundy was unsure of what the back and forth between him and Simone meant.

"Relax, Joe," Broussard said with a smile. "Becca and I are just havin' some fun. You're as good as anyone here." Simone didn't have the heart to tell Bundy that the remark was actually a real barb.

"Let me finish," Broussard continued. "I chose you, Becca, because you have experience that will come in handy in the field. The Quarter is as close to a war battle zone as we have in New Orleans. Its combination of drunk tourists, doped-up musicians, and vagrants makes it look like a crime scene waiting to happen every night."

"Thank you, Captain. I guess." responded Simone.

"And I chose you, Joe," Broussard added, "because you were lucky enough to be Becca's partner. That made you conveniently available." Broussard just couldn't help himself. He loved kidding Bundy, knowing he would take everything he said literally. He enjoyed toying with sycophants like Bundy more than just about any aspect of his job. Which is why he couldn't resist having one more piece of fun: "So don't fuck up, and do whatever Becca tells you to do."

Simone decided to get back to the serious business at hand. The fun with Bundy was over. "Captain, we'll need some foot soldiers. Two people can't solve this alone."

"Get me a list of who you want. I'll spare who I can," responded Broussard.

With that promise in hand, it was time to leave if for

no other reason than to avoid further psychological damage to Bundy. She stood as Broussard relit the cigar he'd been gnawing on during the meeting. While cigars didn't bother Simone, she never could understand why someone would smoke one so early in the morning, let alone chew on it. Bundy, on the other hand, thought the habit disgusting.

As they left the office and walked down the corridor, Bundy remarked to Simone, "What a stink hole with those fucking cigars. And he can be such a prick."

"Don't let him get to you, Joe. He's just busting your chops. It doesn't matter," responded Simone. She could suggest that Bundy should stop sucking up to Broussard and trade a few quips with him. But she enjoyed the show too much.

CHAPTER FOUR

In the two days following their meeting with Broussard, Simone and Bundy put together a team that included four other officers. Broussard also assigned an assistant medical examiner to the Bayou Slasher cases. While designating a specific examiner was unusual and something usually within the discretion of the chief medical examiner, Broussard wanted the same set of eyes on each crime scene to see similarities and differences, both keys to a good investigation. The chief medical examiner reluctantly agreed, fearful of crossing Broussard.

The task force hit the streets in hopes of finding clues and piecing together a way to catch the killer before he murdered again, splitting up people to interview, places to visit, and leads to follow. Basic police work.

A month into their investigation, Simone assembled the team in the room set aside for the investigation. While relatively small at fourteen by twelve, its pale green walls were lined with magnetic, erasable whiteboards for posting evidence and writing notes. The obligatory coffee pot sat on top of a small refrigerator. The table in the middle of the room was surrounded by four government-issued metal armchairs. Two additional chairs were off to the side.

In front of two of the chairs at the table were desktop

computers for the team to use when they needed to retrieve a file in the New Orleans database, check emails, or search for clues on the Internet. The computers were also what they used to find out more about the victims through their presence and postings on social media.

As the team sat at their desks, Broussard interrupted during his morning walk through the station. Simone knew it was really his way of checking in on everyone, particularly her team, since there had been so little progress. But at least there hadn't been another murder.

"Becca," said Broussard, looking around the room at the officers. "Your people are glued to their computers. What exactly are they looking for?"

"Captain, you would be amazed at how people post the most intimate of things on Facebook and other social media outlets. It can shock anyone's sensibilities. With enough surfing of the sites where someone posts, our team can get a very good psychological profile of just about anyone. I only wish we had the technology like servers that ran complex algorithms and used sophisticated web spiders that could analyze massive amounts of data to help find people and analyze clues."

"That's the wish of every police department, Becca. It's just not in the budget. Please carry on as best you can."

"Will do, Captain."

Satisfied with what he saw, Broussard left and continued on his walkabout.

"OK, we've had three murders," began Simone as she stared at the largest of the wall's whiteboards, divided into three columns, each topped with a photo of one of the victims. Below each photo were the clues for each murder: location, key evidence, crime scene photos, dates and times, and associates of the victims. Some of the clues were written in erasable marker, and others were pinned to the board with magnets. Beside the whiteboard was a large map of the city mounted on corkboard. Each had color-coded pins showing the location of the killings and places where the victims were believed to have been just prior to their deaths. Simone, Bundy, and their Bayou Slasher task force were looking for connections that might give them leads to the killer or where the next victim might be.

"Let's go through the facts on each victim," continued Simone. "Jackson Walker. White male, twenty-eight years old. Single. Bartender at Arnaud's. Fit. Murdered on June 26. No signs of a struggle. Throat cut, wooden cross in his hand. He was working that night. No one remembers seeing him leave the bar. So, we can assume he closed the place. People said he was a quiet guy. No known religious affiliation. Inspection of his apartment showed no evidence of enemies or materials that might suggest he might be someone who would be targeted. Believed to be heterosexual but no evidence of a girlfriend. In New Orleans for five years after a three-year stint in the Merchant Marine. Came to New Orleans to work on ships but found no job. So, he tended bar. Originally from Georgia. Father dead, mother alive and living outside Atlanta. No DNA other than his at the scene."

Three red pins on the map showed Arnaud's, Walker's apartment on Toulouse Street, and the last one pinned on a parking lot between Royal Street and Chartres Street, the site in the Quarter where his body was found.

Bundy took up the next victim.

"Maria Benson. A white thirty-year-old female. Accountant with Ernst & Young. Married. No children. Regular at SoBou, a bar in the Quarter that caters to the sophisticated. Not your usual gin mill. A ten-minute walk from her office on Poydras. Witnesses that night remember her talking to several men and women at the bar. The bartender says it was common for Benson, despite being married, to pick up men at the bar. A real harlot from what we know. Bartender doesn't recall her leaving with anyone that night. Husband was shocked to hear of her indiscretions. Right. As if I believe that."

"Joe let's dispense with the editorial comments, please," Simone interrupted sharply.

"Sorry, Becca," responded Bundy.

He continued: "She was liked and had no known enemies and enjoyed working at EY. Lived on Kerlerec in an expensive home. Been in New Orleans for twenty-five years, since her parents moved here from Mississippi. Parents both deceased. Her only sister lives in Dallas. Coroner believes there was some struggle but no DNA and no signs of sexual assault. Killed on August 14."

Green pins on the map identified her home, her office location, and the Quarter alley where her body was found.

Simone turned to the final victim.

"William Hitchcock, Jr. Body found this past Sunday. White, twenty-eight years old. Unemployed. Got fired in April from a job at the Superdome in the maintenance department. Lifelong New Orleans resident. Lives with his parents in the Garden District. Father, a lawyer, has been a councilman for the past ten years. Two brothers, neither of whom live in the city. One is in California and the other in Alabama. Same girlfriend for past two years. Friends say he was quiet and kept to his own business. Always went to church with his parents on Sundays, but folks say he did so only for the appearance his father needed as a councilman. And to make sure his father kept supporting him. No known enemies. No known hangouts. No struggle. No DNA."

Yellow pins noted Hitchcock's home and the back street in the Garden District where his body was found.

"Anyone see some common threads?" asked Simone.

Hearing no response, Simone continued, "OK, I'll start. The obvious things in common for all of them are they're white and young. Only Hitchcock is a registered voter—a Republican like his father. None of them have criminal records. None of them were robbed. They're all in good shape, so the lack of evidence of any significant struggle is a mystery. That tells me they knew the killer. Or trusted him. Any attack had to be sudden, when they didn't expect it. Quick. Bloody. But why no DNA? Whoever did it must have been very careful to make sure we'd find none. No prints."

"Let's not forget the cross and the triple X," added one of the junior officers on the task force. "As the press has said, it points to a ritualistic murder inspired by Voodoo."

"Maybe," responded Simone. "But with someone so careful to leave no DNA, the crosses and scarring could be a ploy to make us think it was Voodoo or religious revenge. Or it may very well be just what you suggest. We don't know yet. But Voodoo does not preach violence despite its reputation. So, I'm not sure that connection gives us any solid clue or motive, but we will run it down."

"Perhaps the killer's victims are just randomly chosen," continued the junior officer. "Maybe they were just in the wrong place at the wrong time. Just bad luck."

"Not likely," noted Simone. "There is too much setup to be random. They were all lured into an alley or dark parking lot before they were killed. That's premeditated. And with three months between the first and latest murder, there's been plenty of time to carefully plan each one. So if we have a serial killer, there has to be something in common between them to make the victims targets of the same killer. We just haven't found it yet."

"Becca," interjected Bundy, "we've been at this for four weeks now. We're no further along than we were on day one except for our pretty whiteboard and map. If we don't make some sort of breakthrough soon, the killer will strike again. Broussard will have our ass."

"Asses, Joe. There's more than one," corrected Simone.

She knew that investigations of complex crimes can take months. Or they might never be solved at all and eventually are relegated to the cold case files. It took years to hunt down some serial killers, and many cases remain unsolved.

"I'm perfectly aware of the reaction we'll get," continued Simone. "Guidry is screaming at the captain, and the press is having a field day. The mayor is asking questions we can't answer. It's a mess. Shit, if the captain decides to take us off the case, I won't cry about it. We've been handed a nearly impossible investigation that will take a long time. And that means, unfortunately, others will probably be murdered until the killer makes a mistake or we get a break. But so far, nothing gives us a hint of who will be next. Or when. The only thing we can be reasonably sure of is that the next murder will be in the Quarter." She paused. "And that there is probably nothing we can do at this point to stop it."

"So why not put cops in every alley?" asked one of the junior officers.

"We've done that as much as we can," responded Simone. "The problem is we don't have that many officers available, and those that are on patrol may be putting the killer at bay but forcing him to find another location. We can't put officers everywhere in the Quarter, much less the city.

Whoever this killer is, he's not stupid. He's waiting for an opening."

"So, what's our next move, Becca?" asked Bundy.

"All we can do, Joe, is follow our leads," responded Simone. "So let's visit Maîtresse LeBlanc, the Voodoo priestess of New Orleans."

CHAPTER FIVE

Maîtresse LeBlanc, respected and well known in New Orleans, was what one might describe as a "classy lady." Fifty-five years old and attractive, she was the leader of the Voodoo community in New Orleans. Her rich black hair, braided in cornrows, her piercing green eyes, long, manicured fingernails and heavy face makeup completed her demeanor as a Voodoo priestess and suggested the misguided belief that she was capable of conjuring up the dead or putting someone in a grave with an evil curse or needle plunged into a Voodoo doll. She fought against those myths every day but never shied away from the look.

Despite her appearance and in contrast to the stereotypical image of Voodoo, LeBlanc advocated for the truth about Voodooists—a people who preach peace and healing. Routinely in the press, she fought against the cultural misunderstandings of the religion. When the local press dubbed the murderer a Voodoo practitioner, LeBlanc was the first to speak out, condemning that assumption as sacrilegious and an insult to Voodoo principles. She claimed it was even racist. LeBlanc preached that Voodoo is a religion of peace with aspects of many other religions, particularly Catholicism.

New Orleans is the epicenter of Voodoo in America. Priestess LeBlanc held court at the Voodoo Temple and

Culture Center. It's one of the local attractions for those who want to know more about Voodoo. While it isn't much to look at from the outside, the site contains many of the relics associated with the movement, some of which have been featured in motion pictures.

Founded in 1990 by Priestess Miriam Chamani and her husband, Priest Oswan Chamani, the Center claims to focus holistically on Voodoo, including traditional West African spiritual and herbal healing practices that are often depicted as spooky in films, an image they believed to be unfair. The temple's stated mission is to "provide service that meets the needs of all mankind, which allows him/her to fulfill their quest in the divine plan of the universe." LeBlanc had now been priestess for three years, continuing leadership precepts inherited generation to generation from Marie Laveau, the first Voodoo priestess of New Orleans, who reigned from 1820 to 1840.

Simone and Bundy were escorted into LeBlanc's office by her assistant.

The massive dark mahogany desk, ornately carved and in immaculate condition, dominated the dimly lit room. Her chair matched the color of the desk. With its high back, the leather of the chair framed her head in a dark aura. The walls were covered with shelves and primitive-style artwork. A photograph of the priestess with the mayor was the only evidence of politics in the room. The carpet was a dark woven Oriental, and the leather chairs in front of the desk were studded on the arms with brass tacks. They were old, and the leather was cracking. Low lighting from a small lamp on the desk and floor lamps in two corners kept the room shadowy. All in all, it felt ominous. Exactly what the priestess wanted.

"We don't kill innocent people," began LeBlanc. "And I don't like the police slandering our religion with racist blasphemy by accusing one of our followers of being a serial killer with no evidence to support it."

Simone was not surprised by LeBlanc's icy reception. Press reports were filled with her disdain at the Voodoo association given to the killer. While Simone didn't practice Voodoo or any other organized religion, she respected LeBlanc as a community leader and shared her concerns surrounding the unfair depiction Voodoo received in movies, such as Yaphet Kotto's role in the James Bond classic *Live and Let Die* or Tia Dalma's portrayal of the Voodoo goddess Calypso in *Pirates of the Caribbean.*

Simone tried to ease the tension.

"Priestess Maîtresse," Simone responded, "we understand why you're upset about the press making this all about Voodoo. We're not here to accuse anyone of being the murderer, much less ascribing his crimes to a religion. But we do have to do our job and have to follow every lead, however flimsy it may be."

"So, you want to determine if this killer of yours is Voodoo or not?" asked LeBlanc.

"In part, yes. But we don't know what, if any, religion he may follow. He has, however, left evidence that might be associated with Voodoo, so looking at it may give us some clues to help find him."

"Like the wooden cross?" asked LeBlanc.

"Yes," Simone said. "And the three Xs carved on their foreheads."

"They're both symbols used in Voodoo," added Bundy. Simone could see the angry reaction in the eyes of the priestess to Bundy's conclusion. Simone wished he'd been quiet.

"A wooden cross?" asked LeBlanc, staring at Bundy. "Last I looked, Officer Bundy, they crucified Jesus on a wooden cross, now the symbol of Christianity. And the triple X? Are you sure they're not symbols for the devil in some religions? What makes you so sure it's Voodoo?"

Her retort set Bundy back. He realized his naiveté to think he knew more than she. After all, she was a religious leader. But no woman, whether a priestess or not, was getting away with insulting him. He put up with enough of that from Simone.

He seemed to noticeably squirm in his chair, but Simone caught the look of defiance on his face—the same look he gives her when she corrects him. The guy obviously doesn't like to be reprimanded by anyone, especially women, and most especially Black women. He was just as misogynistic and racist as all the other white cops in New Orleans, as far as Simone was concerned.

"Three Xs in Voodoo symbolize the granting of a wish," answered Bundy. "I've done the homework, Priestess Maîtresse. They're etched into tombstones in St. Louis Cemetery. While the markings on the bodies might mean something else entirely, the combination of the Xs and cross suggest a strong Voodoo connection. And this is New Orleans. So Voodoo is an obvious suspect."

"Mr. Bundy," the priestess said deliberately, "I doubt very much you would speak to a Catholic priest as you are speaking to me, would you? Perhaps you have done your homework about the markings for Voodoo. Have you done the same for Christian symbols?"

Simone knew she had to retake control of the conversation. "We understand, Priestess Maîtresse, that the triple X can mean many things and that the wooden crosses could refer to any religion, including the Holy Trinity. And we do not mean to imply that the killer is Voodoo. In fact, I was hoping you could help us prove he is not. For me, the clues are too obvious. So even if the reasons for the killings are related to Voodoo, it's a sick interpretation. Help us make that clear."

"I see," responded LeBlanc, now beginning to warm up to Simone. Pointing to Bundy but speaking to Simone, she added, "And I suppose you can convince this one that his views are equally sick?"

Simone chose not to respond to the taunt directed at Bundy, and before he could again add to the tension, she stood. "I think we have taken enough of your time, Priestess Maîtresse. I only ask that you think about how you might help us and let us know if you have any ideas. And, of course, we're happy to answer any questions you might have. Please reach out to your contacts and let us know if you hear anything." Simone dropped one of her cards on the desk. Looking at a surprised Bundy, Simone added, "Joe, let's go."

LeBlanc did not get up from her chair as the two left.

Once outside in the sunshine, Bundy could not restrain his anger.

"What the hell was that about, Becca? We were barely into an interrogation, and you get up and leave? She knows a lot more than she's telling us. We should have pressed her. What did we accomplish?"

"That's the point, Joe. You saw it as an interrogation. As if LeBlanc were a suspect. I'm not surprised she shut us down. If we'd stayed much longer, she would have thrown us both out and cut off any future discussions. As it is, you certainly can't show your face to her again."

Bundy bristled. "So now what? We just ignore the Voodoo connection?"

"No. We don't ignore any evidence. But as far as any Voodoo connection in the future is concerned, I'll visit alone with the priestess."

"Suit yourself, Becca," Bundy said, shrugging. "But as far

as I'm concerned, the killer is one of her psychopath followers or someone who thinks he's carrying out the wishes of whatever god the Voodoo worship."

"They worship the same god as you and me, Joe. If you're going to attack them, at least get your facts straight," Simone said. The conversation was over.

CHAPTER SIX

George Landes loved New Orleans. He particularly looked forward to his annual trip with five of his buddies to enjoy a Saints game and some gambling at Harrah's Casino near the French Quarter or at the Boomtown Casino when it fit their fancy to take the three-hour trip to Harvey, Louisiana. The odds at the tables there were better. That didn't necessarily mean they could win more. It just meant it took them a little longer to lose their money.

The "rule" was to never split up, particularly when they were bar hopping in the French Quarter, where trouble was always brewing. There was safety in numbers. However obnoxious Landes and his friends got, no one wanted to mess with six young guys out for a good time. Tonight, however, Landes, was just not feeling like being part of the gang. When the game was over, he decided to go off on his own, claiming he wasn't feeling well. In truth, he wanted to find some other games to play, without his buddies. He wanted the company of a woman.

He asked the Uber driver to drop him off at St. Ann and Bourbon. As he strolled along Bourbon Street, he was enticed by the music and decided to have a nightcap at the Famous Door just a few blocks from his room at the Four Points Sheraton. It was rally time.

The night was getting late, so the bar wasn't particularly crowded, as it usually was on busy nights. But it was still filled with music lovers and revelers common to New Orleans bistros. Landes sat on an open bar stool and ordered his usual bourbon Manhattan.

"Makers Mark OK?" the bartender asked.

"Sure," replied Landes. He thought of ordering a Jefferson's Ocean, but he reserved that for when he wanted his bourbon neat or on a little ice. At the price of Jefferson's Ocean, it was a crime to ruin it with any additives.

Listening to a cover band singing the Animals' "House of the Rising Sun," an anthem for New Orleans, he noticed a woman sitting a few bar stools away from him. Only she and another man were sitting at the bar. The rest of the forty or so customers were at tables or on the dance floor. The other man at the far end of the bar sat a good distance from the woman. She was very attractive, wearing a short blue skirt and a white deep-cut blouse. The blouse was thin enough to make out the curves and bumps of her breasts. Typical of the day, she was glued to her cell phone busily texting.

As the bartender began to make Landes his drink and the band played on, the woman ordered a Cosmo without looking up from her phone. As Landes looked closer, he realized she was not just texting but also secretly taking photos of customers at tables and on the dance floor.

I wonder if she'll take a picture of me, Landes mused.

He had tended bar in college and had the habit of watching bartenders make specialty drinks, always curious if they'd take shortcuts rather than use the right proportions and premium ingredients. He watched the bartender take the metal cocktail shaker, add ice, and pour in the right amounts of Rose's Lime Juice, Cointreau, and Ocean Spray cranberry juice. The guy was a pro using the best ingredients. Landes wondered when he'd add Tito's or Absolut vodka. Instead, the bartender used the tap at the bar to add the last ingredient. While bars sometimes have house-brand alcohol on tap, it's almost never used in a specialty drink that commands a high price. The bartender shook the drink with flourish and poured it into a martini glass, adding the lime wedge to the rim. A perfect Cosmo with bad vodka or worse, no vodka at all.

The bartender arrived with both drinks.

"A Makers Mark Manhattan for the gentlemen and another Cosmo for the young lady. Enjoy," he concluded as he walked away.

The woman paid no attention to Landes or the bartender, still glued to her phone. Never known to be shy, Landes decided to ask her a question she was not likely to expect. Certainly not the kind of pickup line she had undoubtedly heard time and time again.

"Sorry to interrupt, but you're not going to drink that Cosmo, are you?"

She put her phone on the bar face down without turning

to him, obviously displeased by the interruption but taken aback by such an odd question.

"What do you mean?" she asked without making eye contact.

"Well, I suspect you're either drinking flavored water or rotgut vodka. The bartender used the right ingredients but no decent vodka. Assuming there's any vodka in there at all."

"It tastes fine," she responded with a tone that sent the message to leave her alone as she turned her back to Landes and returned to her phone.

Not one to easily give up, he waved for the bartender to come over.

"What's your name?" Landes politely asked him.

"Jeff," responded the bartender. "Is there a problem?"

"Well, Jeff, I'd like you to make a proper Cosmo for my friend here. One that has vodka in it. Preferably Absolut. Not water from the tap."

The bartender's face didn't hide his guilt. He fidgeted as he turned to the woman looking for guidance. She heard what Landes asked and was now looking in his direction, away from the bartender.

"Don't worry, Jeff, this one's fine," she said, adding, "and when you make his next Manhattan, use some flat Coca-Cola instead of bourbon. That will teach him," she smiled.

"You got it," the bartender responded with a smile. "Thanks for keeping our secret."

Landes, now confused, looked at the woman.

"Our secret?" he asked.

She turned and faced Landes. He was immediately taken in by her beauty. She was spellbinding.

"Where are you from?" she asked.

"Warwick, Rhode Island, just outside of Providence."

"I know where Warwick is," she responded with a tone.

"Sorry."

"So what's your name?"

"George."

She waited for more, looking at him.

"George Landes."

"And what are you doing in New Orleans, George Landes?" she asked with a warm tone that seemed to invite him into a conversation.

He was not used to being questioned. In bars with women, he was usually the one asking them.

"Down here for an annual trip to see the Saints and do some gambling," he answered, deciding to play along.

"Let me guess. You and a bunch of your boy buddies out for a stag outing. Right?"

"Yeah, we come every year. Stay at the Sheraton."

"That's nice," she replied. "And who are the Saints playing?"

"The Patriots. You should have figured that one out if you know where Warwick is," remarked Landes with a grin. "Anyway, the game's over. Pats lost."

"Never been the same since they lost Brady," she responded, looking up at the TV in the bar, airing the post-game recap.

"So why are you in this bar, George Landes, and not with your buddies?"

"I just wasn't into endless bar hopping and decided go off on my own. The music and my thirst brought me here. Could it be that fate brought us together?" Landes joked.

"Be careful what you wish for, George," she responded, dropping his last name.

Now it's my turn, he decided.

"I can guess you're from New Orleans and don't drink. I bet that's water in your Cosmo. So that makes me wonder why you're at this bar. It can't be for the music. It's not that good, and a local would know that. And I get the feeling you're not looking for a hookup unless you're just naturally rude. Which, if you are looking to be picked up, I'd suggest you try another tactic."

She smiled.

"OK, you don't have to tell me if I'm right," continued Landes. "But you can at least tell me your name. And by the way, you're not very good at hiding the fact that you're taking pictures."

She tilted her head a bit and looked at Landes as if she were trying to decide if she'd reply. She decided she would. She was bored and needed some entertainment.

"Rebecca Simone," she responded. "Detective Rebecca

Simone. I work for the New Orleans Police Department and I'm not drinking the vodka because I'm on duty. And I don't like the music and I don't go to bars looking to hook up. So, I guess you're pretty good at guessing, George."

"Shit," he responded. "My apologies. I sure hope I didn't blow your cover. You here looking for a suspect or something?"

"Or something," she responded as her phone vibrated with a message. It was a text from Broussard. After a look at it, she turned to Landes. "Look George, I'm kind of busy and have to make a call."

"You have a lead?" he asked.

"I wish. We'll see. But you have a great night, enjoy the music, and try to behave. When you're done, just take a right out of the bar and you'll find your hotel on the left in three or so blocks." Simone got up from her stool, nodded to Jeff the bartender, and walked over to another seat at the bar away from Landes, continuing to sit quietly, now talking intently on her phone.

As Jeff cleared up her spot at the bar, Landes asked, "So I guess I blew that one, huh, Jeff?"

"Nah. Becca's usually as cold as a fish. Probably why she's such a good cop. I like her. We all do. She plays fair. You at least got her to talk to you."

"So what's going on that she's undercover at a bar?"

"Not sure, but she made sure she looked good. Maybe it has something to do with the Bayou Slasher."

"Bayou Slasher?"

"Yeah. Seems we have a serial killer in the Quarter murdering people with Voodoo rituals. Really cuts them up and leaves them with a wooden cross and three Xs across their foreheads. There's been three dead so far. That we know of. So maybe Becca's on the lookout. I guess. But with her, she's always looking for troublemakers. So maybe she's just doing her job on some other case," Jeff said.

"Well, by the looks of her, I'd say she's inviting trouble," observed Landes.

"You have to put out the bait to catch the fish, George," the bartender responded. "Another Manhattan? We're past last call but I can squeeze one in for you."

"No thanks, Jeff, I'm done for tonight. I've had enough excitement."

He paid his tab and left, noticing Simone was still on her phone.

The streets were less crowded as party goers and drinkers were mostly back in their hotels or in after-hours bars that kept their doors open. So the walk was slow. But he enjoyed watching people act like idiots walking with their yard-long hurricane glasses festooned with plastic flowers and straws. Souvenirs of their visit to New Orleans.

He stopped for a moment to marvel at a teenager performing for spare change as he backflipped down the sidewalk, reminiscent of the scene on a Memphis street in the movie version of John Grisham's *The Firm* where Tom

Cruise duplicated the character by doing a backflip himself. As tempted as Landes was to play Tom Cruise and do the same, he was in no condition for such a feat. So, after watching the street performer entertaining the crowd with backflips, Landes threw a dollar in his hat on the sidewalk and moved on.

It was beginning to rain and the late-night stench of Bourbon Street began filling the air. Rain always brought out the worst of the smells. The sewer system was so deteriorated that even light rain caused the muck to percolate to the surface. Landes continued down Bourbon Street for the three-block walk to the hotel. It was nearly 3 a.m., and the bars were closing. The crowds kept thinning.

As Landes walked past Willie's Chicken Shack, something down the alley caught his eye. He stopped and squinted in the darkness, and saw a body on the ground, hunched over and clearly in a lot of pain. Someone else was in the shadows but he couldn't make them out. Without thinking, Landes ran down the alley, asking if they needed help.

There was no response. Whoever he thought was in the shadows seemed to have gone.

When he arrived, what he saw nearly made him vomit. The man now lying in the gutter was bleeding from a gash across his throat. While Landes had seen such things in movies, it was not the same when witnessed in real life. The man was still alive as Landes knelt beside him. The dying man attempted to speak, but blood instead of words gurgled from his throat. Landes took a closer look, not out of curiosity but because he thought he might be able to help, and saw the three Xs on the forehead.

The next thing he felt was a coldness in the back of his neck. It wasn't painful. Just cold. He brought his hand up to his neck and felt blood. His blood. Sticky and warm. As he started to look up, the next hit was to the front of his neck, straight in through to his spine, followed by a slash to the right. It nearly severed his head.

Landes never felt a thing, not even the final slash across his throat. Everything was too fast. As the rain continued to fall, a single wooden cross lay on the pavement between him and the other victim.

CHAPTER SEVEN

The alley, now cordoned off with the familiar yellow crime scene tape, kept the morning crowds at bay. Forensics was finishing their investigation and confirmed that both victims bled out from their neck wounds. They took samples from under fingertips and searched for items at the scene that might have traces of DNA, but had no confidence they'd find any.

When Simone and Bundy arrived, the bodies were covered and waiting for the coroner to arrive to put them in body bags. Patricia Harvey, the New Orleans assistant medical examiner Broussard assigned to the task force, was already there and reminded Simone to tell the coroner to keep the victims' clothing intact so she could more thoroughly search for clues.

"So what do we have here, doctor?" Simone asked, knowing the question was as routine and hackneyed as they get—the kind Joe Friday of *Dragnet* would ask. *Just the facts, ma'am.*

Harvey was used to the game and responded in a deadpan manner, "Two dead. We think the body on the left is Richard Walsh, from New Orleans. I suspect that's his saxophone case in the gutter. No ID on his body but his name was on a card in the case. Probably a local musician. The guy's ID on the right identifies him as George Landes from Rhode Island. Probably a tourist. We found his wallet on the street, whatever cash that was in it taken. His license was in his pocket, probably because he was proofed at some bar and put it there," responded Harvey.

"George Landes?!"

"Yeah. You know him, Becca?" responded Harvey.

"Oh my God. I met this guy last night at the Famous Door. He figured out I was a cop when he tried to pick me up at the bar."

"What did he say to you?" asked Bundy.

"Nothing important. Just the typical crap," responded Simone. "He was staying at the Sheraton, a straight shot down Bourbon."

"Is it typical for strange men to tell you where they're staying, Becca?" added Harvey with a grin.

"Pat, please," responded Simone.

"Can you estimate the time of death for these two, doctor?" asked Bundy.

"Hard to say, Joe. Probably very early this morning," responded Harvey.

"That much even I can figure out, doctor," replied Bundy. "I meant who died first and the time between."

"That I can't say, Officer Bundy," Harvey said coolly.

Simone could see Bundy crossed the line with Harvey. She needed her on the team and could not afford insults. "I apologize, Pat. Joe meant no offense. Would you agree that they probably died within minutes of one another?"

"Yes," Harvey answered.

"May I look?" asked Bundy as he bent over to lift the blood-stained sheet covering one of the victims.

"Whatever floats your boat," Harvey muttered. "Just don't touch the bodies."

Bundy lifted the sheet, exposing Landes lying on his side, facing toward him and Simone. His face was clearly visible in the pool of blood that surrounded it.

"Any additional thoughts, Dr. Harvey?" asked Bundy, more as an aside than a direct question.

"Well, Officer Bundy, this has the markings of another murder by the Bayou Slasher. The slit throats. The wooden cross. And one body, the musician, has three Xs carved on his forehead."

"But why a second victim? And why doesn't he have the three Xs?" asked Bundy.

"I don't know," she answered. "Maybe the killer is trying to be more efficient, or was rudely interrupted before he could finish the job."

Bundy stared at Dr. Harvey with disgust.

"Don't mind Dr. Harvey, Joe," Simone said. "She can be a bit morbid. Seen too many dead bodies."

"Indeed, I have. But there is another odd thing about this one," Harvey said as she pointed to Landes. "Unlike the other dead guy, this one not only has a slash in the front of his neck but also a puncture in the back. Combined, they nearly severed his spinal cord. That's a first for the Bayou Slasher."

"Severed?"

"Yeah, Officer Bundy. Severed," responded Harvey. "And that's no easy trick. The killer had to know what he was doing to get that right. The force needed to do that is very strong or has to hit just the right spot."

"But why would Landes come into this alley?"

Ignoring Bundy's question and speaking before Harvey could reply, Simone continued, "There was no one at the Famous Door last night who looked suspicious. That's why I left. The captain called and told me to hang it up for the night. Another night with dead ends."

"No pun intended, Becca?" added Harvey.

"Perhaps he saw something," added Bundy. "Maybe he wasn't the target but showed up at the wrong time. Wrong place."

"Possible," interjected Harvey, now with a serious tone. "That might explain the puncture wound in the back of his neck. It could be that the killer had to stab him to kill him quickly."

"But why slit his throat, too?" asked Bundy.

"Maybe because once the killer disabled him to get control, he decided he needed to slit his victim's throat to be sure. Or to make it look like the Bayou Slasher."

"Or maybe he just got pissed off at being interrupted," added Bundy.

Harvey returned to the first victim and continued her investigation, leaving Simone and Bundy to themselves among the cadre of cops at the scene.

"At this point, we can only guess why Landes might have been stabbed before his throat was slit, but we do know we have a double homicide now," observed Simone. "That's a change in the usual pattern. So, we have two more dead bodies with evidence like the others. This time, however, it looks as if the killer took one victim's wallet. If it is the Bayou Slasher who did this, and he changed his routine, then maybe we'll get lucky. If it isn't, then we have a copycat killer."

"We might have something here," interrupted a returning Harvey. "Take a look." She was holding a plastic evidence bag. "This may be foreign hairs on the first body. Could be from the second one, but the color doesn't match."

"Or it could be from the guy's pet dog," sarcastically added Bundy.

"Maybe," responded Harvey with a look of displeasure, "but last I saw, dogs don't drink MD 20/20."

"What?" asked Simone.

"We found an empty bottle of the cheap crap in the gutter about ten feet away. It's probably got nothing to do with the murder, but it will definitely have DNA on the bottle. And if it matches the hair, then we're not talking about man's best friend."

CHAPTER EIGHT

It took the lab less than two days to match the DNA samples collected at the scene where Walsh and Landes were murdered. It found a match with a local named Wallis Manning who had been in New Orleans for a few years.

Broussard wasted no time getting a warrant to search Manning's apartment after they took him into custody to ask him some questions. He wanted the timing to be just right to preserve surprise for Manning if anything was found, so he had Manning detained at 9 a.m., while his team of investigators arrived at his apartment an hour later. If things worked out right, after letting him sit alone in the interrogation room for hours, Manning would be questioned without knowing his apartment had been searched. If incriminating evidence were found, then he'd be trapped into lying or telling the truth. Either one got him in prison for murder.

When taken into custody Manning seemed confused, but put up no resistance. He was taken to an interrogation room at the police station to wait while the rest of Broussard's plan was executed.

When Bundy handed the landlord a copy of the search warrant, he willingly opened the door to Manning's three-room apartment.

"Please don't do any permanent damage, officers. I need to be able to rent this place."

Who the hell would rent this dump? wondered Bundy. The building was a tenement decayed to a point at which Bundy wondered how the landlord even got a license to rent it.

The apartment was a mess. Empty vodka bottles and cans of beer sat on the end tables next to a cheap sofa, and dirty dishes, which looked as if they'd been there for days, were stacked in the sink. Opened cans of cat food were in a corner where a black cat crouched in fear of the commotion. To Simone's amusement, Bundy flinched. He hated cats. Particularly black ones.

"Can you take the cat?" Simone asked the landlord. He nodded, and picked the cat up, carrying him out of the apartment.

"OK, let's make sure we take pictures of everything first, then what we find, and finally how we left the place. We certainly can't make it any messier. But I don't want anyone saying we didn't do this by the book," ordered Simone.

Once the "before" pictures were done, the officers began to randomly search the place with no apparent rhyme or reason, opening drawers and lifting sofa cushions with abandon.

"Damn it. Stop!" barked Simone. "Throwing drawers open and tossing things won't get us anywhere. Joe and Smitty, you two stay. The rest of you leave except for the photographer. He can wait outside and take pictures when

I ask him to. Smitty, Joe, and I will do this." The other three officers left, grumbling.

"Smitty, you take the bedroom. Joe, you take the kitchen. I'll take the rest."

It only took a few minutes before Bundy announced he'd found something.

"Over here," he said as he held up a necklace with a chicken foot dangling on the chain.

"Really, Joe?" Smitty asked with a smirk. "You think our killer ate a chicken first?"

"Fuck you, Evans," answered Bundy. "A chicken foot on a necklace is a Voodoo symbol, you idiot."

"Just put it in an evidence bag, Joe, and keep looking," ordered Simone.

The search continued, with Simone and Evans finding nothing they considered important. Bundy had more luck in the kitchen.

"Hey smartass!" Bundy called to Evans. "Why don't you come out here and tell me if you think this isn't important."

Both Evans and Simone walked into the kitchen to find Bundy holding open a drawer with a Ziploc bag with two small wooden crosses.

"So, Smitty," Bundy asked with a smile, "you think it's merely a coincidence that we found these crosses along with the chicken foot? Sure looks like Voodoo to me."

"Bag it and all the knives you can find in this place," ordered Simone.

The search took about an hour. Bundy was looking forward to confronting Manning with his chicken foot and crosses.

CHAPTER NINE

The interrogation room at the New Orleans Police Department on Royal in the French Quarter was typical: a ten-by-ten room with a metal table in the center and chairs on either side, fluorescent lights above, green walls, and a camera in the corner near the ceiling. While it wasn't exactly comfortable, it was not intimidating. Nor was it meant to be. Interrogators want their suspects to be comfortable but still aware of the serious nature of their plight. Slowly put them at ease, then pounce when the moment is right.

On the morning he was taken into custody, Manning was brought to the interrogation room, not yet officially charged. At that point, however, he was a suspect of high interest, having been found through incriminating evidence. But Simone wanted to get more out of him before a lawyer got involved, so she needed to be delicate and certain not to cause him to stop talking and demand counsel. Simone and Bundy agreed that she'd do the questioning and Bundy would play the bad cop role when Simone gave him the agreed-upon sign to do so by pulling on her left earlobe. It was a routine they often used.

Manning looked as if he'd been on the bad side of an arrest. His left eye was swollen, and he was rubbing his right forearm as if it hurt. His clothes, oversized tan khaki pants and a ragged wrinkled shirt, hung loosely on him. He wore shoes but no socks. He had no belt. From his appearance, he looked like a street bum. Bundy wondered if that was intentional so no one would suspect him of being anything other than someone down and out.

"Mr. Manning," Simone gently began, "we have some questions for you that we'd like to ask. As you were already told, you have a right to have a lawyer present. And if you can't afford one, we'll arrange one for you. Of course, if you want a lawyer, we won't be able to talk to you any more without the lawyer present, but that's your choice. Right now, you're a person of interest, but we haven't charged you with anything. This is your chance to help us unravel some of the confusion."

"Go ahead and ask," responded Manning, continuing to rub his arm.

"Are you hurt, Mr. Manning?" asked Simone.

"Yeah. I got roughed up by the cops when they booked me," he answered.

"Did you resist arrest?" Simone asked.

"I didn't resist no one. They just wanted to beat me up some. That's what cops do around here," he answered.

"If that happened, Mr. Manning, then you should file a complaint. We really don't accept unnecessary force. I'm sorry if that happened."

Manning stared at Simone. "You're sorry?"

"Yes," she said.

"Oh, well, uh, thanks, I guess." Manning settled back in his seat. "You can get on with your questions now."

The file on Wallis Manning described him as a recent local who moved to New Orleans three years earlier. His whereabouts immediately before he came to New Orleans were unknown, although he had been in the U.S. Marines. To make a living, he did odd jobs and occasionally had something more long-term, the last at a local gas station. He knew about repairing cars but couldn't hold a job long enough before his predilection for alcohol got him fired. He had a rap sheet filled with petty crimes and one unarmed robbery, but nothing more serious. He'd been in and out of local jails but never served a long sentence. He was rather short, 5'6", and weighed only about 145 pounds. His face was worn with the ravages of too many drinks and cigarettes, and his unruly brown hair was typical of someone who didn't care about his appearance. On the surface, he seemed an unlikely candidate as a serial killer, particularly one strong enough to overpower his victims.

"Good," Simone said. "I just need to do some technical stuff first and then we'll get started. Do you want a glass of water?"

"I'd like somethin' a lot stronger than that."

"I'm sure you would," interjected Bundy. "But that's not happening, so water is all we can offer. Or coffee. Black."

"I'll take coffee."

Bundy left to get it.

"OK, Mr. Manning, let's get started," began Simone as Bundy returned with the coffee.

Simone turned on the tape recorder, and the video camera over her shoulder automatically started.

"This is detective Rebecca Simone and Officer Joseph Bundy with the New Orleans Police Department. It is 3:25 p.m. on November 18th and we're here questioning Wallis Manning."

Manning took a sip of his coffee as Simone continued. "Mr. Manning, do you consent to our recording this meeting?"

"Fine by me," responded Manning.

"And can you confirm that we advised you that you're entitled to have a lawyer present and that we'd pay for one if you can't afford it?"

"Yep."

"And that you have freely chosen not to have a lawyer present?"

"For now, yeah."

"Good," responded Simone. "And last, can you confirm that we told you we can use what you say against you in a court of law?"

"If you mean did you read me my fuckin' Miranda rights, yeah. I've heard it before."

"Thank you, Mr. Manning," continued Simone. "May I call you Wallis?"

"Sure."

"You can call me Becca, and you can call Officer Bundy Joe."

"My new best friends, huh?"

"I'm not sure we're your friends, Wallis," responded Simone. "But we're not your enemies, either."

"Yet," interjected Bundy. Simone shot a look at Bundy. She hadn't given him the signal. He was playing the bad cop, but getting too aggressive too soon. Manning didn't react, so Simone let it go. Simone wanted to make Manning comfortable with talking to her. That would not happen if he saw her as an enemy. But it would have been a shallow lie to say she was a friend. That would backfire too.

"Where's my cat?"

"Your cat's with the landlord, Wallis. He'll be fine."

"That bastard? He'll let him starve!"

"We won't let that happen, I promise. I know how important a pet can be."

"Yeah? You got a cat?"

"No. A dog."

"What kind?"

Simone wasn't interested in talking about Sully. "Wallis, can you tell us a little about yourself? What brought you to New Orleans? What do you do here?" Typical questions to put a suspect at ease. No one likes anything more than to talk about themselves. Criminals in particular.

"Been here a few years. I wandered around for a while

after I was discharged from the Marines. Did four tours in Iraq. Weapons specialist. Ended up here." Simone could see he was proud of his service.

"Were you honorably discharged?" asked Bundy, even though he already knew the answer.

"Yeah, Officer Bundy, I was honorably discharged," Manning responded with disdain in his voice. "Were you hopin' it was otherwise?"

"Wallis, Officer Bundy means no disrespect." She noticed Manning had finished his coffee. "Joe, why don't you get Wallis another cup of coffee? Would you like one, Wallis?"

"Yeah. Let Bundy fetch me another cup."

"OK," said Simone. "We'll take a pause and return to our questions when Joe returns. In the meantime, the tape will continue running."

Without hiding his displeasure, Bundy left and was met by Broussard outside the interrogation room. The captain had been there watching and listening to the questioning on the computer monitor, which was hooked up to the camera.

"You need to ease up, Joe," Broussard began.

"Ease up?" Bundy responded. "We've got this son of a bitch by the short hairs. Why are we even bothering with the questions? Just charge the asshole and bring this to an end."

"Officer Bundy," responded Broussard, purposefully changing his tone to a formal one, "you have a lot to learn. We never have enough evidence, and keep digging until there's nowhere else to go. If you ever get the opportunity to question a witness, let alone a suspect, without a lawyer present, you take it."

"Fine," Bundy muttered. "But we found his DNA on the hair at the scene, on the bodies, and on the bottle in the alley. Our search of his apartment found wooden crosses, a Voodoo trinket, and knives that are now in forensics. I have no doubt it will show blood from the victims. So, what more are we going to learn, Captain?"

"How about why he's killing people, Joe? Or whether he killed others we haven't discovered? Or if others are involved? You may think you have this neatly packed in a box, but what do you say we let Becca put a bow on it so it's all wrapped up? We may be convinced he's the killer, but we have to make sure we have enough for Harper Gaudet and a jury. OK?"

"Yes, sir," responded Bundy. "I'll get the asshole another cup of coffee."

"Joe, you're a good cop who cares, but you've got a lot to learn. Becca is just the person to help you do that. So follow her lead."

Bundy nodded his head in response and fetched the coffee, returning to the room.

"OK," continued Simone. "Let's get back to it."

"Here's your coffee, Wallis," Bundy said as he sat back down beside Simone.

"You look in pretty good shape, Wallis," Simone lied

as she placed folders on the table hoping Manning would become curious about what they contained.

"I was a marine. I keep in shape," he replied as he looked at the folders.

"No doubt. A few good men, as they say. What exactly did you do in the Marines?" asked Simone.

"Like I said, I was a weapons specialist."

"Indeed. Help me understand what that means."

"I was a sniper."

"A sniper? Wow!" she said. "That's amazing!"

Simone could see she had his attention. And that's what she wanted.

"I used a CheyTac M200 Intervention," Manning volunteered.

"Tell me more about it, Wallis. Why that weapon?" Her question was more about getting Manning comfortable than it was about learning why he chose a particular rifle.

Manning responded as if he'd been programmed to be exact. "The CheyTac Intervention is an American bolt-action sniper rifle fed by a seven- or five-round detachable magazine. It's designed for multiple-caliber ammunition depending upon the distance of the shot and the damage the shooter wants to do."

"That's quite a bit of detail, Wallis."

"The Marines make us memorize it."

"What kinds of bullets did you use?" asked Simone.

"I liked the .375 hollow point bullets. They do more than

enough damage to a target. And the bullet stays supersonic until it hits the victim. Then it's lights out." Bundy observed to himself that Manning didn't sound like some dumb-ass southern boy when he described his weapon.

"Sounds ominous," replied Simone. "I'm not familiar with that weapon. When I did my tours in Iraq, I met snipers with Remingtons mostly. But I know snipers are allowed to use whatever they like."

Manning sat up straighter and actually smiled. "The CheyTac's the one used by SEALs," continued Manning. "Has the longest range of any rifle and holds the record for the longest shot."

"Really? And how far was that?" asked Simone.

"To be exact, 3,871 yards," Manning answered.

"My God, Wallis, that's more than two miles!" Simone said. "Did you ever hit a target that far away?"

"No. That distance was staged. My longest shot was about a mile. Hit some towelhead standing like an idiot on top of a wall."

"That must have been one hell of a shot, no?" asked Simone.

"Yeah, it wasn't bad," responded Manning, looking proud.

"Why hollow points?" asked Bundy, now getting curious himself. Unlike Simone's surprise at Manning's comments, he'd done his homework and read Manning's military record. He knew Manning was a sniper. But nothing else. No details beyond his duty stations and discharge date.

"You ought to be able to answer that, Bundy. It's for the same reason you cops use them," responded Manning without looking at Bundy.

"I thought the military was not allowed to use hollow points under the Geneva Convention," Simone said.

"Yeah, that's what people still think," offered Manning. "I think they changed that. Or we just didn't care."

"So, you wanted to do as much damage as you could when you hit the target," Bundy said.

"Yeah, genius, that's what hollow points do. On impact, they fragment. The more flesh and bones they hit, the more the bullet splatters the person shot. The funny thing is that they don't injure no one around 'em. It's really cool to watch in your scope as someone's chest explodes and those around him are unharmed except for the blood and guts that spew all over them." Manning smiled wider, exposing his decaying teeth.

"So you just blow their heads off from a couple of thousand yards, right?" asked Bundy. "And they never even hear the gunshot or bullet coming?"

Still refusing to look at Bundy, Manning replied, "Yeah, they never see the fuckin' thing coming. And with the silencer on the barrel, the fuckin' towelheads never even hear it. Just watch their comrades' chests blow to shit. They never know where it came from. That's how we wanted it."

Manning finally turned to Bundy with a look that put a chill down Bundy's spine. Bundy knew he was looking at the eyes of a trained killer. "But we don't really want to shoot for their heads, Bundy. We shoot for their chest. Bigger target and a definite kill. Center mass is where you're sure the fucker dies before he can praise Allah." Manning turned back to Simone and added, "But blowing someone's fuckin' head off? That's a real shit show watching blood and brains blast all over anyone standing near the target. And a decapitating kill sends a really good message to the assholes who see it. So yeah, I took some head shots if there were spectators who needed to be given a fuckin' lesson."

"Always make sure they're dead, right?" asked Simone.

"Yeah. I had a weapons instructor at boot camp. When I asked him how many times you should shoot some fucker, he told me that if a person is a threat and you need to shoot them, you shoot them until you set the fucker on fire, or they disappear. I made sure that happened with one shot."

"And to do that, you needed to take into account wind, terrain, and the target's movement, too. Right?" added Simone.

"That's how it works. It's what we were taught. As long as I had my spotter with me, I could take down any fuckin' bastard within a mile. But most of my shots were a few hundred yards."

"I see. And where is your rifle now, Wallis? Do you still have it?"

"Nah. They took it away when I left."

"Why not just buy another one?" she asked.

"I don't have that kind of money."

Simone felt Manning was ready for the tougher questions.

"Did you ever make any kills close up?"

He fidgeted a bit in his chair and answered, "No. I liked bein' far away from the hand-to-hand crap."

"But I thought snipers got hand-to-hand training too in case they were attacked," interjected Bundy.

Turning to Bundy with the derisive stare of an insulted marine, Manning responded, "Sure we were trained. Marines are trained in every kind of fuckin' combat. But I never killed no one close up."

Simone could see Manning was getting uncomfortable, so she decided to dial back her pressure. "I remember during my tours that my biggest fear was getting into hand-to-hand combat. Not that women generally did, but the army certainly trained us for it. They wanted us to be ready for anything."

"Like I said, I was trained in hand-to-hand. So, I was as ready as any marine if it happened."

"No doubt," Simone replied, satisfied with the answer. Continuing, she asked, "And as a sniper, how many targets did you eliminate?"

"In my four tours, I took down thirty-one," Manning proudly replied.

"No telling how many lives you saved, huh?" continued Simone.

"It was my job. Other than my hits, I didn't keep count."

"And how many did you miss?" asked Bundy. Simone looked at Bundy and slightly shook her head. Still hadn't given him any signal.

Manning looked away. "Like I said, I only kept count of my kills."

"Well, all I can say is thank you for your service," Simone said.

"Hold on." Bundy stepped back and pointed to each of them. "You both might have been in Iraq at the same time."

"Looks that way," responded Simone. "For all I know, I was one of the people Wallis saved."

"If you were one of the lucky ones," responded Manning.

Simone could see Manning was warming up to her. Time for some more softening. She fumbled with the folders to make sure she kept Manning curious.

"And I see you're now an auto mechanic, too. Pretty strong hands in that job, huh?" she continued.

"Yeah, I gotta lift a bunch of crap. Just part of the job."

Watching the computer monitor outside the interrogation room, Broussard was impressed. Simone was taking Manning down a path that would establish he had the capacity to commit the murders. He hoped Bundy was learning a thing or two watching her.

"Quite a change from being a sniper," observed Simone.

"Yeah. I suppose. But since I was a kid, I was into cars. So, it was easy. And it's pretty hard to find a civilian job as a sniper," replied Manning.

"I can imagine," Simone continued. "Did you ever think of becoming a cop? We can always use a good shot." She shuffled the folders again. She could see Manning was dying to see what was in them.

"I took the test but didn't make it. Lost out to some affirmative action shit."

"Right. The old affirmative action trap. That must have made you mad, huh?"

"Sure, it did. It would make anyone mad by bein' beaten out of a job by someone less qualified."

"And because they were Black?"

"No. I just think winners ought to be the best. You think Marines pick people to defend this country through affirmative action?"

Simone wanted to reply "no," but the truth was that a disproportionate number of Blacks enlisted. It wasn't a matter of the Marines having a choice. But she could see this agitated Manning, and she didn't want to go there. Not yet.

"No doubt. The few and the proud, as they say in recruiting ads. I guess that only works with the best, too," added Simone, trying to keep Manning calm. She pushed the folders again.

"So what's in the damn folders you keep pushin' around?" Manning asked, as if on cue.

"Right, we'll get to those in a moment," she replied, wanting to further build his curiosity.

Simone leaned back in her chair as if to relax and asked, "Wallis, no doubt you're familiar with the so-called Bayou Slasher." Manning stiffened in his chair and raised his head as if he'd been jerked to attention.

"Yeah, I heard of him. Is that why I'm here?"

"I don't know, Wallis," Simone calmly replied. "I'm certainly not accusing you of anything. But I do want to give you a chance to help us. After all, if you have nothing to do with the killer, then my questions should be easy to answer. And helpful to you."

"I didn't kill no one."

"I want to believe you, Wallis, but there are things we're having difficulty understanding." She tapped one of the folders.

"Like what?" Manning responded, looking at her hand.

"How familiar are you with where the bodies were found? Or the way the victims were killed?"

"Only what I've read in the papers."

"I see. And what did you read, Wallis?" asked Simone.

"That he cut their throats and left a cross," replied Manning.

Simone stared at Manning for a moment to make sure she had eye contact and opened one of the folders in front of her. She took out five pictures, each one a close-up of the faces of the murdered victims, clearly showing their slit throats and, except for Landes, the triple X on their foreheads. She arrayed them in front of Manning, looking for a reaction. The pools of blood, filthy streets, and looks of horror in the victim's eyes were gruesome. Simone intentionally chose the worst photos to display to Manning. Manning stared at them without expression or reaction. A sign of no remorse or emotion is common in killers. An observation she'd want to include in her report.

"Do you know who these people are, Wallis?"

"Sure," Manning replied. "Like I said, I read the newspapers. They're the ones the Bayou Slasher killed."

"All of them, Wallis? Including these last two here?" asked Simone, pointing to the two most recent victims, not waiting for his reply. "That's interesting, Wallis," Simone said. "You identified the two of them as victims, but these photos have never been published. No one other than officers in the NOPD have seen these. How do you explain that, Wallis?" Simone could see Manning again fidget in his seat, a sign that he was uncomfortable. She had to be careful not to push too hard out of fear he'd ask for a lawyer and the interrogation would end before she got what she wanted.

"A lot of shit has been in the papers about the Bayou Slasher, and it wouldn't take a genius to figure out what the photos are about. C'mon, you mixed them with the others. What else was I supposed to think? But I didn't do nothing."

"I really want to believe you, Wallis, but there are a few

other questions as well. Do you mind if I proceed?" Simone gently asked.

"I already said OK. So let's get this over with," responded Manning. Turning to Bundy, he added, "Hey, Bundy, get me some more coffee." Manning paused and grudgingly added, "Please."

Bundy began to rise, but Simone put her hand on Bundy's arm.

"We'll wait on that coffee, Wallis. Let's get to another question first." Simone was now at the point at which she needed to risk Manning getting nervous and asking for a lawyer. She knew she wouldn't get much more out of him. If she was going to get the answers she needed, now was not the time for an interruption that might give Manning a chance to think or to decide he needed a lawyer.

Hearing no objection, she continued.

"Good." Simone gently moved the photos, three to the left and two to the right to make room in the middle of the table. She opened another folder and placed a photo on the table taken at Manning's apartment. It showed a dried chicken foot on a cheap primitive black string necklace knotted at the end.

"Do you recognize this?"

"Yeah."

"What is it?"

"My good luck charm."

"Where did you get it?"

"I don't remember. Probably some fuckin' Voodoo shop in the Quarter. There are a bunch. Lots of us have 'em."

"Us? Who do you mean by 'us'?" Bundy asked.

"My friends. Guys I hang out with."

"So you're into Voodoo, Wallis?" Simone asked.

"Not really. Just because I have Voodoo crap doesn't mean I'm one of those nuts," he replied.

Bundy, in his inexperience, couldn't resist. "Mr. Manning, just tell us. Do you practice Voodoo? A chicken foot is a Voodoo symbol for protection from evil."

"I don't practice no religion," responded Manning, his eyes staying on Simone. His hands were shaking a bit and he began to look more agitated, which Simone wanted to avoid.

"OK, let's calm down and continue," Simone observed as she moved the photo of the chicken foot to the side and opened the next folder, placing two photos of the crosses and a knife in front of Manning.

"And do you recognize these, Wallis? We found them in your apartment."

Manning's voice rose. "I don't know what that shit is. I don't have no knife like that and those crosses ain't mine. You couldn't have found them in my apartment."

"But we did, Wallis," responded Simone. "And I'm sure you have a better reason you have them than to use them to pray to God or slit someone's throat."

Simone was ready for her own version of a kill, but could

sense that Manning would shut down at any moment. She had to be careful. She opened the last folder and took out a piece of paper.

"What's that?" Manning asked.

"It's a DNA report. We found your DNA at the scene where the last two were killed. On hair samples and your bottle of MD 20/20. And we found it on the knife, too. The knife you say you don't own." Bundy looked at her quickly, then up at the camera. He knew Simone was lying. The DNA report was still awaiting completion of the lab tests. The paper Simone had was nothing more than a case report. But he also knew that it is permissible police procedure to lie to a suspect to see how they react and find out if they're willing to reveal more to protect themselves.

Manning jerked upright in his chair and said, "I want a lawyer."

Simone started to close the folder, knowing she'd gotten all she was going to get. Bundy decided it was too close to stop, angry that Simone was backing off. He knew the rules about what it meant once a suspect asked for a lawyer, but also knew the New Orleans police didn't stop if they felt they were close to a confession or statement that could be used against the defendant.

"Why did you kill those people?" demanded Bundy.

"I didn't kill nobody."

"Bullshit, Manning," blurted Bundy. It didn't matter if this outburst upset Manning, and Bundy knew it. Manning had asked for a lawyer, and anything else he said was inadmissible. If Bundy continued, Simone might lose the right to use anything Manning had already said. It was all on camera.

Simone stood and turned to Bundy. "Mr. Manning has asked for a lawyer, Officer Bundy, so we're finished asking questions." Despite that, she decided to take one more chance, wondering if it would keep him talking. "It's really too bad. I was beginning to believe you, Wallis."

She looked at Manning to see if he'd continue. He didn't move; just looked straight ahead. There would be no confession that day, and Simone didn't want to compromise anything on the video tape. The interrogation was over.

"Wallis Manning, you are under arrest for the murder of George Landes and Richard Walsh." She reread him his Miranda warning just to be sure it was on the record. As if on cue, two uniformed officers entered, cuffed Manning, and took him into custody. He offered no resistance as he was escorted out of the room to be fingerprinted and processed before being placed in a cell and allowed to make a call to his lawyer.

By the time his public defender arrived, Manning was charged with two counts of murder for the killings of Richard Walsh and George Landes. Arraignment would be the next morning. He would later be charged for the murders of Jackson Walker, Maria Benson, and William Hitchcock Jr.

CHAPTER TEN

"Well, Becca, you did it," began Broussard as he lit his victory Padron.

"It's not a confession, Captain, but the evidence is solid that he was at the scene. He lied about that. He had no alibi. We saw one hole after another in his story. We checked on timing and his whereabouts. It all pointed to him."

"But what still baffles me, Becca, was his motive. Why was he killing these people?" asked Bundy.

"I wish I knew," responded Simone. "He's a serial killer. And while I'm sure he had some sick reason to murder the victims, we may never know why."

"Perhaps he's just insane," added Bundy. "No one in their right mind would do what he did. Or maybe he suffers from some kind of bullshit post-traumatic thing."

"It's post-traumatic stress disorder, Joe," corrected Simone.

"And if he suffers from it," said Broussard, "that's for his lawyer to argue. It's not our responsibility to establish his defense. He's a killer and it's our job to stop him."

"Yes, sir," Bundy dutifully responded.

"Well, you both did your job brilliantly," concluded Broussard. "Now it's up to Parish District Attorney Gaudet to do her job and put the bastard behind bars permanently.

Or better yet, pinned down on a gurney waiting for a lethal injection." Broussard sat back, took a long draw and blew smoke rings into the air.

"You sure we have enough, Captain?" asked Bundy, still in doubt. "It seems like a lot of circumstantial evidence."

Broussard took another long draw on his cigar and calmly blew more smoke rings in the air in Bundy's direction as he contemplated the question. Simone thought he looked pompous, as if the rings were a spectacle to impress them. They didn't impress her.

Sitting back in his chair, Broussard responded, "Joe, I've never seen a perfect case. It's almost always circumstantial evidence. But we've got enough here so we'll now leave it to Harper to close it out. Our job is done."

"But Captain," Bundy objected, "we didn't find any DNA on the knife in Manning's apartment."

"So what? Maybe he wiped it clean. Or threw the one he used somewhere in the Bayou. We have the DNA in his hair at the scene and on the bottle he left behind. Crosses in his apartment. Voodoo worship. That puts him there with corroborating evidence in his apartment. Absent some compelling evidence to the contrary, that should be enough to send Manning to death row."

"Yes, sir," Bundy responded, knowing he'd get nowhere with further comments.

"Besides, a New Orleans jury already paranoid that there is a killer in town slitting throats will be more than happy to convict on the evidence we have and send that bastard to his rightful death."

Jesus, thought Bundy. *He couldn't care less if the man is innocent.*

Taking another puff, Broussard continued, "And I have to compliment you, too, Joe. I know I bust your balls a lot but you're a good cop. You did well in this investigation. You just need to tone down your negative vigor a bit. You've got the right instincts. Just not the patience and trust."

"Thanks, Captain," Bundy replied. He wasn't sure what else to say. He had his doubts about the adequacy of the evidence but knew better than to push it. He just got a rare compliment from Broussard, so he decided it was best to move on to something else.

"I do have to say, Captain, meeting someone so cold-blooded, with so many kills in Iraq to his credit, was really something."

"Really something?" responded Broussard. "It's guys like Manning who saved a lot of lives in Iraq. Maybe shooting all those people made him into a murderer, but he was probably a hero in Desert Storm. He may have gone wrong when he got back or may have even been a killer before he went, but I wouldn't describe what he did as a sniper 'really something,' Joe."

"Sorry, Captain. I'm just sayin' the guy is scary."

"Joe," said Simone, "it takes a special kind of person to be a sniper. I can't imagine how killing people like they do doesn't screw 'em up in some way. I suppose killing people will do that to you no matter how you kill them."

"So did you ever kill anyone while you were in Iraq, Becca?" asked Bundy.

"Me?" she responded. "No, I was never in the field. I was an MP first at Camp Fallujah and then Camp Baharia. The closest thing I got to combat was breaking up bar fights at the bases' clubs or arresting a soldier who got on the wrong side of some local family, usually over a daughter he assumed was a whore. Luckily, I never had to shoot anyone."

"After listening to Manning, I wonder if I could ever shoot someone," responded Bundy. "I'm not sure I have that kind of cold heart in me to do it. I've never even drawn my weapon."

"I've drawn mine and shot when I had to," Broussard said. "If the time ever comes when you may need to defend yourself or someone else and shoot a suspect, your training will kick in. Just make sure that if you ever draw your weapon, you draw it to use it."

"Like Manning told us, Joe, set the fucker on fire or watch them disappear. Captain, I'll write up our final report and have it on your desk tomorrow," Simone said.

"No, Becca, take a couple of days off. You too, Joe. You've both been working your asses off for two months. I can't give you more money, but I can give you time off. So, the report can wait a few days."

"Thanks, Captain. What's next?" asked Bundy.

“What’s next, Joe, is a press conference with the mayor to announce that we’ve solved the case of the Bayou Slasher,” replied Broussard, taking another drag on his cigar. “And you and Becca will be center stage, so put on your dress blues.”

“Will do, Captain,” replied Simone as she turned to leave the office with Bundy, always the toady, in tow.

CHAPTER ELEVEN

The Bayou Slasher was national news. So, it was not surprising that the press conference to announce that the NOPD had captured the killer drew reporters from around the country. It was broadcast live on CNN, Fox, and other top cable networks. Even ABC television interrupted their afternoon talk shows to go live to the event. To add drama, the mayor's office decided to hold the conference outside on the steps of Gallier Hall, the old city hall on St. Charles Avenue. Built in 1845, its granite façade and six towering pillars presented a grandeur every politician loves.

It was a beautiful November day in New Orleans. With the cameras pointed at the podium on the steps of Gallier Hall, the mayor spoke. "Good afternoon, my name is Alicia Pratt, Mayor of New Orleans."

Elected a year before the murders began, Pratt, a Black forty-eight-year-old Republican, was a popular conservative law-and-order candidate, even in the Black community, where police brutality and misconduct were all too often present. Born and bred in New Orleans, Pratt was a former Miss Louisiana before she enrolled in LSU's medical school, eventually becoming a pediatrician. She entered politics at age thirty-five as a councilperson and never returned to her medical practice again. In her campaign, she promised police reform and had begun making changes, including telling Guidry that he needed to resign. If he resigned, she had the right to appoint an interim superintendent. But then the murders began, and she decided it was not the time to replace him. She decided she was stuck with Guidry until the Bayou Slasher was found. Press conferences such as this one would generally be conducted by the prosecutor who charged the accused, but Pratt was a politician who wanted the limelight when it suited her. While Gaudet was not pleased with being relegated to standing on the steps, she knew better than to cross another Louisiana politician.

"I'm joined here today," continued Pratt, "by our finest from the New Orleans police department and our Parish prosecutor, Harper Gaudet." Behind her, one step up the stairway, was a lineup that included Guidry, Broussard, Simone, Bundy, and Gaudet. On either side of them were the American and Louisiana flags. Some additional uniformed police officers stood on the steps between the other pillars on either side of the podium. It was set up to be quite the show.

The square was cordoned off with red velvet roping typical of bank lobbies. The press was permitted within the ropes, sitting in rows of chairs. Outside the ropes were spectators, standing and trying to jockey for better views. In addition to the fifty or so reporters, the entire crowd exceeded two hundred. For New Orleans, it was an excellent turnout.

"I'm pleased to announce that yesterday we arrested a

suspect who we believe is the Bayou Slasher. I say 'suspect' only because this man deserves his constitutional rights of due process and a trial. Rest assured, however, that we will speed this along as quickly as we can to finally close this chapter once and for all."

Cameras snapped and reporters' hands rose, waving to be recognized by the mayor.

"Before I take any questions, there is one more thing I want to add," continued Pratt. "It dismays me that this murderer has been so associated with Voodoo. Such a conclusion is a dishonor to our Voodoo culture and our law-abiding community members who practice this long-honored religion. It is too often cast in dark shadows and evil practices when, in fact, it teaches love and tolerance, something we could all use more of. So I will not again refer to Voodoo as part of this investigation. For me, he's simply a murderer."

"But what about the Voodoo symbols on the bodies?" shouted one reporter.

Realizing that the last thing she wanted to do was get into a debate with a reporter, Pratt ignored the question and continued, "Now, Captain Raleigh Broussard will take the podium for a few remarks and to answer your questions." She didn't bother to turn around; she could imagine the anger that must have appeared in Guidry's eyes. She had no intention of giving him any forum to claim credit for the good work of her police force.

As Broussard approached the podium, more cameras snapped and raised hands waved for recognition like grade school children anxious to be called upon when they have the answer to a question.

"Thank you, Madam Mayor," began Broussard. "First, I want to acknowledge the fine work of Detective Rebecca Simone and Officer Joseph Bundy, standing behind me. Through their tenacious police work, we were able to capture Mr. Wallis Manning. We have substantial evidence against him and believe he is the Bayou Slasher. While I appreciate the sensitivity, the evidence does suggest a connection to Voodoo. And Mr. Manning had the trappings of a practitioner." Broussard paused, feeling the icy gaze behind him from Pratt for the reference. He had no intention of avoiding it. As far as he was concerned, Manning was at least partially motivated by Voodoo. That was enough for him.

Broussard continued, "But as Mayor Pratt said, we do not want to make any final conclusions and intend to make sure Mr. Manning is afforded all of his rights the same as any defendant accused of a capital crime. Now I'll take your questions." Broussard pointed to a reporter in the first row.

"Joe Catchings, *New Orleans Gazette*," he announced. The *Gazette* was owned by Victor Richards, a seventy-five-year-old gray-haired southern publisher. Cagey and sly when it came to developing sources, he hired reporters who were not afraid of getting their hands dirty. A muckraker, Richards had his run-ins with Guidry, whom he believed was corrupt, though he couldn't prove it. On the other hand, he liked Broussard and hoped to see him become the next chief or superintendent, something he made known privately to both Pratt and Broussard. But as far as Richards was concerned, Broussard had to earn it by solving the murders and catching the serial killer. So he told Catchings to take the gloves off.

"Captain Broussard, Mayor Pratt ignored the question about the Voodoo symbols. How can you explain them without seeing Voodoo as part of the killer's identity and, perhaps, motive?" Richards liked the Voodoo angle to the story. It sold papers.

While Broussard would have preferred to stoke the Voodoo theory, he could not win with Pratt by giving it credence. He decided that despite his intuition, he needed to end that direction of questioning or face the wrath of the mayor, something he very much wanted to avoid. If there was a shot at becoming chief or superintendent, he wanted to preserve that opportunity.

"First, like Mayor Pratt, I'd like to avoid unfair allegations against the Voodoo religion in New Orleans," responded Broussard. "I am trained to follow the evidence, wherever it leads. At this point, the Voodoo symbols are merely facts in a complex investigation. Nor as of yet do we have evidence of any association between Mr. Manning and the Voodoo establishment. There may seem to be connections, but we cannot assume they're true. Even if he practices Voodoo, that does not mean the religion itself has anything to do with the murders any more than any murderer's religion should define their crimes."

"But you can't deny the fact that each victim had Voodoo symbols carved on their bodies and crosses left at the scene. How can that not connect the killer and the victims to Voodoo with such obvious evidence?" Catchings persisted.

"Mr. Catchings, I told you I follow evidence wherever it leads and make no assumptions or conclusions until an investigation is done. I believe that answers your question." He decided any further dialog with Catchings was over.

Broussard pointed to a reporter in the back of the room. He favored folks in the back since they so rarely had an opportunity to participate. In their position as reporters who were lower on the food chain, they were not afforded a front-row seat. Broussard liked the underdog, recalling his days of winning games while at LSU when on the rare occasion the opposing team was favored.

"Barbara Phillips, Bayoobuzz.com." Broussard immediately regretted his choice, believing that Internet publications were sloppy and disregarded conventional norms of good journalism. Bayoobuzz.com was no exception.

"Captain Broussard, we appreciate your views on falsely maligning Voodoo, but it makes no sense that Voodoo is not involved given all the evidence—something you profess to follow. So why do you now discount it?"

"Ms. Phillips," responded Broussard, "there is nothing to

be gained by continuing attacks on Voodoo. Come on, folks. We've had five innocent people murdered by the same person. We believe that person is Wallis Manning. The facts are what they are, and we will pursue every lead. So, if someone else has a question not about Voodoo, I'd be happy to answer it."

"Including Voodoo if the evidence takes you there?" interjected Phillips, unwilling to give up.

"Yes, Ms. Phillips, including Voodoo," replied Broussard, knowing that he had no way to avoid the controversy as long as the press continued with it. They had the last word, and there was nothing he could do about it regardless of the legitimacy of what he had to say about the evidence. They'd never let the Voodoo story go.

"Now, again, if anyone has questions about this case other than any connection to Voodoo, I'd be happy to answer them," repeated Broussard.

Hands were raised again, and Broussard answered questions about the evidence, Manning's past, and whether he'd be charged with more murders. The press conference ended at 1 o'clock.

As the entourage left the steps to return to their offices, Pratt said to Broussard, "Sorry for putting you in such a tough spot, Captain."

"No problem, Madam Mayor. It's my job to take the heat. My apologies for allowing the Voodoo connection to continue after you tried to put it to rest."

"And you think there is a connection?"

"I can't avoid what the evidence tells me. Whatever motivated Manning to kill, Voodoo has something to do with it. We can't discount it out of fear of offending some people," Broussard responded.

"As you wish, Captain. Your job is to solve crimes," Pratt offered. "So, congratulations again for finding the killer. It means a lot to the city."

"Yeah. I suppose so," he responded. "But Manning's not been convicted yet. So, I'll hold off celebrating until he's found guilty and about to be injected."

"Understood," responded Pratt. "Of course, that assumes the drugs will be available. Louisiana may allow a death sentence if Manning is found guilty, but carrying it out is quite another matter if drug companies refuse to produce them for executions."

"True," responded Broussard. "It's strangely ironic that these same drug companies manufacture and sell opiates without restraint, leaving innocent addicts dead in the street. So, who are the real executioners?"

CHAPTER TWELVE

"You have the wrong man," Guidry heard on the other end of the call.

Christopher DiMeglio had been with the FBI ten years as a specialist in its Behavioral Science Unit, whose members were known as the "Profilers." Established in 1974, the BSU uses profiling as a tool in identifying people suspected of serious crimes, particularly serial murders and terrorists.

"That's preposterous, Agent DiMeglio," angrily replied Guidry. "We have DNA, physical evidence. He was at the scene. That's all we needed to close this case."

"Superintendent Guidry . . ." continued DiMeglio.

"I prefer to be called Commissioner, Agent DiMeglio," interrupted Guidry.

"My apologies, Commissioner," responded DiMeglio in as respectful a tone as he could muster.

That confirms the reports I got that this guy is a total asshole, thought DiMeglio.

"With all due respect . . . Commissioner, let me go through your evidence. First, the DNA was found only at the latest murder scene. You didn't even find it on the knife you secured in his apartment. So, it does not link your suspect to the other three. The cross? Any killer could use that ruse. Or someone could have planted it. And the knife?

Don't you think finding it is a bit too convenient for such a careful killer? And with no DNA or forensic examination proving it was the murder weapon, it's not even admissible. Nor does your suspect have any record for violent crimes. Just petty stuff to get money for another drink. And from all indications, he's not on drugs because he can't afford them."

"Agent DiMeglio, you and all your fancy FBI Ivy League analysts can look at this from your desks in Washington all you want. You're not in the field doing the hard work. Down here in Louisiana, we know what we're doing and how to protect the people we look after. Wallis Manning is a murderer. Pure and simple."

DiMeglio was finding it hard to be tolerant.

"Commissioner, I grew up on Arthur Avenue in the Bronx. I saw more than enough crap on the streets. And I didn't go to Harvard or Yale. I got my undergraduate degree from Fordham, my law degree from NYU and a masters from John Jay College of Criminal Justice. I'd say that beats your poly sci degree from Louisiana State. I worked my entire life on the streets, Commissioner, not behind some fucking desk." DiMeglio didn't regret losing his temper.

He was used to the respect FBI agents usually received from local police. But in the South, particularly Louisiana, the sting of civil rights arrests by federal agents was still felt. So, he should have expected a cold reception.

Guidry's ignorance reminded DiMeglio of his early training in Quantico, where FBI agents learn the basics of their trade and where he first met members of the Behavioral Science Unit. More often than not, BSU agents were looked upon as techies and not real agents. Real agents hit the streets and did their jobs pretty much the same way as any beat cop in a city. The difference was that they had the power and resources of the federal government. That meant more tools, including forensics that could break a case wide open when needed. Field agents often looked at BSU members as such tools. DiMeglio had his own ways of dealing with the attitude of BSU outsiders. His job was to educate local law enforcement about profiling techniques and to assist them in investigations of serial murders even when they didn't welcome him with open arms. He came to accept that as part of his job. But Guidry was more than he was willing to tolerate or respect.

"If you know better how to protect your citizens," DiMeglio countered, "then how do you explain that only Chicago has a higher murder rate than New Orleans? Your city shares the number two spot with Baltimore. Forgive me, Commissioner, but I'm somewhat at a loss how that indicates your policing is successful."

DiMeglio resolved that Guidry would never be his friend, so to hell with professional etiquette.

"As for Manning," DiMeglio continued, "my bet is his IQ is above average, a trait common in snipers but not an attribute of serial killers. In other words, he's probably too fucking smart to be one. I suspect he's just a poor alcoholic looking for his next drink. Even if he did kill the latest victims, I can assure you he didn't kill the others."

"He knew things about the other murders, Agent DiMeglio. Things only the killer would know."

"And who told you that, Commissioner? The officers who interrogated him? I'll bet you they mentioned every one of those facts you think are unique before Manning repeated them. It's a classic interrogation trick. Plant the idea and then get them to repeat it. Damn, I've used it myself to confuse suspects. But not to build a confession for something they didn't do."

"This is nonsense," replied Guidry as his temper rose. "And besides, we didn't ask you to look at our investigation and give us an opinion on how we did. Your office here in New Orleans interferes enough with our work. What the fuck would you know from your ivory tower in Washington? You think you can just divinely investigate a case? We didn't ask for your help and don't want it. Frankly, this is none of your business or the business of the FBI. I'd be obliged if you and your fellow agents butted out of Louisiana and our business."

"Butt out of your business, Commissioner Guidry?" replied DiMeglio, now at the end of his patience. "That's how you see my effort to help? OK, Commissioner, I'll move on. God knows I'm busy. But when the killer strikes again—and he will—you give me a call. Perhaps then you'll be ready to listen."

"He won't strike again, because we have him behind bars, Agent DiMeglio!" Guidry hollered.

"What you're missing here, Commissioner, is a motive. Serial killers don't murder on a whim. What was Manning's motive? As far as I can see, you don't have one."

"Good day, Agent DiMeglio." Guidry abruptly hung up the phone as he shouted to his assistant, Nancy Garland, "Get me Broussard. Tell him to get his ass over here right now!"

"You don't have to yell, Mr. Guidry," Garland calmly responded in her rich southern drawl. She was never one to back down to Guidry. Or anyone else for that matter. She knew she'd outlast Guidry. In reality, her job was more secure than his. She knew far more than Guidry did about the political secrets of New Orleans. Guidry was the third superintendent she served. And he would not be the last.

CHAPTER THIRTEEN

"What does he need to talk to me about that he can't do on the phone?" Broussard asked Nancy Garland when she called.

Garland was no stranger to Broussard's dislike of Guidry. And she didn't blame him. Guidry was the worst superintendent she'd ever worked for. She knew he was racist—everyone did, including Broussard. But Guidry was not the first racist appointed to a political position in New Orleans and most likely would not be the last.

While that made it hard for Broussard and Guidry to work together, for the most part, Broussard did as he pleased, knowing that given his popularity and respect in the community, there was little Guidry could do. But Broussard also knew Guidry's core racist beliefs motivated Guidry to do his best to find a reason to get rid of him. It was getting harder and harder for Broussard to tolerate the insults. His patience remained only because the mayor kept assuring Broussard that she would find a way to get rid of Guidry.

Garland continued, "I'm not sure what bug he's got up his ass, Captain Broussard, but he blew up just after he hung up with a man from the FBI."

"The FBI? Who?"

"A nice young man named Christopher DiMeglio. He

called this morning before the superintendent was in. When Mr. Guidry got here at ten, I connected him to Mr. DiMeglio. He just hung up with him. And he's not in a good mood. So you'd better get over here before he decides to go home and just get madder," Garland responded, smiling to herself.

"Raleigh," she continued, "you know the bastard is always late to the office and early to leave. So if you want to know what's buggin' him, you'd better get over here right away."

"Tell the asshole I'll stop by this afternoon," responded Broussard.

"He wants to see you now. C'mon. You need to find out what's going on."

"Nancy, I couldn't care less when he wants to see me. And as for what's going on, I think you want to know it more than I do. So tell him three o'clock so he has to stay and put in an honest day's work. I've got a lot to do, and listening to him bitch about a call from some guy at the FBI is the last thing on my to-do list. I'll be there this afternoon."

"OK, I'll tell him," responded Garland, grinning. She was looking forward to seeing the fit Guidry would throw.

Broussard searched on Google for DiMeglio. It didn't take long to find him and see that he was a specialist in profiling and finding serial killers. He looked to be in his late thirties, average height, dark hair, and in decent shape. The glasses he wore made him look more like an accountant than a cop. Although Broussard held no love for the FBI, he grudgingly respected the FBI and how it trained its agents. Ever since the Feds sued the New Orleans police department in 2010 for poorly enforced policies and police brutality, Broussard had no liking for any federal agents, particularly one who was second-guessing his detectives and officers. So even though Broussard knew that DiMeglio would be smart, formidable, and someone you'd rather have on your side than not, the last thing he wanted was an FBI agent looking over his shoulder. He wasn't surprised that a blowhard like Guidry played him all wrong and now made Broussard's life more complicated.

Dammit, thought Broussard. *I don't need federal eyes looking at our work. I don't need this to turn into a public relations shit show.*

As Broussard sat at his desk chewing his cigar and fuming over Guidry's interference, his cell phone rang. The caller ID revealed that the call was from Harper Gaudet, the Orleans Parish district attorney. At the age of thirty-six, she succeeded famed New Orleans DA Leon Cannizzaro Jr., who chose not to seek a fourth term in 2020 after eighteen years in the role of defending the city. A former public defender now in office for a short time, Gaudet chose to leave private practice and run for DA when Alicia Pratt ran for mayor. She was the first woman DA in New Orleans history. She and Broussard got along well. He regarded her as a fair and even-handed prosecutor, just as she had been when she was a public defender and in private practice. It was easy for him to vote for her.

"Good morning, Harper. What can I do for you?"

She didn't waste time. "I just got an irate call from Guidry. Seems he got a blind call from some guy at the FBI saying we charged the wrong man for the Bayou Slasher killings."

"Yeah, Christopher DiMeglio. He's an FBI profiler."

"How do you know that?"

"Nancy Garland called me. I assume this is a stunt by Guidry to get some press touting the FBI as part of our investigation. My bet is it wasn't a blind call at all, and Guidry set it up for show, as if he's bringing in the cavalry. The last thing I need is some FBI agent second-guessing my detectives and officers. That will only complicate the situation."

"You're not even close, Raleigh. It's not a publicity stunt. He's freaking out that this case may go south, and Manning will go free. DiMeglio insists we have the wrong man."

"We've got the evidence, Harper. What are you worried about?"

"Manning's got Armand Percy in his corner," Gaudet responded.

Broussard took a breath. "I see."

"That means he's got the best public defender in Louisiana, maybe the country. Or the best criminal defense lawyer, period. And now Guidry's got doubts because he got a call from some Boy Scout from the FBI. Percy will smell that and turn it to his advantage."

While he grew up in New Orleans among its most wealthy southern blue bloods, Armand Percy chose to eschew his family's oil and shipping business for a career in law. Knowing that his trust fund would give him all he'd ever need to lead a very comfortable life in the Big Easy, he opted to be an underpaid public defender and represent the most heinous clients he could get. From his perspective, the worse the person, the better. He put fear in most prosecutors. Percy knew how to persuade juries and spin the worst evidence to his client's advantage. He was right out of central casting with bright white hair left a bit too long, a thick southern drawl, and piercing blue eyes. Adding to his legendary status were his flamboyant suits, southern personality, and the love affair he had with the press—and the press had with him. No matter how good the case was, it could be lost if Percy was on the defendant's side.

"So what?" responded Broussard. "You've been up against Percy before and won."

"And lost," added Gaudet.

"Fine, Harper. Relax. We've got you covered. Did Guidry tell you what else the FBI agent said?"

"Yeah. Claimed he said DNA only at the scene and not on the knife or crosses didn't support connecting Manning to the murders. Claims Manning was probably just looking for money and decided to riffle through a couple of dead bodies. I'm sure Percy will make that the centerpiece of his defense—that it was a setup, and casting your investigators as incompetent. And he claims that without a motive, we've got the wrong man."

"I understand. But we searched his apartment and found enough evidence to implicate him. The lack of DNA does not absolve him. He's no fool. He probably wiped the knife clean. And as for a motive, he's a serial killer. Want a motive, Harper? How about he just likes to kill people?"

"Are you sure you did enough investigation, Raleigh?"

"We did enough to make at least a circumstantial case, Harper. We've got a killer on the loose and if we wanted to be perfect, we'd end up with more bodies. Even you admitted that when you indicted him," Broussard snapped.

Gaudet was not going to back down. Her reputation was at stake.

"Raleigh, my concern is that we might have jumped the gun. If we'd done a more thorough job, maybe we would have found more. I might have had enough to indict him, but as the saying goes, any prosecutor worth their weight could indict a ham sandwich."

The expression, however hackneyed it was, held some truth. Before a grand jury, only the prosecutor presents evidence. There is no defense counsel. It's an entirely one-sided presentation of the evidence the prosecutor decides to put before the grand jury. Any good prosecutor can make a case that will win over a grand jury and garner enough votes to press ahead with an indictment. In Louisiana, all they need is a majority of the twelve jurors who hear the case. And Gaudet was good. She'd never failed to get an indictment she sought.

"Look, Harper," continued Broussard, "I know we've got some holes in the case we need to fill in. And we will. But you had more than enough to charge Manning. Don't start doubting yourself."

Gaudet, resigned to agree, added, "What really pissed off Guidry was DiMeglio pointing out that the only city with more murders every year than New Orleans is Chicago."

Broussard smiled. "How did Guidry leave it with the agent?"

"Told him to go fuck himself."

"Really? He actually had the balls to say that to a federal agent? As much as I dislike the bastard, that was a good response. We don't need the FBI."

"But that's not where it ended, Raleigh," responded Gaudet. "The agent said he'd wait for Guidry to call him when the next person is murdered while we're holding a petty thief in jail. So, you better be right about Manning."

"I trust my officers, Harper."

"I'm glad you do, but we're running out of time. You need to fill those holes. I'm not so sure a trial jury will buy what we have once Percy's through with them. All Percy needs is one holdout to hang the jury."

CHAPTER FOURTEEN

"I'm your public defender," Armand Percy announced, as he sat down across from Wallis Manning in the reception area of the jail. The room was large, with an array of tables. The other tables had defendants talking to their lawyers or visiting with their families. Guards were stationed on the perimeter, watching closely to see that nothing was passed to an inmate that might be used as a weapon or ingested as drugs.

As a public defender, Percy often pushed the limits and had been found in contempt by judges on numerous occasions for skirting court rules and getting too close to the edge of a proper defense. But Percy didn't care. He survived four bar investigations, acquitted on each. Even the bar association was afraid of him. He was one of New Orleans's most notorious characters and publicity hounds. He played the part well with his white linen suits and blue fedora, brim down in front. He was handsome and perfectly fit the stereotype of the southern lawyer. Percy loved the comparison, almost as much as he loved the idea of defending a serial killer—a dream come true.

"I didn't do it," responded Manning.

"I didn't ask, and I'm sure you didn't, Mr. Manning, but that's not the point," continued Percy. "And I do not care whether you did it or not. My job is to make sure the State of Louisiana proves its case against you beyond a reasonable doubt. They have to prove your guilt. I don't have to prove your innocence. All I need is one juror to agree with me. One in twelve. I'll take those odds any day."

"Straight out of the rule book, huh?" observed Manning.

"Were it not for those rules, Mr. Manning, you'd be swinging from a rope by now."

"So what's your plan, Mr. Public Defender?" asked Manning with a sarcastic tone. His experience with lawyers was not a good one. To Manning, lawyers were a bunch of lazy bastards more concerned with getting paid than defending clients. But Manning didn't know Percy was an enigma. He didn't know that Percy didn't care about money. Just fame.

"I don't know yet," Percy responded. "That all depends upon what you tell me and how honest you are with answering the questions I ask. Lying to me, Mr. Manning, will get you nowhere. Do you understand that?"

"Yeah."

"OK. So first, may I call you Wallis?"

"Sure."

"Good. You can call me Armand." Percy could see the smile on Manning's face at his name. Percy never understood why so many people thought his name was funny.

"So, *Armand*, what happens next?" asked Manning with a smile.

"Well, they've set bail at a million dollars and I suspect there is no way you can raise the cash for it," responded

Percy, knowing that clients of public defenders never do.

"So, I have to rot in this fuckin' hell hole until they get around to trying me?"

"I don't know that yet, either. That's why the first thing I'm going to do is file a motion to reduce your bail. How much can you afford to pay?"

"I ain't got a pot to piss in," replied Manning. "Maybe a couple of thousand bucks. And if I borrow from my sister, I can maybe raise $5,000 at the most."

"OK, that's a start. Five grand can cover about $50,000 in bail from a bondsman. So I can work with that."

"If I'm found innocent, do I get my money back?"

"No, Wallis, you do not. Whatever you pay for the bond is lost money. The bail bondsman keeps it. That's how he makes a living. But I suspect you know that. So please dispense with stupid questions. Ask me something important like whether I think I can get it lowered?"

"Think you'll win?" asked Manning, for the first time showing concern.

"Honestly, no," replied Percy. "We're sitting on five murder counts. But a bail hearing gives me a chance to learn more about the prosecutor's case."

"Figures," responded Manning with dejection in his voice. "And how soon will you try?"

"I'll file the motion tomorrow. Don't lose faith in the system yet, Wallis. No one knows how to work it better than I do. So let's get started, OK?"

He didn't bother to wait for an answer. It wasn't as though Manning had any choice.

"First, tell me about yourself. I want to know as much as possible. Where were you born? What were your parents like? How many siblings do you have? Where did you go to school and where do you work? Tell me that kind of stuff."

For the next hour, Manning told the story of his life to Percy. Born in Alabama, his parents moved the family around the South wherever his father, a preacher, could find a church, while his mother cleaned houses for extra cash. He and his sister were well cared for and he felt his childhood was, in his words, "like any kid's." He occasionally got into trouble in school for petty things that got a beating from his father on more occasions than he could recall. After high school, he enlisted in the Marines to get away. When discharged, he came to New Orleans and settled down. He had a few girlfriends, but nothing ever worked out. His parents were dead, and his sister lived in Baton Rouge. He was still close with her and enjoyed spending time with his two nieces. Manning thought his brother-in-law was a fine enough guy, but Manning had no real use for him.

"Interesting life you've led, Wallis. In truth, I suspect it was pretty boring except when you were in the Marines."

"Yeah, boring."

"OK, so let's get to the reason you were in the alley that night."

"Who says I was there?"

"Your DNA says you were, Wallis. So, unless someone planted it or it's capable of walking around on its own, which I seriously doubt, you were there. So don't bullshit me."

Manning stared at Percy for a few seconds and then confessed, "Yeah, I was there."

"And you touched the bodies, presumably to look for their wallets?"

"You're a regular Sherlock Holmes, *Armand*. Real genius." Manning's attitude did not sit well with Percy. For someone who was likely to end up on death row, Percy thought Manning had a very blasé attitude.

"Cut the crap with how you pronounce my name, Wallis. Do you understand that you're probably facing the death penalty if you get convicted?"

"I suppose," responded Manning, as if the potential consequences were no worse than a slap on the wrist. "How many of your clients have been executed, Armand?"

Percy thought for a few seconds and responded, "None. Yet."

Percy had two clients awaiting execution and he was doing everything he could to prevent that outcome with appeals. While his record was perfect so far, he knew that sooner or later he'd run out of appeals.

"So, I'll take those odds, Armand," replied Manning. "Just like you like the odds of convincing one out of twelve jurors."

"OK, Wallis, but you need to understand that you may

well get a death sentence, not that you 'suppose' you will. So, I need you to ditch the attitude and start answering my questions without all the bullshit. Unless, of course, you want to die. Some serial killers welcome death. Is that what you want, Wallis? 'Cause if it is, you can do this on your own."

"OK, OK." Manning held his hands up in surrender.

"Now why were you in the alley that night?"

"Because I got a text," responded Manning. That got Percy's attention.

"A text? On your phone?"

"Yeah."

"Who was it from?"

"I don't know. It didn't have a name."

"Did it have a number?"

"I suppose," responded Manning, then realized Percy looked angry again. "I mean I don't know much about how phones work."

"You don't text a lot?"

"Only sometimes with my sister."

"Where is your phone, Wallis?"

"I don't know, they took it from me."

CHAPTER FIFTEEN

DiMeglio was not one to back down when he smelled a case going in the wrong direction. Angered by Guidry's attitude, he dove deeper into the Manning investigation from public records and confidential information available to the FBI, including the suspect's military record. The more he looked into Manning, the more he was convinced that he was not a murderer. While he exhibited no remorse for the kills he had as a sniper, every personality test he took to become one didn't fit the profile of a serial killer. There was just too much missing. He decided to call the prosecutor, a move he knew was outside protocol, but DiMeglio was never known as one who played by the rules when it meant a killer might be caught. Or that the wrong man was charged with a crime he didn't commit.

"Ms. Gaudet, my name is Chris DiMeglio. I'm with the FBI."

"I'm aware who you are, Agent DiMeglio," responded Gaudet, "and I can guess what you're calling about. If all you want to do is tell me the same thing you told Superintendent Guidry, you're wasting your time and my time."

"Ms. Gaudet, I only ask that you listen to what I have to say. We're on the same side and no one wants to stop and solve the murders more than I do."

With an audible sigh, Gaudet responded, "OK, Agent DiMeglio, give it your best shot."

For the next hour, the two spoke about the evidence and the holes in it. DiMeglio also gave Gaudet a crash course on serial killers. The more she listened, the more concerned she was about her case.

"I also noticed Manning is being defended by Armand Percy," added DiMeglio.

"I see you do your homework, Agent DiMeglio," responded Gaudet. "And what is your point about Percy?"

"We both know he's as good as it gets. Maybe the best, at least in New Orleans. The stuff I've seen about him on YouTube makes me think I'm watching Matthew McConaughey, except with white hair."

Gaudet laughed and added, "Apparently *Lincoln Lawyer* is Percy's favorite movie. With his linen suits, fancy hat, and a southern accent as thick as molasses, Percy looks like an actor. Juries eat that stuff up."

"And rest assured they'll eat up every word he says about the holes in your case," responded DiMeglio. "You really need to face the possibility that you've got the wrong man or that you need to do a lot more work to plug the gaps."

"We've got excellent evidence, Agent DiMeglio, and we're filling those gaps. I have complete faith in our police captain and his team," Gaudet said.

"Yes. I'm sure you do. And you should. But that's not enough, and you know it. All you have is excellent evidence that Manning is a petty thief who took advantage of the situation when he found two dead bodies in an alley. That's the only good case you have. The rest is sheer speculation. In the hands of a guy like Percy, you're dead in the water."

"Not every jury believes Percy, Agent DiMeglio."

"No doubt. But think about it. If you do have the wrong man—as I believe you do—there's a killer out there planning his next murder. Your police department and detectives need to be looking for him, not waiting for a trial of an innocent man."

"So what are you recommending I do?"

That was the opening he needed.

"Let me come down and help in the investigation. If we turn up more evidence on Manning, so be it. It can only help your case. But let me look at the entire case. We can do two things at the same time. It's what I do, Harper. And I do it well. May I call you Harper? Please call me Chris." DiMeglio wanted to move away from formal ground to the familiarity of being on a first-name basis with Gaudet in hopes of more easily winning her over to his argument.

"OK, *Chris*, but do you have any idea how much shit I'll get from Guidry if I invite you into the case?"

"That depends on how you spin it with him, Harper. Even though we're not generally asked to help with murder investigations, it's relatively common to involve us in serial killer cases. We're experts. And we provide cover. So I have the distinct impression that he'll do anything he believes will help him to keep a political edge that ensures he keeps his job. I also understand that the mayor would like to see him go, and the press is all over him. Having friends at the FBI volunteering to be by his side in putting Manning—or whoever the killer is—in prison to die can only help him in a popularity contest."

DiMeglio assumed that the silence was Gaudet thinking about the proposition. He was right.

Finally, Gaudet spoke. "If I agree to this, you have to tell me everything. And Raleigh Broussard, too. He's in charge of the investigation. He's a good man. I want the two of us to know everything before anyone else does, and particularly before Guidry does."

"Agreed," DiMeglio said. "When can I start?"

"Give it a couple of days. I need time to explain it to Raleigh. He's not going to like it."

CHAPTER SIXTEEN

Broussard didn't take it well. Were it not for the relationship Gaudet had developed with him, it might have caused a fatal rift. But she assured Broussard that the investigation was his and that DiMeglio was there to help, not take over.

Broussard chose the Olde Nola Cookery on Bourbon Street for DiMeglio's first lunch in New Orleans. The long-established New Orleans eatery gave DiMeglio a taste, literally and figuratively, of New Orleans. The two were joined by Simone and Bundy.

The Cookery is casual, with simple chairs and wooden tables. Some outdoor seating among palm trees and a fire pit are also available in a courtyard in the back of the restaurant, a feature common to many French Quarter eateries. The four sat outside at one of the wooden tables with a top painted by a local artist. Every table had a different painting, DiMeglio noticed, and the walls of the restaurant—inside and out—showcased more paintings and metalwork by local artists.

"Beautiful place," the agent said. "So what should I order? I should make my first taste of New Orleans authentic. Right?"

"Try the Crawfish Etouffée or Blackened Bayou Duck,"

Broussard suggested. "Both are specialties of the house and thoroughly Cajun."

DiMeglio chose the Etouffée, a stew made of crawfish, onion, celery, and green pepper in a sauce on top of rice. Broussard ordered Cajun sausage with red beans and rice. Bundy ordered a shrimp Po Boy, a traditional New Orleans sandwich, and Simone chose a chef's salad with chicken.

"C'mon, Becca," Broussard chided. "Have something better than a fuckin' salad. You afraid of getting fat?"

"Captain," responded Simone with a sly smile, "I'm not the one here who should worry about getting fat."

"Ouch!" laughed Broussard.

Broussard turned his attention to their guest.

"Agent DiMeglio," he began. "While we appreciate your coming to work with us, you need to understand we do things here our own way. New Orleans is not Washington."

DiMeglio smiled. "Captain Broussard, I promise you I'm not here to tell you what to do. I just want to help. It's my job to work with local law enforcement in apprehending criminals. Particularly serial killers. I've studied their habits and traits since I first joined the Bureau."

"And you think we have a serial killer who murdered all the victims, Agent DiMeglio?" asked Simone.

"Based upon what I've looked at so far, I'd say yes. But we can't be sure until we find some connection between the killer and the victims, some common reason they were targeted, before I can be sure. Otherwise, it could just be a bunch of copycat killers. The fifth victim, Landes, was probably in the wrong place at the wrong time. Most likely a good Samaritan who got in the way of the killer."

"If that's what they teach you at the FBI, you're not going to be much of a help, Agent DiMeglio," Bundy said. "We already figured that out and don't need no fancy FBI agents to tell us how to do our job."

Broussard glared at Bundy. "Agent DiMeglio, please excuse the exuberance of our young Officer Bundy. He's a bit territorial. I'm sure he meant no disrespect. Right, Officer Bundy?"

"Sorry, Captain," responded a red-faced Bundy. "Agent DiMeglio, I was born and bred here in New Orleans and we can sometimes be a bit standoffish to outsiders. The captain is right, I meant no disrespect. Just a Cajun talkin' too much." That was as close to an apology as DiMeglio was going to get.

"No problem," replied DiMeglio.

"So how can we help you?" asked Simone.

"Mostly the ordinary. I've read some of the file, but I'd like to see all the evidence, of course. Probably interview some folks who might have information. The Voodoo priestess is one. And if possible, I'd like to interview Manning, too. While I'm not sure he'll cooperate, it's worth a try."

"But we interviewed him thoroughly. You can watch the video. What makes you think you'll learn anything we don't already know? And if you think his lawyer, Armand Percy, is going to let a federal agent anywhere near his client, you're nuts," Simone replied.

"I'm sure you covered everything, Detective Simone," DiMeglio responded. "But the more I learn about what he saw firsthand, the better I can do my job. I'm not questioning whether you were thorough or not. Just coming at it with a new set of eyes. I've interviewed a lot of serial killers and have some idea of how they think. I might see something new."

Simone smiled wryly. "We'll see if we can arrange it."

"But more important," continued DiMeglio, "I'd like to get a feel for New Orleans and the scene here. I'm staying at the Royal Sonesta so I could be in the middle of the French Quarter. The Bureau wasn't too happy with the cost but I convinced them I needed to immerse myself in the neighborhood. I've obviously read a lot about the city and the French Quarter, but seeing and knowing more firsthand will help me better understand the killer. I need to know more than what I've seen watching *CSI: New Orleans.*"

"I've lived here all my life," responded Bundy, "and I'm not sure I even understand the scene, Agent DiMeglio, but we'll do what we can."

"And by the way," added Simone, "it's *NCIS New Orleans.* If you want the real scene from TV, try *Pitbulls & Parolees.* That will give you the real flavor of the Bayou. You need to get your TV shows right if you're going to fit in here."

Turning to Simone and Bundy, Broussard interrupted

with his instructions.

"Detective Simone, show Agent DiMeglio the city. Officer Bundy, show him some of the seedier places where we seem to find most of our criminals."

"But Captain," objected Simone. "I can certainly join them. Just because I'm a woman doesn't mean I can't handle any place here. You know that."

"OK, Becca, if you'd like to join them, that's fine. But explain to me why you think some of the people in those places will be willing to talk to two men accompanied by a woman? I'm not trying to protect you, Becca. God knows you can do that all by yourself. I just want to make sure Agent DiMeglio gets what he needs most efficiently."

Simone nodded.

"Don't worry, Becca, there are some places I wouldn't dream of going into without you," laughed Bundy.

"Agent DiMeglio," Broussard continued, "we might have been a bit too anxious to arrest and charge Manning. But I remain convinced he's guilty and I'm honestly not sure what you'll add to our case."

"He may be the right man, Captain, but we can't be sure," responded DiMeglio. "So, let's continue to look at the evidence we have against him. And if he turns out to be guilty, then I'll be as happy as you in seeing him fry. But on the other hand, if he's innocent, we don't want to let the killer know we believe that just yet. We need some bait, and Mr. Manning may be our unwitting offering."

Broussard nodded with a smile. “Use Manning as bait? All right, then, I just might get to like you after all, Agent DiMeglio.”

“And how do you think we make him bait?” asked Simone.

“I have some ideas,” responded DiMeglio.

CHAPTER SEVENTEEN

"Your Honor, at this point in time, the State of Louisiana is withdrawing the charges against Wallis Manning without prejudice," announced Gaudet, knowing this would set the suspect free for the time being. But that's what DiMeglio suggested should be done so Manning could be watched on the streets, where he might make a wrong move. He was of no use to DiMeglio behind bars. At least not yet.

When Gaudet told Guidry she wanted DiMeglio to help build the case and confirm they'd arrested the right person before they went to trial, Guidry immediately saw an advantage for himself. He agreed to call in DiMeglio for help, making it clear to Gaudet that he'd take full credit for the idea, and she'd take responsibility if it didn't work. Gaudet didn't care. Her reelection prospects were enhanced by victories, not press conferences.

Judge Bertrand Enfield, a white, sixty-three-year-old trial judge now in his fourth six-year term, was well respected but hard on anyone charged with a crime. He was even harder on prosecutors who brought cases before him that needed to be dismissed for sloppy police work.

His courtroom was ornate. He liked it that way. The bench from which he ruled was elevated so he loomed over the courtroom like the Wizard in the *Wizard of Oz*. When he was first elected, he had modifications made that raised the bench five feet. He also had alterations made to the courtroom itself, including new dark wood benches for spectators and black leather chairs for jurors. He was known to carry a .45 Smith & Wesson under his robe. No one fooled around in his courtroom.

"Ms. Gaudet," Judge Enfield responded. "Can you explain to me why, after all the press I've been reading and the myriad allegations in your indictment, that the State of Louisiana has suddenly decided that the charges against Mr. Manning for multiple counts of first-degree murder should be dismissed?"

Gaudet could feel the pit of her stomach churn, knowing that Enfield would give her no slack.

"Your Honor, the State is not saying Mr. Manning is innocent. We're simply dismissing the charges at this time without prejudice. While we feel we have probative evidence, we feel we need more time to develop the case and do not believe it is reasonable to hold Mr. Manning in jail for what could be an extended period of time."

Under Louisiana law, a prosecutor may voluntarily dismiss a case without prejudice and seek another indictment on a later date. While unusual, it is generally invoked when a prosecutor believes that the State may have other, more serious charges to bring or if it believes it is simply not ready for trial. In other words, it needs more time. The problem, however, is that a criminal defendant has a constitutional right to a speedy trial, so the prosecution cannot simply drag a matter along while a person sits in jail and the State does investigative work to better prepare a case. So, when the State is not ready, as Gaudet had to concede was the case with Manning, a prosecutor requests delays or, in the worst-case scenario, permission to dismiss the case without prejudice, which allows the suspect to go free until new charges are brought. If a trial jury hasn't been assigned or a witness called, it's not double jeopardy, and the defendant can be recharged at a later date.

"And you trust Mr. Manning will stick around while you try to find a better case against him than you already have?" sarcastically asked Enfield.

Letting Manning back out on the streets was risky. There had been no murders since he was arrested. DiMeglio was quick to point out that lulls in murders when serial killers saw someone else arrested wasn't unusual. Serial killers often lay low in such times, hoping to learn more about what the police might have on them. But the main reason Gaudet asked for a dismissal was because she suspected she very well may have the wrong man and she agreed with DiMeglio's plan to watch Manning once released. Her conscience didn't let her keep a man under the cloud of a murder conviction when she had doubts as deep as she did about Manning. Increasingly, she also knew that others, including Broussard, shared her concerns.

"We will keep him under reasonable surveillance, Your

Honor," responded Gaudet. "It is a risk we are prepared to take." She silently hoped Broussard's promise not to let Manning out of his sight would work.

"Let me get this straight, Ms. Gaudet," continued Enfield. "Despite the fact that your indictment claims to have secured the defendant's DNA at the scene of the crime and recovered additional incriminating evidence at his residence, you believe you have an insufficient basis to proceed further at this time and you want to let Mr. Manning, a potential murderer, run free in our streets?"

Armand Percy, Manning's public defender, rose and addressed Enfield. "Your Honor, if Ms. Gaudet is not prepared to proceed, then I ask this court to dismiss the charges with prejudice. It is a complete abuse of Mr. Manning's constitutional rights to have this continue to hang over his head."

"Mr. Percy . . ." Enfield turned his glare toward the public defender, not holding back his long-held disdain for Percy and his histrionics. "Counselor, I don't recall asking you for your opinion. Please sit down and be quiet until I call on you. Your job is not to interrupt me but to do your best to get the charges against Manning dismissed with prejudice. Your problem is that it is solely my decision. So as much as you'd love to turn this into a front-page article, I can assure you that will not happen in my courtroom." Percy sat down.

Turning back to Gaudet, Enfield asked, "Just how long does the State need to be ready for trial?"

Gaudet hesitated. She could not give Enfield a precise time. There were simply too many loose ends and open questions, many of which she did not want to disclose to Enfield, much less Percy.

"I'm unsure, Your Honor," Gaudet said, deciding the truth was the only way to go with Enfield to avoid his wrath.

The judge turned to Percy. "OK, Mr. Percy, give it your best shot, but be careful to stay within bounds."

Percy smiled as he rose. He stood tall, confident, and completely unintimidated by Judge Enfield.

"Thank you, Your Honor," Percy began. "While I understand Ms. Gaudet's dilemma, the State brought it all upon itself by hastily charging my client, Wallis Manning, for crimes he did not commit."

"Last I looked, Mr. Percy, you are not in a position to determine the guilt or innocence of Mr. Manning. That's my and the jury's job. And we don't have a jury yet." Enfield glanced surreptitiously at members of the press sitting in the back of the courtroom. He wanted to avoid opening a door to Percy's manipulation.

"That's unfortunate, Your Honor. Because I have no doubt I'd do a fine job if I made such decisions," retorted Percy. There were a few snickers from the audience. Percy smiled even more broadly.

"That's enough showmanship, Mr. Percy. Get to the facts that support your request that the charges be dismissed with prejudice. I'd like to understand why your client would be unfairly treated if the State put this all off to another day when it's ready."

"I beg the court's indulgence, Your Honor," Percy persisted, "but last I looked, the Sixth Amendment, the one that guarantees someone charged with a crime a speedy trial, is not served if the State can turn such charges on and off on a whim when they're not prepared to proceed. Your Honor denied my client bail, and he has already sat in jail for nearly two months while the State played its games. And so far, all I've seen is a lot of circumstantial evidence and very questionable DNA procedures."

"Whether the State has a good case or not is insufficient basis upon which I'm prepared to dismiss the charges with prejudice. From where I'm sitting and based upon what I read, there is ample evidence to proceed and put the State to its proof. If you disagree, you'll have to do better than you've done so far. And I would also caution you not to lecture me on constitutional rights."

"Forgive me, Your Honor. I just wanted to be sure the court had not lost sight of my client's constitutional rights," Percy said, bowing his head slightly.

"Mr. Percy, you are trying my patience. As usual. So, unless you have something enlightening to add, I will make my ruling."

"I have nothing further to add at this time, Your Honor," responded Percy. "But I do reserve my right to comment further depending upon the Court's decision."

"I have no doubt, Mr. Percy," responded Enfield, "that you will have lots to say, particularly when the press is present, as you apparently made sure was the case today."

Percy began to speak again with an air of objecting to the insult.

"Sit, Mr. Percy!" ordered Enfield, as if he was commanding a dog. Percy sat.

Enfield continued, "I am going to deny the State's motion to dismiss. Instead, I am going to give the state ninety days within which to either proceed or face a dismissal with prejudice."

Enfield turned his gaze to Gaudet as she rose and said, "Thank you, your Honor." She knew better than to argue with the judge. He'd made his decision and nothing Gaudet could say would change his mind. She sat down.

"Your Honor," Percy said as he rose, "I object."

"You object, Mr. Percy? I'm so surprised," responded Enfield with a smile. "And once again, you choose to speak before spoken to. You really need to work on that, Mr. Percy. Now sit back down again. I'm not finished." Percy retook his seat, intentionally doing so with a theatrical huff intended to impress the reporters.

"As for the continued incarceration of Mr. Manning, I also find it would be unfair to keep him behind bars because the State is not ready. As such, I am reversing my earlier decision denying him bail and now release him on his own recognizance. No doubt you like that part, Mr. Percy." Percy rose, getting ready to speak.

"Before you speak, Mr. Percy, there's more, so sit down," continued Enfield, turning his gaze to Manning. Gaudet heard a reporter say that Percy was like a jack-in-the-box, popping up only to be put back down and wound up to try again. She delighted in the image.

Addressing Manning directly, Enfield continued, "I will assume you understand that I have not dismissed the charges against you and that you are still a defendant in a capital murder case. The fact that I am releasing you on your own recognizance should not give you any impression that I believe you are innocent. At this time, I have no opinion on whether you are guilty or innocent. In the end, that will be for a jury to determine, not me, nor Ms. Gaudet and, most certainly, not Mr. Percy. Do you understand that?"

"Yes, sir," answered Manning, rising from his seat.

"OK. You can sit down. Now for the conditions of your release," continued Enfield. "First, you may not leave New Orleans without this court's permission, which you are highly unlikely to get. You will turn in your passport, assuming you have one, over to the bailiff. You will wear an ankle bracelet so we can track your whereabouts at all times. If you try to disengage it, you'll immediately be arrested and go back to jail, where you will sit until trial. You will see a court-appointed officer every day. It will be up to him or her if they want you physically in front of them or whether they'll let you call them. You can work that out. If you want to leave your house for any reason, you will call the court officer. And any reason needs to be related to your health or well-being. Or a job. In other words, you're not going to any bars or out on dinner dates. If you need to see a doctor, that's a good reason. If you want to take a stroll in the park, that's not likely going to happen. For all intents and purposes, Mr. Manning, you are under house arrest. Do you understand these limitations, Mr. Manning?"

"Yes, sir," Manning repeated.

Turning to Percy, he added, "And, Mr. Percy, I suggest the only thing that should come out of your mouth now is 'Thank you, Your Honor.'"

Percy gave Enfield a disapproving look and said, without rising, "Thank you, Your Honor."

Manning was released that afternoon and returned to the streets of New Orleans. Or at least to his house, assuming the NOPD could keep him inside.

CHAPTER EIGHTEEN

Wallis Manning stumbled into Percy's office, his right arm still in a cast from a beating his fellow prisoners gave him, a sort of going away present. He was late, as had been his routine during the month since his release from jail. The booze on his breath reached Percy the moment Wallis sat down across from him.

"You're late again, Wallis," Percy said. "And you've been drinking. Again."

"Yeah, so?"

"Look, Wallis, I want to help you. There are some gaping holes in the State's case, but I need your help in figuring them out. If you're not going to be serious about this, then I'm not going to waste my time."

"Sure. I'll help. Why not? I've got no fuckin' life. The press is hounding me. They're camped outside my apartment all day. I can't get a job. Soon, I won't have any money to pay my rent. So, what am I supposed to do, live in the street? Don't suppose I'll be much use to you there, Armand."

Percy had a soft spot for people who were given the short end of the DNA stick and ignored by society. It was no wonder so many of them resorted to crime. It was as if the environment gave them no choice. But whatever sympathy he had, if Manning was a serial killer, Percy would rather see him rot in some prison awaiting an injection. But he was convinced that Manning was not the Bayou Slasher. To prove that, he needed to find as many missing elements in the State's case as he could. For that, he needed Manning's help.

"Don't worry about being homeless, Wallis," continued Percy. "We'll work something out. And did you register for welfare assistance like I told you to?"

"No. I ain't no beggar," responded Manning.

"Jesus, Wallis, cut the crap. Look at it this way. You've paid taxes your entire life. The government did nothing for you when you left the Marines. Think of welfare as a payback you've earned and are owed. It's not a handout to someone who contributed for as many years as you did."

Percy could see his words had an impact.

"Look, Wallis, I see no difference between those who contributed with their taxes and those who never did when it comes to getting welfare. I only care you get some semblance of dignity, because a trial is going to weigh heavily on you. I need you in a decent frame of mind."

Manning shifted in the chair, rubbing his hand below the cast on his arm.

"So how's the arm, Wallis?" Percy asked.

"Shitty," responded Manning. "Hurts all the time. The jailhouse doctors did a lousy job. They didn't care. I was leavin' and all they wanted to do was get rid of me."

"When does the cast come off?"

"I'm told in two weeks. I don't know."

"Tell you what," Percy said. "I'm going to make you an appointment with a doctor I know who will take a look. It shouldn't be hurting at this point."

"I can't pay no doctor."

"Don't worry about that, Wallis."

For the next hour, Percy and Manning went through what they had. DNA at the crime scene. That made sense. Manning admitted he was there. A knife found in his apartment. Manning claimed it wasn't his and had no idea how it was found in his apartment. Same thing with the crosses. The chicken-foot necklace was his but was just a silly trinket Manning stole in the Quarter.

Percy could deal with the DNA evidence. No one was better than Percy in attacking DNA experts. As much of a science the public might think DNA matching is, creating doubt in a juror's mind was not that difficult. O.J. Simpson proved that. The science was so complicated that many jurors, when told about it, came to the conclusion that it was fake science. Just too impossible to believe. And Percy always found mistakes by the police. If the initial officers at the crime scene didn't tamper with evidence, the crime lab might have. He could always find mistakes. So even though the DNA evidence was powerful, it did not daunt Percy.

But the mystery around the cell phone was troubling.

"Wallis, let's get to the cell phone," continued Percy. "You say you got a text telling you to go to the crime scene."

"Yeah, it said 'opportunity knocks.'"

"Right. But you don't know who it came from?"

"No, like I said, it didn't come with no name. Just a number. And I don't remember the number."

"Or you just happened to be there and took advantage of the moment and never received a text," suggested Percy.

Manning stared at him, silent.

"Well, the problem is there is no text saying 'opportunity knocks' on your phone, Wallis. We recovered it from the evidence room and saw no texts at all that night. We saw some the week before and a couple the next day to your sister, but nothing else. Can you explain that?"

"No. All I know is I got the text. Someone must have erased it."

"Indeed. That might explain it, right?" Percy said, doubtfully. "Assuming you're telling the truth, and I want to believe you are, someone did delete it. But who?"

"Had to be the cops. They're the ones who took the phone from me when I was taken in."

"That's what I think, too. And that is something we need to look into."

"The good news," Percy continued, "is that a text is never really deleted. They're all stored by the telephone company in the cloud. So, if such a text exists, we'll find it and bust the New Orleans police department wide open." Percy leaned back, grinning. The thought of tying an overzealous police department to trying to find a dupe to charge for a crime was enticing. He could stick it to Harper Gaudet, someone he felt was in way over her head and just another New Orleans political hack.

But Manning was shaking his head.

"What's the problem? I've asked Verizon for the backup and should have it any day. So that will tell us when you got the text, what it said, and the number it was sent from. From there, I can get a name. It's the key to our defense, and once we have it, it's the key to your freedom."

"If someone erased it, you ain't gonna find it," Manning said. "I use Signal for my texts. It's got some kinda security on it that stops hacking unless you have one of the phones that still has a copy of the text on it. If the text I got was erased, that's a dead end. You need to find the phone used to send it. But chances are, that's a burner phone. So it won't be easy to trace to the owner."

Percy's excitement deflated. How did this drunk know so much about encryption? "Shit, that is a dead end," he agreed. "How'd you know about Signal?"

"Military uses it," Manning explained. "That's where I heard of it. All of the snipers used it. Kept our messages secret. I've used it for years now."

Percy would look into what Wallis told him and learn that Signal, a texting program that encrypts messages end to end was indeed impossible to reconstruct on a cell phone on which it had been deleted. Signal was growing in popularity among people fearful of having their privacy invaded by the government and was particularly popular among conspiracy theorists. It was also used in the intelligence and military communities, where hacking was a legitimate concern. Other groups who loved it were criminals. It let them traffic in illicit communications with relative immunity so long as the phones were secure or destroyed when convenient. The expression "burner phone" arose just for that reason. Use it and burn it. No trace for police.

"Well, that makes everything a lot harder," Percy sighed.

"Find the other phone," Manning pleaded, "and you find the Bayou Slasher."

CHAPTER NINETEEN

DiMeglio assembled the entire investigative team in the briefing room. He knew he was an outsider but also knew he'd get nowhere with them if he didn't show he was qualified to do the job. He didn't expect to win over Bundy, but he needed allies, including Broussard and Simone.

"So, what do we conclude about serial killers?" asked DiMeglio, as if he were teaching a class.

Not waiting for an answer, he continued, "First and foremost, they lack remorse or guilt. To them, what they're doing is justified. Their reasons may be insane, but their insanity is their solace in committing murder. In fact, most of them feel compelled to kill."

Bundy was taking notes, as were most of the officers in the room. Simone was listening.

"They're also smooth talkers but insincere. Listen to them closely. Like I said, smooth talking but insincere." DiMeglio wanted to be sure that sank in. "Unlike just about anyone else, they can hide their true emotions. Take Ted Bundy, for example." The smiles in the room were widespread as heads turned to look at Officer Bundy. DiMeglio wanted that, hoping it would lighten the moment at Bundy's expense.

"Ted Bundy looked the role of a real charmer," DiMeglio

continued. "A real ladies' man. He had no problem talking beautiful women who ought to know better into getting into the car of someone they'd just met. That takes a strong personality."

"I guess that rules you out, Bundy," Officer Smitty Evans laughed. His colleagues joined in.

Bundy frowned. "I can assure you, Evans, that if it was me, you'd be my next victim."

DiMeglio continued, "And they have egos that don't stop. We often see that in the grandiose way they describe their lives. Manson was a good example. He quite literally thought of himself as some sort of god."

"That makes Superintendent Guidry a suspect," Evans again said with a smile. "He's got the biggest ego I know!" The room erupted in laughter.

DiMeglio decided the joking had gone far enough. He needed to reassert his control.

"So, Officer Evans," DiMeglio said, "you find this humorous?"

"No, sir. Sorry." Evans looked back down at his notes, his face reddening.

"They also like to brag," DiMeglio continued. "They brag about their victims. Or how the police are inept because they can't capture them." That caused some officers to look up from their notebooks. DiMeglio knew they were all unhappy with an outsider like him interfering with an investigation they felt was under control, even if the killer had not yet been found. They didn't appreciate criticism, implied or otherwise.

DiMeglio decided to move on.

"Let me read you something Jack the Ripper wrote to the local press on September 27, 1888."

DiMeglio picked up a piece of paper from the podium and began to read.

> Dear Boss: I keep on hearing the police have caught me but they won't fix me just yet. I have laughed when they look so clever and talk about being on the right track. That joke about Leather Apron gave me real fits. I am down on whores and I shan't quit ripping them till I do get buckled. Grand work the last job was. I gave the lady no time to squeal. How can they catch me now? I love my work and want to start again. You will soon hear of me with my funny little games. I saved some of the proper red stuff in a ginger beer bottle over the last job to write with but it went thick like glue and I can't use it. Red ink is fit enough I hope. The next job I do I shall clip the lady's ears off and send to the police officers. My knife's so nice and sharp I want to get to work right away if I get a chance. Good luck.

"Now that's in your face, huh?" added DiMeglio.

No one responded.

DiMeglio moved on. "Let's continue. Serial killers are also deceitful and manipulative. How else do they do such a good job of conning so many people?"

He could see the officers thinking, fixing in their minds the faces of suspects who might fit the profile he was building.

"But worst of all, the best serial killers are impulsive and truly enjoy what they do. They're driven by a need to feel fulfilled by killing what we would consider innocent people. They fail to see their victims as innocent and honestly believe they are getting what they deserve. We see that most acutely among serial killers who target prostitutes, killing them because of what they consider to be the immoral ways their victims lead their lives. It's exciting for them to kill. It actually gives them sexual gratification even if they don't get laid. Son of Sam used to kill and then go home and masturbate."

"But we're not talking about dead prostitutes, Agency DiMeglio," offered Bundy. "These were well-respected people in the city."

"Precisely, Officer Bundy. That is what makes this case so interesting. But there has to be some connection between the victims. There almost always is with serial killers. They need a reason to kill. Otherwise, they won't get the gratification they need. So, since prostitutes are not involved and it's a mix of several men and a woman, we can probably omit sexual gratification as a motive. It just doesn't fit," concluded DiMeglio.

"Then what does fit?" asked Evans.

"Our killer, Officer Evans, is killing for a reason. Once we figure that out, we'll be well on our way to finding him. That's why we need to discover the connection among the victims. It's there. We just haven't seen it yet."

"So, if we compare him with other killers, we can eliminate reasons that way as well," another officer called out.

"Precisely," DiMeglio said, pleased. "So, we can also eliminate sociopaths who kill and eat their victims. Serial killers like Jeffrey Dahmer."

"And that gets us closer to the killer?" asked Bundy.

"Every time we eliminate a motive, Officer Bundy, we get closer to the truth," responded DiMeglio.

"So where do we go next?" asked Evans.

"We first need to find the connections between the victims. Then we need to look at suspects who display antisocial behavior toward people with those connections. It could be a result of abuse when they were young. We find that in many serial killers. Or it could be something else that triggered them in their lives. Many serial killers driven by religious beliefs fall in that category."

"Like Voodoo?" offered Evans.

"Yes," responded DiMeglio. "That's one motive we have not eliminated."

But that was enough for his first day.

"Let's all start thinking about possible connections. Or things we can eliminate. We can get back at it tomorrow."

DiMeglio planned to assemble everyone before the whiteboards again the next day to go through everything. Again. And again. There had to be a connection. He intended to find it.

CHAPTER TWENTY

"This discovery request is outrageous, Your Honor," began Gaudet at a hearing in Enfield's chambers, equally ornate as his courtroom.

Percy had asked for the personal cell phone of every police officer who handled Manning's phone from the time of his apprehension to the time the phone was turned over to Percy for inspection. His motion, filed under seal so no one on the police force would know about it, was unprecedented.

Enfield turned to Percy, looking forward to his response. The idea clearly fascinated the judge.

"Your Honor," Percy began, "my client claims he received a text that gave him the location of the crime scene with the message 'opportunity knocks.' Yet when we looked at his phone, no such message was found. If there was one, it was deleted. And unfortunately, the defendant uses a messaging service that cannot retrieve deleted messages. So the only way we can determine if our suspicion that the New Orleans Police Department is trying to frame Mr. Manning is correct is to get access to their cell phones." While Percy knew that the likelihood of a bad cop being stupid enough to use his own cell phone and not a burner was poor, Percy had seen as many stupid cops as he'd seen stupid defendants. As he liked to say, quoting Forrest Gump, "Stupid is as stupid does."

"And the Tooth Fairy may have left some clues under the pillows of the police officers as well," interjected Gaudet. "Would Mr. Percy like to look through their linens, too?"

Enfield remained silent and let Percy and Gaudet go at it. He looked at one, and then the other, like a fan at a tennis match. After a dull morning of arraignments and defendants pleading innocence, this back-and-forth was delightfully entertaining.

"Your Honor, Ms. Gaudet may like to treat this as frivolous, but I assure you it is not. My client has been charged with killing five people in what the press is calling one of New Orleans's worst serial killing sprees. He deserves to look at whatever evidence is available."

Enfield turned his gaze to Gaudet. "OK, your turn."

"Your Honor, even the most permissive court would refuse to allow Mr. Percy to chase such speculation. If you were to allow this, then every insane theory his client might come up with to put the blame on someone else will be yet another frivolous request for evidence that does not exist."

Enfield turned to Percy. "Mr. Percy?"

For just a moment, Percy hesitated, expecting Enfield to come down hard against him. But the judge raised his eyebrows and nodded, encouraging him. He hid his surprise and answered, "I don't deny this request is a bit out of the ordinary, Your Honor. But so is this case. The court should allow me to go down some unordinary paths."

"More like extraordinary, Mr. Percy," replied Enfield. "But interesting." Enfield wanted the show to continue.

"Unordinary or extraordinary, Your Honor, I believe my request is consistent with affording Mr. Manning a fair defense," argued Percy.

Gaudet looked fit to be tied. "Your Honor, haven't we had enough of this? The request to invade the privacy of officers of the New Orleans Police Department on some cockamamy theory is ludicrous. Can't we put an end to this foolish pursuit so that we can all get back to the serious business at hand?"

Enfield took a breath, and nodded at Gaudet. He liked her and thought she had potential to be a good prosecutor. He knew he shouldn't push her too hard. But he agreed in a way with some of what Percy said.

"I must admit," Enfield began, "this is an unprecedented request, at least in my experience as a judge. And I would generally dismiss it as fishing in an empty pond. But as hard as it is for me to say it, Ms. Gaudet, Mr. Percy has made an interesting argument."

Percy took the insult as a compliment.

"That said," Enfield continued, "I am concerned about the privacy of the officers. What they say in their texts is their business and no one else's. So, Mr. Percy, assuming I grant you this request, how will you ensure the privacy of the officers?"

"To be honest, Your Honor, I had not given the privacy

issue much thought," Percy truthfully replied. "I will of course guard their privacy."

Gaudet jumped up, and began angrily pacing around the room, stopping behind her chair with her hands on the backrest. "Your Honor, there is simply no way the State can condone a public defender, much less Mr. Percy, being given access to the private conversations of police officers. They may not only contain information that is no one's business but might also have discussions about active investigations. None of that can be shown to anyone under *any* circumstances."

"Good point, Ms. Gaudet," Enfield replied. "But you need to control your emotions when you are in my chambers or my courtroom. So sit down."

"Sorry, Your Honor," Gaudet said. She sat down, but still scowled at Percy.

Enfield turned to Percy. "Mr. Percy, any thoughts?"

Percy wasn't sure his idea would work, but it was worth a try.

"Yes, Your Honor," Percy answered. "I suggest you alone examine the phones in camera. I can give you the approximate time, and what my client claims the text read. You can easily go to the date and check. If you find nothing, then we're finished with this request. If you find such a text, then you can admit it into evidence."

Gaudet was now nearly apoplectic. Heeding the judge's warning to her, she tried to sound calm, but her voice shook with fury. "Again, Your Honor, I have to object. While I certainly respect your integrity, you too cannot be permitted to inadvertently see matters relating to ongoing investigations or communications of a personal nature. It just can't be permitted. It might raise objections in future cases that you must recuse yourself." Exhausted, Gaudet leaned back in her seat.

Enfield knew Gaudet was right. As much as he believed the New Orleans Police Department had too many corrupt cops that he'd love to see outed, he realized that as novel as the request was, he could not grant it.

Percy saw what was coming. Frankly, he had expected it.

"Mr. Percy, as much as I'd like to grant your request, the phones of the New Orleans police officers are not relevant evidence in this matter on what is only speculation on your part. Nor can I allow you to go on a fishing expedition simply because your client has made an accusation that so far is unfounded. There is no evidence to support it. So, I am denying your motion. If you get better evidence in the future, you may renew the motion."

Percy knew he'd tried his best and actually got further than he thought he would. "Thank you, Your Honor." But he wasn't done. "I have only one request."

"I can't wait to hear it. OK, Mr. Percy, what would you like?"

"Because Your Honor will permit me to refile my motion at a later date, I request a court order directed to

Ms. Gaudet and the New Orleans Police Department that no one is to erase anything from their cell phones until this case is resolved. If any officer who might be involved used the encryption app that Mr. Manning uses, any text deleted can never be retrieved."

"I thought everything was backed up," responded Enright.

"Me too," replied Percy. "Until Mr. Manning explained to me that there are certain texting applications that are totally secure and cannot be hacked without possession of one of the two phones with the message intact."

"Really?" asked Enfield. "I'll have to look into that for myself."

"I've already started using it, Your Honor," replied Percy.

Enfield sat quietly, thinking. He then addressed Ms. Gaudet.

"I am not going to issue such an order, Ms. Gaudet. Assuming Mr. Percy is correct, and an officer could delete a text once he or she heard of the order and it would never be discovered, then my order is meaningless. And chances are, if such a text exists on an officer's phone, they already erased it. I will not issue a meaningless order. I strongly caution you, however, that if Mr. Percy later renews his motion with sufficient support, I will hold you personally responsible if we discover any tampering by your officers. Is that clear, Ms. Gaudet?"

Gaudet stayed in her chair as much out of contempt for the game Enfield was playing as she was just too spent to get up. "Your warning is clear, Your Honor, but entirely unreasonable. I cannot babysit my officers. Nor can I monitor their cell phone use. Making this my responsibility is not reasonable."

"Perhaps not, Ms. Gaudet. But it is my right to hold those I believe are responsible in matters before this court. And as I see it, you have responsibility for any officers who tamper with evidence you might owe the defense. It is your right to appeal my decision should disciplinary action be undertaken against you."

He turned to Percy. "Anything further, Mr. Percy?"

"No, Your Honor."

"Ms. Gaudet?"

"No, Your Honor."

"Then this hearing is adjourned."

CHAPTER TWENTY-ONE

"OK," began DiMeglio, "let's take another look at the whiteboard." It was 3 in the afternoon—the hour when the crowds on Royal and Bourbon began to build.

The whiteboard with all the victims' names hung on one wall, and a blank one hung on another. DiMeglio had already spent the better part of the day looking through the evidence files. He also pinned some posters to the walls with pithy sayings about police work and believing in success. He knew they were hokey, but he always believed that there was wisdom in every cliché, however hackneyed it might be. He had many hanging in his office. Among his favorites were "People sleep peacefully in their beds at night only because rough men stand ready to do violence on their behalf," attributed to George Orwell, and "When you think about quitting, remember why you started," author unknown. Also, from Michael Jordan, "I've missed more than 9,000 shots in my career. I've lost almost 300 games. Twenty-six times I've been trusted to make the game-winning shot and missed. I've failed over and over again in my life. And that is why I succeed."

DiMeglio knew that Simone and Bundy's investigation into the murders would never pass FBI muster, but he knew better than to say so. He still needed them to cooperate and see him as an ally before he decided where fault for a shoddy investigation lay. If he'd learned anything as an FBI liaison with local police departments, it was how poorly most were trained in complex investigations. He suspected this case was no different.

Sitting in the conference room set aside as the investigation war room, DiMeglio stood before a task force that now had twelve officers assigned to it full-time. That impressed him, since he rarely saw that many policemen dedicated to a single investigation. It gave him hope that the odds were in favor of one of them finding the killer.

"So let's start out with the obvious similarities among the victims," began DiMeglio. "And remember, everything is fair game. So, every suggestion is a good one, regardless of how obvious or idiotic you think it might be."

DiMeglio pointed to one of the officers. "What do you see?"

The officer, caught off guard, looked around like a kid in a class called on for an answer. DiMeglio could see his apprehension.

"Look, everyone, this is not a test. It's a process where no one fails and every contribution is appreciated. And important. Play this through and I assure you you'll understand why."

"They're all white?" asked the officer. DiMeglio could see derision in the expressions on the face of the other officers. It wasn't exactly the most profound of observations. That didn't matter to DiMeglio. The process was one step at a time and every step, no matter how obvious, was important.

"Good," responded DiMeglio as he wrote "White" on the clean whiteboard. He pointed to the next officer.

"They all live in New Orleans," she volunteered.

DiMeglio wrote "Locals" on the whiteboard.

The interchange went on for more than an hour. By its end, the officers had compiled a long list.

Commonalities among the victims:

- White
- Locals for years
- Born outside Louisiana
- Young
- Liked by others
- No criminal records
- No scandals
- Heterosexual
- No sexual assault
- No signs of resistance
- Ritualistic Voodoo symbols
- Slit throats
- No evidence of robbery except at the killing of Landes and Walsh

Commonalities among the crime scenes:

- All but one in the Quarter
- All in alleys or unlit parking lots
- No DNA except at one crime scene
- No witnesses yet located
- Nothing on city cameras

Uncommon items:

- One victim—George Landes—bore no Voodoo markings
- One woman
- Jobs varied significantly

"This isn't telling us anything," offered Bundy, frustration in his voice. "Sorry, Chris, but I don't see where the list leads us. We need to be on the street squeezing our CIs and doing the basics."

"And what has that gotten you so far, Joe?" asked DiMeglio. "You've been doing the basics, as you like to call them, for well over three months. You've been pushing your CIs, all to no avail. I don't object to pushing them more, but the killer is still killing, no doubt planning his next murder as we speak."

Confidential informants, known as CIs, are losers that cops develop to get the inside scoop on what is happening in the criminal world. The officers usually have something on the CI and use it as a threat that if they don't cooperate with the police and become an informant, they go to jail. Most often, it starts out with a simple piece of information. As it escalates and gets riskier, a CI sometimes wants out. That's when the cops pull in the line and tell the CI that if they quit, the word will go out that they were an informant. Once the street learns that, the CI is as good as dead. So once hooked, a CI is a cop's property. Developing CIs is an ugly but necessary process to keep cities like New Orleans safer.

"I understand that cases aren't solved overnight, Chris," replied Bundy. "We keep pushing, but I feel we're getting nowhere. I still say we have our killer. Why are we wasting our time chasing windmills? Let's build a better case against Manning."

"Your right, Joe," responded DiMeglio. "Crimes are not solved overnight. Particularly serial killers. But unlike most cases, where the victim knows the killer or has talked to someone about them, serial killers are outside that mold. They're loners. I have yet to see a case where a confidential informant gave us a tip worth shit. Don't get me wrong, we followed up every one of them. But in the end, what caught the killer was figuring out why he was killing and where he'd likely strike next."

"And you don't think Manning is the killer?" asked Bundy.

"I have my doubts, Joe. But if we have the wrong man,

then we need to know how to stop the killer from adding another victim."

"We know where he'll strike," offered another officer in the room. "In the Quarter."

"You're probably right," responded DiMeglio. "That's why we're beefing up patrols. It will either deter him and save a life or, in the worst case, challenge him to beat us at the game and strike under our noses."

"Or move somewhere else," suggested Simone.

"It's true that serial killers often move. But this one strikes me as a killer who wants to stay local."

"Like Son of Sam," another officer said.

"Right, like Son of Sam," replied DiMeglio. "Every one of his kills was in a borough of New York City."

CHAPTER TWENTY-TWO

At the end of DiMeglio's first week on the job, Simone had offered to take him to a traditional breakfast spot in the Quarter. Now she was delivering on her offer.

DiMeglio was waiting for her outside the Royal Sonesta entrance, dressed in a pair of jeans and a light tan linen shirt to keep cool. Simone, ever the detective, was wearing her usual conservative pantsuit, a look DiMeglio had come to expect.

"My, my, Chris, you look so casual," commented Simone.

"It's Saturday. We are allowed to relax every once in a while, even at the FBI. But it looks like the NOPD doesn't share that view." He smiled.

"Always on duty, Chris. Always on duty."

As they began their stroll down Bourbon Street, DiMeglio said, "So tell me more about the restaurant and bar scene here in New Orleans."

"It's pretty much what you see. We have our typical split between locals and tourists, even in the French Quarter. It's expensive to live here, so the homeowners and renters tend to be reasonably well-heeled. That's sometimes a problem when the kids from rich families up north come down here on spring break or Mardi Gras to celebrate. They get drunk and act like idiots all too often. And now we're seeing a lot more drugs, too."

"I want to know more about other parts of town," responded DiMeglio. "Local neighborhoods. It's likely the killer came from one of those areas."

"If you're rich and still want the French Quarter feel, you live in the Garden District. Otherwise, neighborhoods are mostly locals except around Tulane and LSU. That's where you'll find a lot of student bars and hangouts. Your typical college crap with kids acting stupid at times. But the real crime is here in the Quarter and in the 9th Ward, where we're still trying to dig out of Hurricane Katrina. Some parts of the city just can't seem to bounce back, particularly the 9th Ward, our poorest part of town. And Ida didn't help with all the damage it caused. The poverty and slow rebuilding continues to attract the problems."

"Slums will often attract crime," suggested DiMeglio.

"Perhaps where you come from, Chris. But New Orleans doesn't have slums like you see in DC or New York. We're a proud people here, and while we've got our share of poverty and run-down neighborhoods, there's a lot of brotherhood and sisterhood here. We care about one another. It's the Cajun way to reach out and help without waiting to be asked."

"I meant no insult, Becca. That's why I'm trying to learn more about the city. Crimes that are done by killers are sometimes easier to explain in a violent city, where major neighborhoods are controlled by gangs and drug dealers. They're breeding grounds for crime that spills over into the rest of the city. If you want to see it firsthand, just visit Chicago or Philadelphia."

Simone came to a stop and announced, "Here we are, the Café Beignet." She guided him into a courtyard lined with trees and accented with paintings and mosaics by local artisans. "It's like an oasis," she said. "The courtyard is a perfect spot to start the day and do some people watching. That's one of the things you need to learn to do here, Chris. Relax and watch people."

As they walked to a metal table with matching chairs, they passed life-size bronze statues celebrating New Orleans music legends Al Hirt, Fats Domino, and Pete Fountain. DiMeglio found the chairs a bit uncomfortable, but he didn't complain. The atmosphere of the café delighted him. The more DiMeglio saw of New Orleans, the more he liked it. The city was art in itself with architecture, music, and crazy characters. The entire lifestyle appealed to him in contrast to the never-ending pressures of Washington and its armies of backstabbers looking to trample anyone on their way to the top. And the mysterious nature of New Orleans' past, strewn with tales of Voodoo and vampires, only made it more appealing. But most of all, people in New Orleans seemed genuinely happy just to get along.

The first thing that struck DiMeglio was the aroma of the coffee and pastries. The mouthwatering smells brought back his best memories of childhood treats when his mother made pies and other confections on holidays and special occasions. His favorite was brownies, a regular on his birthday. The reminiscent waft of chocolate from brownies fresh out of the oven filled the café air.

"We'll have two orders of beignets, lightly sugared, and two cafés au lait," Simone told the waiter.

Looking at the posted menu board, DiMeglio added, "And a chocolate brownie."

"That officially makes you a tourist, Chris," responded Simone with a smile.

"What can I say? I like brownies. So, tell me more about New Orleans and why you like it," he said as they waited for their coffees.

"It may surprise you, but I don't love New Orleans. Mind you, I like it and most of the people here, but it's no love affair."

"Then why do you stay?"

"Mostly inertia, I suppose. I'm comfortable here and have a good job. The social life leaves a lot to be desired, but the cultural scene keeps it interesting. You can learn something new all the time here in the city. And some of it's pretty exotic."

"Like what?"

"Well, lately I've been getting into Voodoo."

"Voodoo!"

"Relax, not to practice it, but to understand it," replied

Simone. "With the recent murders and the possible link to Voodoo, I wanted to learn more. I found out quickly that I was pretty ignorant about the religion. My impressions were that it was what we used to see in old movies with people sticking pins in dolls and conjuring up curses from the graves."

The coffee, beignets, and chocolate brownie arrived. DiMeglio took a bite of the brownie, and sighed, closing his eyes. Smiling, Simone said, "Before you take another bite of your brownie, Chris, try a beignet."

DiMeglio took a bite of the beignet. Then another. He quickly forgot about his brownie. "Someone has to get bakeries in Washington to make these. They're wonderful."

Simone smiled. "I'll see what I can do."

She returned to the discussion, "As for Voodoo being akin to a cult, it is not. That's the Hollywood version. And just about anything out of Hollywood isn't even close to the truth. In fact, Voodoo is one of the largest and oldest religions in the world. And it's what you'd expect from a traditional religion. It preaches peace and kindness, not dark magic and spells."

"But isn't it a bit odd that they collect trinkets like decorated chicken feet, crude dolls and human skulls to symbolize their religion?" DiMeglio asked. "I'm not sure I understand how that promotes peace and kindness."

"Really? Are Christianity's horned man-goats or grim reapers with sickles any different? And the Inquisition with judges cloaked in hoods? How was that an exercise in sympathetic religion?"

DiMeglio shrugged. "Well, my only interest is in what connection, if any, Voodoo has to our killer. Do you believe there is one?"

"I don't know yet. But if there is, the killer is not someone who practices the religion but someone who is using its dark side to justify killing these people."

DiMeglio was starting on his third beignet with a fourth waiting on his plate. He noticed that Simone had stopped after only one. He was impressed by her willpower. The things were addictive.

"That's possible," DiMeglio said between mouthfuls. "It's not unusual for serial killers to be motivated by a perverse view of religion. It's often a convenient excuse they use to kill for god or say that they're ordered by god to do so. Or worse, that they are god. We've had a string of them. Charles Manson. Jim Jones. Marshall Applewhite. Perhaps our serial killer falls in that mold."

"Perhaps. But we need to dig deeper," responded Simone.

"I couldn't agree more, Becca," he replied. DiMeglio decided to change the subject and learn more about New Orleans and Simone. "So, tell me about the darker side of New Orleans."

Simone waved to the waiter for another coffee.

"It's much like any city in the South," she began. "Racism and bigotry are always under the surface. It's a simmering time bomb that we have to deal with every day. It can get tense. With all the emphasis on police brutality across the country, we're always on guard. That sometimes makes us hesitate when we shouldn't. People get hurt. Or worse. We lost more than fifty cops in New Orleans last year in gunfights. It's just too easy for things to get out of hand."

"I don't think racism and cop shootings are unique to the South," responded DiMeglio.

"Perhaps. But racism started in the South when the first slaves were bought and sold like livestock. And it's been deeply rooted in southern families for generations. So, while it's a problem elsewhere, it's worse here."

DiMeglio sensed some discomfort and chose to again change the subject. "And how about you? Have you ever had to use your service revolver?"

"Thank God, no. But I wouldn't hesitate to do so if I thought I or a colleague was in the line of fire. What scares me is I'm not so sure I'd be prepared to shoot unless I was sure they were aiming at me or another police officer. It's a terrible decision to have to make."

"So what's the solution?"

"I wish I knew. But I do know that until we take care of those who hold racist views, both in the department and in the community, we'll never change. We'll never get the community to trust us as much as they need to."

"And how do you do that? How would you take care of the racists?"

"Another good question that haunts us every day. Education is one way. But dealing with racists under our laws is a challenge, including those among our fellow officers. Look at Guidry. He's as racist as they come and he's the top cop. We all too often give him and others like him embedded in society rights beyond what they deserve, even electing them to office."

"You sound frustrated."

"Find me a cop who isn't."

CHAPTER TWENTY-THREE

Bar Tonique on Rampart Street is on the outskirts of the French Quarter and a popular hangout for locals, including off-duty police. Some would say it was a dive bar with some class. Regardless, they serve generous pours that patrons appreciate. And unlike most bars in the Quarter, Bar Tonique has special happy hour drinks at just five bucks apiece, a price a cop's salary can afford.

Bundy, Evans, and a couple of other officers on the task force sat together at a table in the bar.

It had been five months of frustration for Bundy and his fellow officers since Walker's murder, and more than a month since DiMeglio arrived on the scene. They were growing impatient with the plodding way DiMeglio approached the case by concentrating on paperwork and psychological theories rather than the streetwise way beat cops approached investigations. Cultivate sources and squeeze CIs. Pound some heads.

"I don't know, Smitty," said Bundy as he twirled his shot glass. "I'm pretty much fed up with the FBI 'do it by the book' approach. And that means by their book. That ain't our book. DiMeglio does not understand New Orleans. We're getting nowhere and the killer—if it isn't Manning—is going to strike again. All we do is sit around talking about what the victims all have in common. How about they're all dead, that's what. And we're going to add more to the pile if we don't do something."

"I don't think any of us disagrees with you, but Becca and the captain seem to be supportive of having the FBI guy here. So, what else can we do?" asked Evans.

"I think you're right about the captain but I'm not so sure you are about Becca. She may be a detective, but she was a street cop first, just like the four of us. The captain's been behind his desk smoking those rancid cigars too long. He's soft and has lost touch."

"Ever since the FBI investigated the department in 2010," Officer Robert Shannon said as he waved to the waiter for another round, "we've had to put up with the settlement and the fuckin' monthly meetings with Broussard and Dickenson. We've been under the cloud of being racists ever since." Shannon, a third-generation cop from an Irish family, regarded any oversight of the police as a personal insult.

"Yeah," agreed Bundy. "That was before my time, but I know how you feel. Those racial education meetings are a pain in the ass. And all they do is make us nervous doing our jobs. We're forced to treat criminals with velvet gloves. Our hands are tied too often."

"So what are you proposing?" Shannon asked.

"I say we do what we do best. Hit the streets. If Manning's not our guy, the killer is out there walking through the Quarter deciding which alley or parking lot he'll use next. Right under our noses."

"But we can't just stop anyone we want and push them around," responded Evans. "And besides, I doubt the killer is anyone we know, and our CIs have proven to be worthless."

"That doesn't mean we sit on our asses," argued Bundy. "I say we all do some overtime and dig deeper. Someone knows the killer. That's the connection we need to find. Not some bullshit about the victims."

"Overtime?" asked another officer. "Why should I put in more time when I won't get paid for it? I don't need more time off."

"That's your decision. As far as I'm concerned, I want to catch this bastard," responded Bundy. "If that means I put in more time without pay, that's fine. I'm a cop and I'm going to do my job."

"Does Becca agree with you? Have you talked to her?"

As if on cue, Simone joined them.

"Hey, boys. Sorry I'm late. I had some paperwork that needed to get done."

The waiter brought her a boilermaker—a shot and a beer—without having to ask.

The officers remained quiet for a while until Simone broke the silence. "So what's bugging you guys? It's obvious you've been talking about something."

"Becca," Bundy said, taking the lead, "we're sick and tired of sitting in the conference room playing DiMeglio's games. He may be from the FBI, but he doesn't understand New Orleans any better than a tourist. He has us playing idiotic games of connect the dots while a killer might be running free. It just won't work."

Simone was quiet for a moment. "Joe, you may be right. And I tend to agree with you. But orders are orders. If this is what the captain wants us to do, then that's what we'll do."

In unison, the officers shook their heads in disappointment. Evans signaled the waiter for another round.

The low morale concerned Simone. "Look, guys, that doesn't mean our hands are tied. We can investigate our way as well. We just have to be discreet. I don't want to piss off Broussard."

The waiter brought the next round.

"I'm beginning to think he doesn't care if we catch the killer or not," said Evans.

"Yeah," added Bundy, "my bet is he's got his eye on Guidry's job. Or wants to be chief. And the mayor would like nothing more than to replace him with Broussard. So the captain has checked out on basic police work."

Simone did not hide her anger. "Wait a minute! That's just plain stupid. Look, the truth is Broussard hasn't checked out on anything. And if you're right that he wants Guidry's job or becomes chief, then he wants to solve this case as much as we do."

"You could've fooled me," concluded Bundy.

Simone was outnumbered, and grew tired of the complaining. She said good-bye and left for home as Bundy and the others ordered yet another round.

CHAPTER TWENTY-FOUR

Before coming to New Orleans, all DiMeglio knew about Voodoo came from horror movies with ominous depictions of Caribbean men and women casting curses or inflicting pain on others by putting needles in rag dolls. But Simone's description of the religion inspired his curiosity. He wanted to know if the killer had Voodoo connections or was somehow perversely motivated by the religion to kill. He suggested to Simone that they meet with Maîtresse LeBlanc, even though Simone had told him of the rather disappointing results from her first meeting with the priestess.

"Priestess Maîtresse, please let me introduce you to Christopher DiMeglio, an agent with the Federal Bureau of Investigation. He's helping us investigate the recent murders in the Quarter." Maîtresse, not rising from her desk, nodded her head but showed no expression indicating she welcomed the visit.

"Chris, this is Priestess Maîtresse LeBlanc." DiMeglio extended his hand. LeBlanc did not reciprocate. It was abundantly clear that the priestess took no pleasure in the introduction, much less the meeting. DiMeglio and Simone assumed their seats in front of the desk.

"We're hoping you can help us understand the Voodoo symbols that the killer has been leaving at the crime scenes.

I know we talked about it a bit when we last met, so I don't mean to be repetitive, but it's important Agent DiMeglio understands it as well. The more we understand how the killer thinks, the more likely we will find him before he kills again."

"And you think I have some divine ability to conjure up your killer?" asked LeBlanc.

"Not at all, Priestess Maîtresse," responded Simone. "We mean no such thing. But you are the most knowledgeable person in the city when it comes to interpreting Voodoo symbolism. We just need some help," Simone answered.

LeBlanc turned to DiMeglio. "So, Agent DiMeglio, I've read a bit about you. You seem to have quite a reputation for finding serial killers."

"Thank you. I've been studying them most of my career, Priestess Maîtresse," responded DiMeglio. "If you spend enough time on one subject, you can't help but learn a lot and have some success. I can assure you, however, that for every killer I have helped find, there are far more who continue to roam the streets. If people truly understood the numbers, they'd live in fear every day."

"And do you live in fear, Agent DiMeglio?" asked LeBlanc.

"No, I can't say I do," DiMeglio answered. He was beginning to wonder if this was more of a meeting with a psychologist than a priestess. "I block it out so I can do my work. I think that's what makes me suppress whatever fears I have. But others live in constant fear of the streets. They live in tough neighborhoods. Crime is on the rise. All we see on TV is how evil mankind can be. And that fear, even if it is sometimes irrational, is heightened when a serial killer is on the prowl."

"And you think a member of my congregation is responsible for these murders, Agent DiMeglio?" LeBlanc continued.

"No, Priestess Maîtresse, I'm not saying that at all," DiMeglio objected. This was not going to be an easy conversation. Simone's warning was correct. "The truth is we don't know one way or the other. Much of what we do to identify suspects is a process of elimination until we have assembled irrefutable facts that can lead us to the killer. Or at least explain to us why he's killing. So, there is as much a chance that he holds no religious beliefs as there is that he practices Voodoo. Or that he's Christian, Jewish, or Muslim. We just don't know."

"So, what can I tell you that you don't already know?"

"I have to admit I knew nothing about Voodoo before I came to New Orleans," DiMeglio began. "I ignorantly assumed it was some African religion of spell makers and curses."

"Our form of Voodoo, Agent DiMeglio, was founded in Haiti. It's a variation of Vodun, a branch that originated in Africa. Over time, believers made a pilgrimage to America. But in essence, we here in New Orleans are of a belief born in the Caribbean."

DiMeglio was tempted to make some sort of remark

about the wonderful weather and seas in the Caribbean but wisely chose not to. He surmised that LeBlanc did not have much of a sense of humor.

"Simone has given me something of a crash course in the past few weeks," continued DiMeglio. "I now understand that the core values of Voodoo are really like most religions."

"That is true," responded LeBlanc. "We worship one God—Bondye—although unlike Christians, we believe in other deities as well. We call them Iwas. You can think of them as saints. And while we have some rites like the seven sacraments of Christianity, ours are far fewer. So rather than believing in baptism, confirmation, communion, marriage, and others, we welcome our followers through initiation and then teach them to lead a life of healing."

"But there are some elements of what some believe, correctly or incorrectly, to be a form of witchcraft," Simone added, somewhat hesitantly. "I don't mean to offend, but there is that, yes?"

LeBlanc smiled. "Detective Simone, what you and others like to call witchcraft is our belief that prayers and incantations can bring about healing."

"And harm, too?" suggested Simone.

"Yes, harm," conceded LeBlanc. "But what you describe as the darkness in Voodoo is really no different from Christian teachings. An eye for an eye. Have not your kings and popes waged wars and killed thousands under the banner of their God?"

DiMeglio didn't like the direction the conversation was going, and fearing that LeBlanc would shut down if Simone continued, he interrupted. "So I guess we can conclude that every religion—Voodoo included—has its dark side."

"Yes, Agent DiMeglio, we all do," responded LeBlanc.

"And it is the dark side, Priestess Maîtresse," offered DiMeglio, "that I want to better understand. At this point we have two possibilities. Either the killer believes he is acting within the teachings of Voodoo as he understands them, or he is using the symbols for some other reason."

"What other reason would he have, Agent DiMeglio?" she responded in a softer voice.

I think I'm getting to her, DiMeglio thought.

"There could be any number of reasons," DiMeglio answered. "Perhaps he likes to put fear in people that he is a ritualistic killer. Jack the Ripper is an example of a serial killer who tried his best to convey that ritualistic image. Or he might be using it as a ruse to cover up his real motives. All we know is that the bodies of all the victims except one had three Xs carved in their foreheads and a crude wooden cross put in their hands. That led us to wonder if there was a connection to Voodoo"

"Yes, I understand. But as I told Detective Simone and her partner, three Xs could mean many things. None of this is unique to Voodoo, Agent DiMeglio."

"You may be completely right, Priestess Maîtresse. But please indulge me with an assumption, solely for argument's sake, that the killer intended to conjure up Voodoo."

"For argument's sake only, Priestess Maîtresse." Simone tried to insert herself into the conversation. After all, this was her investigation.

"Very well," responded LeBlanc. "Ask me whatever you'd like."

"OK, let's start with the Xs. What might they mean in Voodoo? What message do they convey?"

"As Detective Simone knows, Agent DiMeglio," began LeBlanc, "the most famous New Orleans Voodoo priestess was Marie Catherine Laveau. She died in 1881 and is buried here at the St. Louis Cemetery. She lies in the tomb of her husband's family, the Glapoins. To this day she is revered, and our version of a Hadj is to visit her grave. Go there yourself and you'll see that the tomb is covered in groups of three Xs."

LeBlanc explained further that if a believer broke a stone or brick off another grave, spun around three times in front of Laveau's tomb and then scraped three Xs onto the tomb with the stone from the other grave, and finally taped the stone on Laveau's tomb, the wish he or she made would be granted.

"And if I am correct," added Simone, "if you see an etching where the three Xs are circled, it means that the wish came true."

"That is correct, Detective Simone. It is believed that Laveau had power to cure the ill, solve romantic situations, and even aid condemned prisoners. It is the only way one can conceptualize the many occult occurrences attributed to the priestess. It's like Christianity's belief in the miracles of Jesus."

"Interesting," responded DiMeglio. "The Xs are symbols of hope, not pain or suffering."

"More like symbols used to heal the pain and suffering," added LeBlanc.

"Regardless, they are something positive, not negative," responded DiMeglio.

"Correct. They relate to the Rada of Voodoo."

"The Rada?" asked DiMeglio.

"In Voodoo, we refer to positive spirits of our beliefs as the Rada. In contrast, we refer to the evil spirits as the Petro Iwa. If the killer's message was based on Voodoo, then the three Xs are most likely meant to call upon the Rada, not to conjure up the evil of Petro Iwa."

"So if we assume the killer understood that, he'd be calling on the Rada to help those he killed. Perhaps to heal their souls," suggested DiMeglio.

"In Voodoo, we do not heal souls through death, Agent DiMeglio. Like Hindu, we believe in reincarnation and that life is continuous. To kill someone is antithetical to those beliefs. No true understanding of Voodoo would see it the way you describe."

"Then perhaps we can assume that the killer does not understand Voodoo," offered DiMeglio. "And if he does not understand it, his message, whatever it is, has nothing to do with Voodoo, even if his sick mind thinks it does."

"And the cross, Priestess Maîtresse?" asked Simone.

"Yes, the Voodoo cross. Another misconception. It has nothing to do with the message behind the cross in Christianity. In Voodoo, the cross symbolizes what supports the universe. It represents the necessary balance between what is vertical and what is horizontal. It is really more of a plus sign, rather than a cross. It originated in the Dahomean religion practiced in Benin, a small country in West Africa. Those who practiced Dahomean also came to the Caribbean and contributed to Voodoo symbolism. The cross is their symbol for strength, not for the crucifixion."

"And another message inconsistent with the killer's motives if they were truly based on Voodoo," concluded DiMeglio.

"So you can see, Agent DiMeglio, that whoever your killer is, he does not practice Voodoo. He either misunderstands it, is simply stupid, or he's smart enough to use it so you waste time like you are today with me. And I suspect you will tell me that serial killers are not stupid."

"No Priestess Maîtresse, they might put up an act like they're stupid, but they know exactly what they're doing and why, even if the 'why' is totally psychotic," replied DiMeglio.

LeBlanc's assistant walked in and informed LeBlanc that she had another appointment. The interruption was likely pre-planned so LeBlanc could keep the encounter short.

Simone rose. "Thank you, Priestess Maîtresse, for your help. It's been invaluable. We apologize for the inconvenience."

DiMeglio rose, as did LeBlanc, this time extending her hand to DiMeglio. "Agent DiMeglio, I will say a prayer for you that you are blessed by the Rada and protected by the spirit of Priestess Marie Catherine Laveau."

Taking her hand, DiMeglio replied, "Priestess Maîtresse, I need all the prayers and blessings you have to offer. I just might have to visit her grave. Thank you."

LeBlanc showed them to the door and shook Simone's hand, wishing them a safe day.

CHAPTER TWENTY-FIVE

"Where were you going, Chris, with the fear thing with the priestess?" asked Simone as they strolled down North Rampart Street on their way back to the Royal Sonesta on Bourbon Street. "You know as well as anyone that the odds of someone being murdered by a serial killer are about as remote as being hit by lightning. More people die getting out of bed than those murdered by serial killers."

"That's true, but tell that to the families of the victims. The reaction is an actual condition called foniasophobia—the fear of being murdered. It gets worse among the population if there is a serial killer loose. If people let their phobias heighten, there could be panic in the streets and mobs of vigilantes hunting down suspects and likely killing innocent people," responded DiMeglio.

"Foniasophobia?" asked Simone. "Why is it that everything needs a name? And one you probably can't pronounce. All I can tell you is that the fear is mounting, as you said it would."

"And it's only going to get worse when he kills again," observed DiMeglio.

"Assuming Manning is innocent, yes. So where are we now?"

"Well, as far as I'm concerned, Voodoo is a red herring

in this case. There's no logic to any connection even if there is one in the mind of the killer. Chasing down theories that Voodoo motivated him will lead us nowhere."

Simone shook her head. "But why? If he was compelled by Voodoo spirits, why not run that down? Is it that easy for you to drop a lead?"

It was only midafternoon and young people already filled the streets with their drinks, barhopping from one bistro to the next. New Orleans never stopped the party.

As the two of them dodged the crowds, their conversation continued. "Becca, if a murderer was a practicing Catholic and drowned his victims in holy water, would you start chasing religious zealots or just plain old criminals? Every serial killer who killed in the name of God lived in his or her own religion. Trying to connect their paranoid ideas to legitimate religion requires time we don't have."

"OK, you're the expert. But I still believe Voodoo is connected in some way. I'm not dropping it."

"I'm not telling you to drop it. What I'm saying is we keep missing something. It's right in front of us. We just see past it. Let's get back to the whiteboard. That's where we'll find our answer."

"It's late and I can't call everyone in at this point. They're exhausted. They're all sick of the whiteboard. Just last week a bunch of them were bitching about it at a local bar. But if it's important to you, go ahead and have your whiteboard. Let's just take it up again tomorrow," Simone replied.

"OK, I guess you're right. So what's next?"

"How about I make you a proper Cajun dinner, Chris?"

"Dinner? Broussard told me you're quite the cook. But are you asking me for a date? We need to keep this professional, right?" DiMeglio replied with a smile.

"It's not a date, Chris. I just thought it would be nice for you not to eat at another restaurant."

"OK, tell you what. If I'm going to learn about New Orleans food, I have to learn to cook it, too. So let's do it together. I can't think of a better teacher."

"Great," Simone smiled.

The two continued their stroll until they reached Bourbon Street.

"OK, Chris, this is where you go to the hotel, and I go shopping."

"Should I go with you?"

"No. Let's not spoil the surprise. But you can pick out a nice red and a nice white wine. Preferably a heavy Cabernet and an oaky Chardonnay."

"Damn! You're a sommelier, too?"

"I just like wine. And I'm picky."

CHAPTER TWENTY-SIX

DiMeglio carried a bottle of Silver Oak Napa Valley Cabernet Sauvignon and a bottle of Peju Chardonnay. Both wines were recommended by the wine store, since he had no idea what wine to pick. His preferred bourbon or Irish whiskey. He almost choked on what the wines cost and hoped the meal would be worth it.

They agreed it wasn't a date, but DiMeglio dressed as if it were. In his light brown shoes patterned with what looked like caning over the front, white linen pants, and a loose-fitting blue linen shirt, he looked like he was out to impress a girlfriend. But he reminded himself that it wasn't a date.

In fact, he hadn't been on a date since arriving in New Orleans, and even back in Washington he rarely dated or had any long-term relationships. He was the classic professional married to his job. He was happiest solving complex problems. Solving the complexities of women was not on his agenda. Most of his outings were blind dates set up by co-workers who felt sorry for him. DiMeglio would usually acquiesce in hopes they'd then leave him alone with his work. He enjoyed the dates and actually had a couple of short-term romances. But nothing lasted. His job always got in the way. He wondered if Simone might be different. She was as focused on her job and solving crimes as he was.

Strangely, he found that particularly alluring despite the adage that only opposites attract.

Simone's apartment was just a ten-minute walk from the Royal Sonesta. DiMeglio decided to take Dauphine Street to Iberville even though he could have walked straight down Bourbon. But it was nearly seven and the partiers were filling Bourbon Street. He'd seen enough of them.

As he sauntered along Dauphine, slightly swinging the bag of wine, he thought about what the team was missing in the evidence and the facts they knew. He was sure there were connections they were not seeing. He just had to figure it out. DiMeglio was convinced the killings were not random. With random serial killers, their methods changed victim to victim. Or they didn't discriminate on who they killed. Black, white, Hispanic. It didn't matter. All of the Bayou Slasher's victims were white. And young.

It would have been easy to assume a racial motive and that a person of color was the killer. But something told DiMeglio that that scenario was too simple. He knew in his gut there was more to it.

Just before Iberville, he passed the Museum of Death, a New Orleans tourist spot since 1995. Rumor had it that people passed out when looking at the museum's exhibits and some of the ways people were murdered and tortured. It was just closing, and DiMeglio could see from the expressions on the faces of those leaving that they enjoyed themselves looking at the macabre. Just as serial killers enjoy it.

He decided to visit the museum someday. Maybe something inside would spark an idea on the missing link to the victims of the Bayou Slasher.

The Museum of Death? Seriously? DiMeglio continued to marvel at the ever-pervasive macabre of New Orleans.

He arrived right on time. Simone's apartment complex was known as the Annex on Iberville Street, just a short walk to the police station. On the outside, it looked like a misplaced gem among the filth of the neighborhood it was in. But DiMeglio had come to realize he should not judge a book by its cover in New Orleans. Behind every façade was a hidden jewel.

DiMeglio was impressed by how nice Simone's building was once inside. Nicer than he'd expect on a detective's salary. She buzzed him in and he took the elevator to the fifth floor.

When he rang her bell, he heard the bark of what had to be a big dog and Simone ordering, "Sully, down." The barking ended immediately.

Simone opened the door, and DiMeglio was stopped short. Not by the sight of her dog, but by Simone. It was the first time he'd seen her not wearing a conservative outfit befitting what she thought was a proper look for a detective. And while DiMeglio was certainly capable of appreciating beauty, this was the first time he realized how beautiful Simone was. She wore a white, sleeveless cotton dress with a plunging neckline that allowed him a substantial view of her cleavage, and enticing details of her inviting breasts. DiMeglio wondered how she had managed to hide such a gorgeous figure. Her auburn hair, usually pulled back in a tight ponytail or in a bun, was loosely touching her tan shoulders. Her makeup included the most inviting red lipstick DiMeglio could ever remember seeing. He'd dated a few women, some very attractive, but none he could remember as beautiful as Simone looked that night. She sure looked like someone on a date as much as DiMeglio did.

But it wasn't a date.

"Come in, Chris. You look very comfortable," she said with an approving gaze.

Smiling, she added, "Don't mind Sully. He's all bark and no bite. Named him after Chesley Sullenberger, the pilot who landed the plane on the Hudson River in New York City. Because like the pilot, my Sully is all about love. Unless, of course, I tell him to look at someone another way."

"I'm sorry, what's your name?" asked DiMeglio.

Looking confused, Simone replied, "Huh, what do you mean?"

"Well, I thought I was supposed to meet a police officer here tonight, not a gorgeous model. So do you know where Rebecca Simone might be?"

Simone smiled wider. "Let's keep it professional, Chris. But I'd have to admit, that's not a bad pickup line. We're off duty, but let's keep it straight."

"Then I'll have to shut my eyes the rest of the night, Becca."

"And I'm not an officer. I'm a detective," Simone reminded DiMeglio.

"Whatever you say, Detective," DiMeglio laughed.

"Just open the wine, Chris, while I work on the hors d'oeuvres. Both bottles. And put the white in the ice bucket. Everything you need is there on the island." Simone led him into the kitchen.

DiMeglio put the Peju in the bucket, already filled with ice, and poured two glasses of the Silver Oak, making sure he turned each bottle so Simone could read the labels. He didn't intend to spend that kind of money without impressing someone.

"Hey, Chris, come here and join me. And bring me my glass of wine while you're at it."

The aromas coming from the stove were a wonderful mix of pungent Cajun spices with a mix of sweetness. Smells far nicer than the stench that too often invaded the French Quarter in the late-night hours. DiMeglio wondered why, with all the restaurants and cookeries in the Quarter, the smell of vomit and sewage was so often overwhelming.

"What is that I smell?" asked DiMeglio. "It's wonderful."

He handed her the glass. In the sink was a colander filled with a couple dozen oysters.

"You're smelling a bunch of stuff," Simone answered. "It's the combination of boiled crawfish and jambalaya. They say the best jambalaya is served at Remoulade in the Quarter. But I make mine a little different, with conch instead of shrimp. I add the sausage and chicken with some special spices, too. Their smells all combine nicely. The crawfish is to go with the oysters."

"But I haven't see you order Cajun food. You usually get the typical healthy stuff," observed DiMeglio.

"A girl's gotta keep her figure. But when I make Cajun, it's good Cajun," responded Simone. "I don't swamp it in sauce and too many spices. My recipes let the meats and fish come through."

"Well then, let me toast the chef," said DiMeglio as he raised his glass. Simone raised hers and they each took a sip. An awkward moment followed with what to do next.

"Would you like to shuck with me?" asked Simone to break the silence. "I'm pretty good at shucking, but there are a lot of oysters here." DiMeglio smiled.

"Chris, don't get any ideas. This is not a date. Just shuck some fucking oysters," she ordered.

"Yes, Ma'am." DiMeglio saluted. "I'd be happy to start shucking fucking oysters with you."

"Here," she said, handing him an oyster knife and a kitchen towel. "Start shucking. I have to check on the jambalaya."

The sink was immediately across from the stove, so the two were back-to-back. DiMeglio wasn't sure, but it seemed to him Simone was intentionally backing into him. The smell of her perfume was driving him up the wall. *Screw the jambalaya*, he decided.

He turned just as she did. Their faces met, inches apart. As if frozen for a moment, they stared at one another.

DiMeglio broke the ice and said, "I've never done this before."

"I find that hard to believe," responded Simone with a look of inviting puzzlement in her eyes.

"Honest, I never shucked an oyster. You'll have to show me how."

She smiled and moved to his side, grabbing a knife and towel.

"Now watch closely," she began. "I'll teach you how to be a good shucker."

"No doubt," responded DiMeglio as he tried to pay attention to the oysters and not the shucker.

"First gently hold the oyster, cupped in your hand, rear to the back of your palm. Like this. See?"

"It looks so fragile," DiMeglio observed.

"Don't worry, it was born for this. Now thrust your knife between the slit in the oyster. Like this." She gently pushed and wiggled the knife between the halves of the oyster's shell.

"Ouch!"

"I often wondered if this was the painful part. But they don't seem to object."

"And if they did?"

"You keep pushing," Simone remarked coyly. "Then move your knife up and down until the oyster loosens. Like this." She slowly separated the shell.

"I can see that's effective."

"Once parted, just pull out your knife and it's ready to eat. It's worth the wait for how they taste. Can you do that?"

"I can do this, too," he responded, turning to face her, putting down the knife and meeting her lips. The kiss was deep and inviting.

Simone began unbuttoning DiMeglio's shirt as he undid the zipper on the back of her dress. As they continued, Simone maneuvered them over to the couch. By the time they arrived, her dress was off, and his shirt lay on the floor.

DiMeglio unclipped her bra and wondered again where she was hiding her figure at work. Simone worked on his belt and loosened his pants, her hands finding their way to him with a gentle squeeze. Together they lay down on the couch, disposing of the last of their clothes and their inhibitions.

DiMeglio would never look at an oyster the same way again.

CHAPTER TWENTY-SEVEN

"I can't imagine what this night might have been if it were a real date," joked DiMeglio as the two shared a shower to clean up.

"Just scrub, Chris."

Once dressed, they returned to the kitchen to find the oysters unshucked, the crawfish overdone, and the jambalaya boiling over. Sully was happily lapping up the cooling fish and meat concoction that dripped on to the floor.

"Well, at least someone's cleaning the floor," quipped DiMeglio.

Simone laughed. "Yeah. My big vacuum cleaner. He's such a mush. All he cares about is being walked, petted, and fed. Get between him and his dog biscuits and you're putting your life in danger." She kissed DiMeglio again.

"Now what do we do about dinner?" asked DiMeglio. "Or do we keep shucking?"

"No more shucking for now, Chris. I'm too hungry."

"Then we need to get you something to eat."

"So let me show you a wonderful burger joint here in the Quarter. SoBou."

"That sounds familiar."

As the two strolled past the stores and restaurants on Iberville, Simone said, "If you recall, SoBou was a regular hangout for Maria Benson, victim number two. I go there at least once a month and don't remember ever seeing her there. But it's not as if I was looking," she continued. "Maybe if you see the place, something will come to mind."

They turned left on Chartres.

"It's up a block on the right just past Bienville. Have you ever heard of Owen Brennen?"

Chris shook his head. "No, don't think so."

Simone took his arm as they walked, and he enjoyed the warmth of her touch.

"Well, as your tour guide, I'll give you some history."

She explained how SoBou was part of the Commander's group of restaurants founded in 1946 by famed New Orleans icon Owen Brennan. Passed on generation to generation in the southern tradition, the restaurant group remains in the same family that now runs more than fifteen eateries in New Orleans with outposts in five other cities, including Memphis and Las Vegas. The well-known Commander's Palace and Brennan's attract the tourist trade as well as the locals. SoBou, however, was more a local favorite.

When they arrived, the maître d immediately showed them to a table near the rear, a good distance from the small combo playing for those gathered. It was crowded despite it being past eleven. New Orleans never really sleeps.

A waiter appeared immediately.

"Detective Simone, good to see you again," he began.

"And good to see you, too, Phillip."

"I hope you're here to enjoy yourself this time. I'm still upset about what happened to poor Maria."

"Yes, that was tragic, Phillip. But tonight, I'm here to enjoy a big burger with my friend, Chris DiMeglio."

"Well, Mr. DiMeglio, you're most welcome here at SoBou and you are in very good company with the detective. But before I take your dinner order, let's start with cocktails. What will you have, Detective?"

"A cosmopolitan, of course."

"And you, sir?"

"Basil Hayden bourbon on the rocks please," responded DiMeglio. He felt like celebrating.

"And can I start you with some wonderful grilled oysters?"

The two smiled and Simone replied, "Not tonight. We enjoyed some back at my place before we arrived. Just bring us some cracklins to start. An order of plain and spiced. Then we'll order dinner."

"Cracklins? Those are the pork skins, right?" asked DiMeglio, looking a bit put off.

"You describe them that way in Washington, but they're much more. One of the purely Cajun dishes I like. Each one is a delicious piece of crunchy fried pork skin, a little fat, and a tiny piece of meat. Think of it as deep-fried bacon bits. I got both plain and spiced. I like them with a little salt. But we'll see if you like them spicy."

"Well, I always like spicy."

"Yeah, I noticed."

Phillip arrived with the drinks and cracklins.

DiMeglio raised his glass to Simone, "Well, here's to the best date I was never on!"

"I'd say you were on it pretty good, Chris." Simone clinked her glass to his.

Not realizing the waiter was still there, they came back to the moment when he asked, "And have you decided on what to have as a main course?"

"We're famished. So I'll have whatever she's having."

Simone smiled. "Bring us two SoBou burgers, fully loaded."

The waiter walked away and DiMeglio wanted to bring the conversation back to business. But first, he bit into some cracklins.

"Wow! These things could become addictive!"

"Told ya. Some of the stuff down here is worth savoring. And like beignets, cracklins are one of them," responded Simone. "Try the spicy ones."

Two bites into it, DiMeglio understood what Cajun spice meant. He was happy the waiter also brought some water.

After finding his voice again, DiMeglio hoarsely said, "So I have to ask, Becca, and I hope I'm not being too forward but . . ." began DiMeglio.

"It's a little too late to think about that, Chris," interrupted Simone with a smile.

"Maybe," DiMeglio said, "but may I ask how a detective

on the New Orleans police department can afford such a beautiful apartment?"

Simone's smile never wavered as she looked at him. "I've got my daddy to thank for that, Chris. He died five years ago and left me a little nest egg. I decided to spend it on the condo at the Annex. God knows a detective's salary would have kept it out of my reach. So, I got lucky when my father died."

"I'm sorry for being presumptuous." DiMeglio was a bit taken aback by her answer. "And sorry about your father."

"It's OK. Ancient history, as far as I'm concerned. And being presumptuous goes with the territory. You and I aren't very different. We share the same antisocial trait of every cop. We ask too many questions."

Now DiMeglio smiled. "Yeah, we do."

"So, what else do you want to know?"

DiMeglio found himself a bit out of his comfort zone questioning a woman he'd just made love to, who was now sitting across from him in a romantic restaurant. So he started with the typical.

"Tell me about your childhood, Becca. Where did you grow up? What did you parents do? I know what brought you to New Orleans, but tell me what you did before that."

"Well, there's not much to tell. I grew up outside Selma, Alabama. It was a white enclave of well-off southern families. I was blessed with all the privileges that came with that. Good schools. Safe neighborhoods. All of it."

"Sounds idyllic," observed DiMeglio.

"It was when I was young, but my mom passed when I was seven. Then my world changed."

"How so?" asked DiMeglio.

"My father was a cotton farmer. Big spread. He kept me away from the fields and the cotton gin. But when Mom died, he changed. Too cheap to pay for a nanny, he dragged me to the farm every day."

"Did he make you work the fields?" asked DiMeglio.

"No. I wasn't strong enough for that and he'd never let me work alongside Black men or women. For him, that would be demeaning. So when I got old enough, he'd have me keep books or fill out paperwork. I could do a lot of that from home once I was old enough to take care of myself."

"And when did you leave?"

"As soon as I could. I graduated high school and ran off to the College of Charleston in South Carolina. It was an eight-hour drive; far enough that my father never visited. I worked part-time jobs for spending money. But I never went home again and haven't been to Selma since."

"So, you never saw your father again?"

"No. He sent money for tuition but once I graduated, that ended."

"So that's when you enlisted?"

"No, not at first. For a while after Charleston, I bounced around California until I ran out of money. I saw a part of America I'd never seen. It was the first time I'd met a liberal!" smiled Simone.

"You could have come to Washington for that!" remarked DiMeglio.

"True, but Washington doesn't have the weather. So, when I finally ran out of money, I enlisted."

"That's a tough road. I'm sorry."

"Don't be. I managed to inherit a cotton farm, sell it, and became a rich woman. It might be dirty money off the back of the remnants of slavery, but money is money, right? I'm not complaining."

DiMeglio let the slavery reference pass for the time being. "So why remain a cop if you don't need the money? It can be a thankless job."

"Not for me. I love it, solving one crime after another," she sarcastically responded.

DiMeglio smiled. "Yeah, maybe we're all masochists. If I can ask, why do you see the money you inherited as dirty?"

Simone's expression became serious. "In case you didn't already figure it out, my father was a racist. He had dozens of Black men and women working for him and treated them like cheap property. Slavery may have been over, but you didn't know it in Selma. He and his cronies used to sit in the house and talk about them while getting drunk and smoking cigars. I grew up listening to a bunch of bigots lamenting the loss of the Civil War."

"And that's why you never went back?"

"Exactly. I wanted to get as far away from the hatred as I could. And while I moved here to be with a guy who became an ex, I've stayed here in New Orleans because I like to think I'm contributing to ending bigotry in my own little way. NOLA is a diverse city where people essentially live in harmony regardless of race. We're not perfect, and there's way too much violence here, but we respect the Black community. And welcome their contributions to the city. Their food, music, and pride. Each day, we get a little better."

The waiter arrived with the burgers. Simone pointed to their two glasses. He left to bring another round.

"So is your story of moving to New Orleans typical of folks here?"

"What do you mean by typical?" asked Simone.

"To get away from something they didn't like."

"Isn't that why most people move somewhere else rather than stay where they were born?" Simone asked. "All I wanted to do was distance myself from my past as much as possible. And New Orleans is a good place to do it."

The waiter brought the drinks.

The two devoured the meal, pan-seared Hudson Valley foie gras burgers topped with a sunny-side-up yard egg, duck bacon, and mayo on caramelized onion brioche. As decadent a burger as one could find. They both devoured their meals without speaking.

When they were done, Simone announced, "And to finish, we'll split a Pecan Pie Not Pie."

"A what?" asked DiMeglio.

"It's what SoBou is famous for. You might not know it,

but pecan pie was invented in New Orleans. It was one of the first collaborations between the French and the Native Americans." Simone waved to their waiter. "But what they've done here is ditch the crust and serve it in a jar with lots of chocolate, peanut butter, and whipped cream. Trust me, you'll love it."

He did.

Over a pair of espressos to end the meal, Simone asked, "So, I told you about my life. Tell me about yours."

"Sure," he responded. "Grew up in the Bronx. Tough Italian neighborhood. Like you, I was an only child. Dad was a construction worker. Mom worked at a local dress shop as a seamstress. I did some construction work with my dad and other odd jobs around town until college."

"What made your neighborhood so rough?"

"On Arthur Avenue, you had two choices. You either became a gang member or a cop. In a way, I guess I chose becoming a cop in a roundabout way."

"And why didn't you go the gang route?"

"Mostly because of my mom. If I ever did anything remotely questionable, I got a whap in the side of the head. I was more afraid of her than I was of any local gangster!"

"So in the Bronx, I guess you saw your fair share of racism."

"Not really. On the avenue and in school we white kids pretty much kept to ourselves. I had more problems with Irish thugs on the street than I did with any Blacks. I went to the Bronx High School of Science, one of the best schools in the city. It was big. Over 2,500 students. But it was far from diverse. Of the kids in my class, less than twenty were Black or Hispanic. Everyone there knew it was tough to get in and wanted to stay, so troublemakers were rare and quickly thrown out. My parents made me work my ass off for the entrance exam."

"Your parents must have been proud to see you go off to college and the success you have now," observed Simone.

"Yeah, they're pretty proud. Retired now in Florida. I see them a few times a year. Less than I should, but that goes with the job."

When they returned to her condo, they actually finished shucking the oysters and enjoyed them. And then enjoyed each other as the night led to morning. DiMeglio left early to avoid being seen. The two decided to see where the relationship might go, but to keep it between themselves at this point.

CHAPTER TWENTY-EIGHT

It was the first time DiMeglio was able to inspect an active crime scene since he had arrived in New Orleans. Two nights after his non-date with Simone, the Bayou Slasher struck again. The coroner's report would later describe the victim as Samuel Beckett, a thirty-six-year-old white male who fit the profile of all the others. Local and respected. Decent job as a manager of a Hertz dealership. Married, no kids. No record of any criminal activities. Moved to New Orleans nineteen years earlier to attend Tulane. He never left.

"Well, Chris, it looks like you're probably right about Manning. He was home all night," Simone observed.

"Or his ankle bracelet was home all night," added Bundy with a sarcastic tone.

"Your thoughts, Dr. Harvey?" asked DiMeglio, ignoring Bundy.

"Looks like the Slasher is back, Agent DiMeglio," responded Harvey. "Throat cut, three Xs in the forehead, and a wooden cross in his hand. No signs of a struggle. Clean like the first three scenes. The good news is that it looks like an innocent bystander was spared on this one."

DiMeglio took a closer look at the victim, noticing that the cut was clean. It had to be a very sharp knife. He also assumed that the same knife was used for the Xs.

"Make sure you match the blood to see if there is any foreign DNA in it. I want every inch of his body and clothes tested with particular attention to the hand with the cross. This time, we're doing a complete DNA panel. I want samples of the water in the gutter. The dirt on the street. I want the video from every street camera within ten blocks." DiMeglio was ordering, not asking.

As Simone was about to remind DiMeglio just who was in charge, he looked past her to the officers who were combing for evidence, concerned that they not spoil the scene with the kind of incompetence he'd seen too many times with local police.

"Everyone please stop. We need to get this right."

"We're getting it right, Chris," responded Simone. "Let us do our job." The other officers could feel the tension.

DiMeglio ignored Simone and continued. "And tonight I want hidden cameras set up that point to the spot where the body was found. And I want two more, one on each end of the alley, recording anyone who so much as looks down the street. Serial killers are known to come back to the scene of their crimes, particularly during the days that immediately follow and during an active investigation."

DiMeglio turned to the officer who had been taking photographs of the scene, now frozen and waiting for orders.

"I'd like you to take pictures of the crowds at either end of the alley watching us. Do it discreetly. There is a high probability that the killer is within a hundred feet of where we're standing. We'll use facial recognition to compare your shots with the camera footage."

DiMeglio was on a roll. He'd be damned if the investigation wasn't done by the FBI's book this time.

"And put an undercover officer here tomorrow night and every night this week watching who goes by this alley," DiMeglio added. "We may miss something on the cameras. And if anyone goes down the alley, arrest them. I'll want to ask some questions before we release them."

Simone finally grabbed his arm and made him look at her. "Chris, you can't just issue orders and do whatever you'd like. All this has to be OK'd by Captain Broussard. This is a New Orleans Police Department investigation, Chris, not the FBI's. You're here to help us, not order us."

DiMeglio looked at Simone in surprise. Then, realizing he had crossed the line, said, "I'm sorry Becca, I didn't mean to suggest otherwise. It's just that now that we know Manning is not the Slasher, we have an active killer on our hands. And the FBI has technology that New Orleans does not. Let's tap into whatever we can get."

The two stared at one another and the moment grew tense. They were not on the same page.

Simone spoke first, conceding, "OK. We'll do that. On condition that everything, and I mean *everything*, is shared with me. Understood?"

"Absolutely, Becca." What difference did it make if he shared with Simone what he already promised to share with

Gaudet and Broussard? "That's the only way to do it." He turned to Harvey. "So, when you're done, Dr. Harvey, send everything to the FBI lab in Quantico. The samples, the clothes, the reports. Everything." The FBI's laboratory was the best in the world. "Dr. Harvey, do you have any questions?"

"No. None." For Harvey, the orders were refreshing. She was thrilled with the prospect of working with the FBI. Any forensic coroner knew that the FBI was the gold standard.

Turning to Simone and Bundy, DiMeglio continued, "Becca and Joe, let's start getting all of this on the whiteboard. We have to find the connection this victim has with the others before the Bayou Slasher kills again."

Simone wondered if DiMeglio heard a thing she said about not ordering her and her team around.

CHAPTER TWENTY-NINE

As it happened, a status conference before Judge Enfield was scheduled the day after Beckett was found murdered. It was clear to everyone that Manning was not the Bayou Slasher.

"Your Honor," Gaudet announced, "the state is dropping all charges against Mr. Manning, including the lesser charges of interfering with a crime investigation and theft."

Percy, sitting next to Manning, could not suppress his Cheshire cat grin as he placed his hand on Manning's arm.

"I assume," asked Enfield, "that this change of heart is related to the victim found last night?"

"Yes, Your Honor," responded Gaudet. "The victim found last night fits the Bayou Slasher's methods, and it was impossible for Mr. Manning to be involved. He was at home."

"I see," observed Enfield. "But how can you be so certain he did not have an accomplice or that he was not involved in some other fashion?"

"Per your order, Judge, we had an officer outside his apartment around the clock and monitored all of his calls. The only exit from the unit was to the outside walkway. So, we could see his every move. He never left his apartment except to see Mr. Percy. On those visits, an officer drove him there and back. He never saw anyone else. All his food was delivered."

"And you're sure he could not have fooled you in some way?"

"Before he was released, we thoroughly searched his apartment. So, unless by some magical ability he conjured up a burner phone, he's as clean as can be."

"Another case of overzealous police work, Ms. Gaudet?"

"No, Your Honor," responded Gaudet. She was not about to let Enfield malign her team of police officers. "Our officers had every reason to believe they had caught the killer. And they convinced me, too. Otherwise, I would not have brought the charges in the first place."

"So who am I to blame, Ms. Gaudet? You? Your officers? A Voodoo curse?" Enfield's tone could not have been more condescending. "This city has incarcerated and maligned an innocent man only to realize that innocence in the discovery of another victim, this time one that might not have been killed if the police had not thought their case was solved. If it were the first time, I might excuse it. On whose hands should the blood be borne, Ms. Gaudet?"

She was not at liberty to tell the judge the investigation never stopped and that an FBI agent had joined the task force. That would have only angered him.

"If you need a scapegoat, Judge, use me," Gaudet responded.

Enfield turned to Percy and Manning.

"Mr. Manning," he began as both Percy and Manning stood. "Mr. Percy, you sit down. I did not call upon you." Percy sat, frowning.

The judge continued, "Mr. Manning, on behalf of the City of New Orleans, I would like to apologize for your false arrest and all the misery you've suffered. While I'm sure Mr. Percy will be advising you shortly on who to sue over this, I believe whatever reparations you receive will never be enough to compensate you for the erroneous charges that branded you in this community."

Were it not that she feared being held in contempt, something a future political opponent would use against her, Gaudet would have objected to the diatribe from Enfield. It was not his place to suggest that Manning sue the city, much less apologize for the harm done.

"All charges against Wallis Manning are hereby dismissed, with prejudice," announced Enfield with a loud rap of his gavel. Turning to an officer in the courtroom, Enfield ordered the officer to remove Manning's ankle bracelet.

As the court officer was removing it, Percy rose. "May I be heard, Your Honor?"

"Very well, Mr. Percy, but please keep it brief. You won today. That should be enough for you. But I know you'd like to make sure the press appreciates it as well. So go for it."

Enfield never hid his dislike of media-hungry lawyers, and no one was hungrier than Percy. As a public defender he couldn't take out ads like all the other ambulance-chasing lawyers in New Orleans. Instead, he used the press like no one else. All the money spent by private criminal defense lawyers didn't come close to the value of the ink the press gave Percy.

"If I may speak for Mr. Manning," Percy began. That was a mistake.

"No you may not, Mr. Percy," interrupted Enfield. "Mr. Manning is a free man. He can speak for himself." Enfield turned his gaze to Manning.

"Mr. Manning, is there anything you'd like to say before I adjourn for today and release you from custody?"

Percy had not briefed Manning on saying anything. It was clear to Enfield that Percy's request to speak on Manning's behalf was nothing more than a publicity stunt. He was not going to let that happen.

Manning rose, "No, Your Honor, I don't. I ain't sure what Mr. Percy was gonna to say either."

"Somehow, I'm not surprised," responded Enfield. "But this is a moment for you to speak for the record. To say how you feel. And unlike the warning you received months ago, nothing you say will be used against you." While Enfield knew he was incorrect, since anything Manning said would be admissible in the eventual civil suit he'd bring against the city, the judge wanted to hear what he had to say that might help him in the press, where he'd already been tried and convicted. Now only the press could truly exonerate him.

"Well, I guess you would say I'm pretty pissed off," began

Manning. His bluntness actually brought a smile to Enfield.

"I had a decent job before this happened. That's gone now. I don't have a job at all. And my drinkin' has only gotten worse. You probably should have banned booze, Judge. You'd be surprised what gets delivered today."

"I'll try to remember that, Mr. Manning," responded Enfield. "Please continue."

"I guess that's about it, Judge. I'd like my life back. Maybe I didn't have the best reputation, but I never hurt nobody. I served my country. And now I'm unemployed and broke. I'll have to leave New Orleans and try and start again."

"You've certainly suffered enough, Mr. Manning. Again, I apologize for the city. And I'm pretty sure you won't be broke long if Mr. Percy has his way. Listen to him."

As much as it pained Enfield to suggest anyone listen to Percy, he wanted to make sure New Orleans felt some pain for its mistake. Otherwise, the system would never change, and rushes to judgment would remain the norm. In a city with one of the highest murder rates in the nation, something needed to change, and better police work, as far as Enfield was concerned, was a good start.

Hearing nothing further from Manning, Enfield announced the hearing was adjourned.

Although Percy was denied his moment with the press in the courtroom, he more than made up for it on the courthouse steps in front of a horde of reporters. After all, he alerted them before the hearing that there would be something big to announce. On the steps beside him and Manning was Stephen Miller, one of the most successful plaintiff's lawyers in Louisiana. Percy gleefully announced that Miller would be bringing a multimillion-dollar lawsuit against the city on behalf of Wallis Manning. As a public defender, Percy could not moonlight nor share in any award. His satisfaction was seeing the city pay. That was more important to him than any cash in his pockets. Nor did he need it.

The reporters obliged Percy's wish that afternoon with headlines announcing that the city would be sued for millions.

CHAPTER THIRTY

The task force once again gathered in their conference room, their frustration clearly mounting. DiMeglio's insistence on finding connections was wearing on the younger officers, who wanted to be out on the street pressuring their CIs or interviewing witnesses. Sitting in a classroom being instructed by an outsider from D.C. was not why they became cops. They wanted action, not debate.

DiMeglio sensed this and decided to have Broussard join the meeting. He hoped that would send a message to the task force members about the importance of the basic work.

After everyone arrived and crowded into the room, DiMeglio began. "I just can't put my finger on it, but I know what we're looking for is on that board."

Bundy saw the opening and took it.

"We've listed everything the victims have in common, Chris," Bundy interjected gruffly. "We've been at this for months and have nothing more today than we did when we started. With all due respect, it's beginning to remind me of the old saying that the definition of insanity is doing the same thing over and over again and expecting different results." Judging by the reaction in the room, most of the task force felt the same way.

"I understand your frustration, Joe," responded DiMeglio. "I understand everyone's frustration. I sometimes question the process myself. If it weren't for the fact that others a lot smarter than me have proven this works, I might agree with you. But what would be insane is to not keep at it, however frustrating that may seem to be."

"So, what do we know about their families?" asked Broussard, sensing the tension in the room.

"They're all local, Captain," responded Bundy. Simone smiled at how Bundy, the one to criticize DiMeglio so quickly, was the first to reply when a question was posed by Broussard. *Such a toady*, she thought, for the thousandth time.

Broussard continued, chewing on his cigar, "That's not what I asked, Officer Bundy. I asked about their families. What about their siblings, parents, grandparents? From what I see here, none of them was born in Louisiana."

"That's what we might be missing," DiMeglio told the group, a stunned look on his face. "Nothing like a fresh set of eyes to see the obvious. Thank you, Captain."

DiMeglio knew that many people, like Simone, came to New Orleans to escape their past. He and Simone had talked about it. He wondered whether that might be a key to what was common among the victims. What were they running away from? While DiMeglio thought it was a stretch, any idea that might lead to a solution to the puzzle was worth pursuing. Particularly if it brought him a new angle with the frustrated members of the task force.

"Just doing my job, Chris," responded Broussard. "Keep up the hunt before this son of a bitch kills again." With that mike-dropping conclusion, Broussard left the room.

DiMeglio continued. "OK, I want to know everything about their families. Where were they from? What did their parents and grandparents do? If they have siblings, what do they do? Was there anything in their past that would show a connection?"

"I can take the lead on that," offered Bundy.

Of course, thought Simone. The suggestion came from Broussard so Bundy, the toady, wanted to track it down.

"No, Joe, we need you and Becca on the street with me. We still have to see some crime scenes and interview potential witnesses. We also need to run down some of your CIs. They're a source we have yet to tackle." DiMeglio had reluctantly agreed to pursue CIs even though he thought they were a dead end. Simone convinced him that he had to let the task force members do what they found comfortable.

"So, who do you want to head up the family investigations?" asked Bundy, disappointed he didn't get the assignment.

DiMeglio turned to Smitty Evans, the young officer who got under Bundy's skin at the first briefing. "Officer Evans, I'd like you to head this up."

"Yes, sir," replied Evans.

"Smitty," DiMeglio continued, "I want you to find out if our victims came to New Orleans to escape something.

What is it in their past, if anything, that would make them settle in New Orleans?"

Simone, quiet until now, spoke. "Chris, that sounds a bit like a wild goose chase. People move to New Orleans for lots of reasons, including the weather, the lifestyle, and taxes. Those are different reasons and clearly not a thread. I'm not sure I see the need to go down that road when we can be doing more work on the streets."

DiMeglio did not appreciate the criticism. Particularly from a woman he had deep feelings for. It hurt. He chose to ignore her comments.

"I know you all want to get there. And we will continue doing that," DiMeglio promised. "And I know you all are frustrated by how many of our leads or ideas turn out to be empty. I get it."

Pointing to one of the quotes on a print he'd mounted on the wall, DiMeglio concluded, "And he's one of the people a lot smarter than me who also gets it." The quote read: "Negative results are just what I want. They're just as valuable to me as positive results. I can never find the thing that does the job best until I find the ones that don't. Thomas A. Edison."

"OK, then," Simone said, rising from her chair. "Let's get going before Chris reads every quote on the wall to us."

And besides, she was in the mood for oysters.

CHAPTER THIRTY-ONE

"That son of a bitch," screamed Guidry. "Where the hell does Enfield get off telling the world that he thinks our cops don't do their jobs?"

While the question was rhetorical, Broussard felt obligated to reply.

"Commissioner," he said, "Enfield has been a blowhard since taking the bench. But overall, he's been fair. This time, however, I agree with you. He crossed the line. My officers can put up with the insults, but to encourage a suit against the city is too much."

"Harper, what can you tell us about Stephen Miller?" asked Guidry.

"He's from Baton Rouge. A real money hound. Sues at the drop of a hat. Wins most of the time, and big. He's got the southern swagger juries love. He should have been a criminal lawyer, but there wasn't enough money in it for him. At least that's what he says when asked."

"Arrogant son of a bitch," Guidry replied.

Takes one to know one, thought Broussard. And he could see Gaudet was thinking the same.

"So now he'll jam up our courts with this shit," Guidry continued.

"No, Commissioner, he won't file suit here. He'll file in

the federal court in Baton Rouge, his hometown. He wants a jury of folks who look on New Orleans as sin city. He's far more certain to get the jury pool he wants there."

"Can't we ask that it be moved to New Orleans?" asked Broussard. "That's where all the evidence and witnesses are."

"We will certainly try, Captain Broussard," replied Gaudet. "And there's a good chance we'll win such a motion. But losing it doesn't hurt Miller against even the long odds of winning it. So it's a good tactic on his part, win or lose."

"So we're fucked no matter how we look at it?" offered Guidry.

"No, Commissioner, not at all," replied Gaudet. "He still has to make his case, and we had good evidence to go on when we arrested Manning. We don't have to be perfect, just reasonable. I didn't bring the indictment on a whim."

"And it won't matter that Simone lied to him about finding DNA on the knife?" asked Guidry.

Jesus, thought Broussard, *and he's in charge of the police?*

"That's perfectly permitted in police interrogation as a method to root out the truth and to see how a suspect reacts," Broussard replied angrily. "It's a basic rule every police officer knows," he added, to make sure Guidry knew he was insulting him.

Guidry saw it differently. "So you tell a jury that it's OK for the police to lie? Where is that going to get you today? Like I said, we're fucked no matter what. And that bastard Enfield only added gas to the fire."

Sitting quietly through the debate was Mayor Pratt. She called the three of them to her office to discuss how best to proceed. She'd heard enough.

"So perhaps our smartest move is to feel Miller out for a settlement," Pratt calmly suggested.

Guidry just about exploded as he rose from his chair. "Settle! With all due respect, Madam Mayor, I'd rather you didn't throw us under the bus so soon. Manning may be innocent, but he's still a scumbag. Certainly not someone a jury would feel sympathy for. Let's go on the attack rather than cower."

Pratt remained calm. The last person who would tell her what to do was Guidry. In fact, she had every intention to use this mistake to put the blame on him and get him to resign. Or she'd make it even worse for him. It was just a matter of time.

"No sympathy, Superintendent? I beg to differ," responded Pratt, using the true title Guidry held. She was not about to give him any more respect than she thought he deserved. "This 'scumbag,' as you like to call him, is a veteran who proudly served this country. He may not be the most literate person on the street, but neither are most New Orleanians. And while he may well be a drunk, what we did to him made him all the more justified to stay one. No, Superintendent, he will get more than enough sympathy from a jury. And Miller will no doubt make sure of that as well."

Guidry sat back down with a thud.

Gaudet looked directly at Pratt and cautioned, "We'll also have to check how we do this under the 2012 consent decree the police department entered into when it was sued by the U.S. Attorney for poor police work. The decree sets up a labyrinth of procedures we need to be sure we complied with. Otherwise, we could be looking at something a lot worse."

Broussard turned to the mayor. "I'm familiar with the decree, Madam Mayor," he said. "We have regular training under it." He was a beat cop when the city settled with the federal government after a yearlong investigation. In its report, the U.S. Attorney concluded that the NOPD violated the constitution and federal law, showing what the report described as a disturbing pattern and practice of using excessive force, making illegal stops, searches, and arrests, committing gender discrimination in its failure to properly investigate violence against women, applying discriminatory policing based on racial, ethnic, and LGBT bias, and failing to provide police services in languages understood by some minority communities. It was a scathing indictment of the police force and the city's administration. Although Broussard was not personally a target of any allegations of misconduct, the blue wall of silence made every cop hypersensitive during the investigation, wondering if any colleague would break that silence. The settlement rocked New Orleans. The city began a systematic process of improvement that, ironically, helped Broussard succeed. In private, the U.S. Attorney gave the then mayor a confidential list of officers he thought capable of making a difference and bringing about meaningful change. Broussard was on the top of that list.

"I understand you are well versed in the consent decree, Captain," responded Gaudet, "but we need to be absolutely sure we followed it without question. No doubt Miller will go through everything with a fine-toothed comb using the consent decree as his guide. So, let's get ahead of this from the moment Manning was a suspect to the day the case was dismissed."

"Madam Mayor," added Broussard, "if there is any officer who should take the fall, let it be me. Detective Simone and Officer Bundy are among my best. They're important to the city. I'm expendable."

"I don't think you're expendable at all, Raleigh, however noble you might be." Her use of his first name did not go unnoticed by Broussard, a familiarity he was not used to hearing, but welcomed. "I'm sure Harper can make a deal with Miller that will protect everyone. I'm not looking for any scapegoats. We'll all take some heat but no one needs to lose their job. Yet." It was the "yet" that caught everyone's attention.

"Harper, reach out to Miller and see what you can do," Pratt continued. "And try to do so before he files suit."

"I'll try, but I doubt he'll agree. He's going to want to

make some headlines with a dramatic complaint and press conference. That ups the ante."

"All he cares about in the end, Harper, is money," Pratt said. "I know how men like him think. Offer him enough and he'll gladly take it and go back to his cave. I've never met a plaintiff's attorney who wouldn't sell his client's soul for the right fee. And I've seen many well-intentioned doctors have their lives ruined over frivolous malpractice cases brought by such money-hungry lawyers. They're not very different from politicians."

Gaudet smiled.

CHAPTER THIRTY-TWO

The weather was unsettled. DiMeglio's morning walk with Sully was shorter than usual and didn't give DiMeglio the chance to explore different neighborhoods, as he had been doing most mornings. It was his way of learning as much about the city as he could. Sully didn't like bad weather, and the distant claps of thunder made him pull on the leash toward home. For such a big, powerful dog, he was pretty much a wuss except when it came to his dog biscuit, his reward after a walk. God help you if you forgot to give him one. He'd drag you to the cabinet where the goodies were stored.

Simone was still in bed, so DiMeglio gave Sully a couple of treats and left a note that he'd gone to the office and would see her there later.

Later that day, DiMeglio stood in front of the whiteboard yet again and studied it. *There isn't a lot but at least something might provide a clue*, he thought.

As DiMeglio took a sip of his fourth coffee for the day, Officer Smitty Evans walked up to him. "Agent DiMeglio," he said, "do you have a moment?"

"Sure, Smitty." DiMeglio put his cup down and motioned for Evans to sit down.

"I may have something. But it's pretty slim. And maybe

crazy," said Evans as he put the manila folder he was holding on the table.

"Any lead's a good one, Smitty," replied DiMeglio, pointing to one of his posters on the wall, a quote from Alfred Nobel, and adding, "If I have a thousand ideas and only one turns out to be good, I am satisfied."

Evans grimaced slightly. DiMeglio's obsession with the posters was getting old.

"So what do you have in that envelope?"

Removing the paperwork, Evans said, "Well, I looked into the families like you suggested, and they're from all over the South. But only the South. So that got me to thinking . . ."

"Smitty," interrupted DiMeglio, "I appreciate all the investigation you must have done, but what connection have you found? If it's only that they're all from the South, it tells us nothing."

"Every family, except Landes, has a connection to the Klu Klux Klan," responded Evans.

CHAPTER THIRTY-THREE

"Show me," said DiMeglio, as he cleared off the conference table. He could feel his heart beating faster.

Evans laid out six sheets of paper, each with a crudely hand-drawn family tree. The names of the victims were at the top, labeling each of the pages. Pointing, one by one, Evans recited: "Jackson Walker. From Atlanta, Georgia. Family been there for generations. His father, Earl Walker, was a Grand Wizard, and actually did some time in jail. Suspected of leading lynch mobs but never charged or convicted. Grandfather also in the KKK.

"Maria Benson. From Biloxi, Mississippi. Father died young, but grandfather was a card-carrying member of the KKK. He was arrested several times and did a stint at the state penitentiary for attempted murder of a Black man.

"William Hitchcock. The Councilman's son. I can't prove it, but I think William Sr. is a KKK member. He's been seen a lot with other known members. But he keeps it pretty quiet. Family has lived in New Orleans for generations. But I did find an uncle, Fredric Hitchcock, who was arrested in a KKK rally in 1955 for resisting arrest. The charges were later dropped.

"Richard Walsh. Also from Atlanta. Daddy seems clean. Lost his mother when he was three. His grandfather, however, was a really bad dude. Charged three times with murder. Each victim Black. Once for raping a Black woman. Acquitted every time. Liked to brag about it. Looks like he pretty much brought up Richard Walsh from the age of fourteen, after Richard's father died.

"George Landes is the only victim with no KKK connection. Grew up in Rhode Island. Looks like his family never left. Pretty boring. He was the one found with Walsh. The one Becca figures was in the wrong place at the wrong time.

"Samuel Beckett. Our last victim. Family is from South Carolina. His family is considered royalty in the KKK. His great-great-grandfather was Robert Beckett, Grand Wizard and in the South Carolina Klan that President Grant attacked in the 1860s."

"President Grant? You mean Ulysses Grant?"

"Yes, sir. The one and only," responded Evans.

Evans explained that in 1871, Congress passed the Ku Klux Klan Act to protect Blacks from being abused, beaten, and lynched in the Deep South. But until the Civil War ended, little was done.

"President Grant began a scorched-earth campaign against the Klan and any white supremacist groups throughout the nation," continued Evans. "Because Grant believed he couldn't trust local police whose prior job was to catch slaves trying to escape their owners, he sent in federal soldiers and arrested Klan members left and right. It was a real shit show. He then had U.S. attorneys try the cases, and federal judges started handing down harsh sentences."

DiMeglio appreciated the history lesson. "I'm beginning to understand the hatred so many southerners have for the Feds, Smitty."

"It got worse. In South Carolina, a stronghold for the Klan, Grant suspended habeas corpus. That gave the Feds the power to imprison suspected Klan members without a trial. In the end, Grant's campaign had hundreds of Klan members rotting behind bars, where they met some harsh receptions from Black inmates. It decimated the Klan in South Carolina and throughout most of the South, but the embers of discontent never went away. They just went underground, where they simmered only to rise again decades later. Grant's efforts were laudable, but they didn't last."

"This is great stuff. How did you find it so quickly?"

"Google," Evans responded.

"Bullshit, Smitty. You have to be using a lot more than Google. What's your secret?"

"If I told you, Agent DiMeglio, it wouldn't be a secret." With that, Evans left the room.

CHAPTER THIRTY-FOUR

The sun shining through the window awoke DiMeglio and Simone early. In their passion the night before, they forgot to shut the shades. Sully was sleeping on the floor at the foot of the bed and as soon as he sensed movement, he was up on the bed licking DiMeglio's face. Sully and DiMeglio had become close, and it didn't take long for the dog to figure out that Simone was the disciplinarian and DiMeglio the easy touch. Bad cop, good cop.

"Geez, Sully, get down," ordered Simone. The dog reluctantly obeyed.

"He needs a man in his life," responded DiMeglio.

Simone responded, "Just get him a dog biscuit. He'll do anything for them. And why did you leave the blinds open last night?"

"Me?" DiMeglio retorted. "You were the one who turned out the light."

"What's that got to do with it?" Simone asked, smiling.

"I don't know. But I'm in the mood for oysters."

As if on cue, Sully let out a soft whine and quietly walked out of the room.

Finished with his shower, DiMeglio joined Simone in the kitchen, where she had made some coffee, wearing only a loose silk robe. It gave DiMeglio some ideas, but he knew better if he was ever going to get to work. *Can you have too many oysters?*, he wondered.

Taking a cup of coffee, DiMeglio decided to tell Simone about what Evans had told him. It was his promise to keep nothing about the investigation from her. And he meant to keep that promise.

"That sounds insane, Chris," reacted Simone.

"I know. But it is a connection, crazy or not."

"Do you have any idea how many families in the South have a past that is in some way connected to the KKK? At one time, there was barely a town that didn't have a chapter. I'm surprised Ancestry.com doesn't have it as an inherited gene. Christ, back in the day, sheets in the South were used more for hoods than beds!"

DiMeglio wasn't sure if Simone thought the comparison was humorous, but chose not to ask.

Simone continued, "Racism and bigotry still infest the South, Chris. So, it's no wonder that the victims might come from racist families. After all, they're all white and privileged in some fashion."

"I know that, Becca. But I also know we can't ignore it."

"Well, I guess you assume that the Slasher is Black then. Right?"

"I suppose," responded DiMeglio. "But that might be too easy. I don't want to assume anything."

"C'mon, Chris, let's go with the stereotype," Simone

derisively continued. "Angry Black man killing anyone connected to the KKK."

"Becca, I'm not trying to convey any stereotype by saying the killer is Black."

"Yet you're willing to assume that the KKK is involved in this in some way? That conclusion, based upon what you know, isn't just not easy, it's preposterous and has no foundation in the evidence we've seen. Tell me where I'm wrong, Chris."

"So far, Becca, you're right. But it might be a start to connecting the dots. I want to pursue it further. We need to understand why their members may have become targets of a serial killer. As Steve Jobs once said . . ."

Simone raised her hand to signal *stop*. "Please, Chris, not another one of your corny quotes. I think we've all had enough of them."

DiMeglio couldn't resist. "Jobs said, 'You can't connect the dots looking forward; you can only connect them looking backwards.'"

Simone raised her hand again. "So where does this now lead us?" she asked. "On the facts you have, do you honestly want to start suggesting to the KKK that there is a killer out there stalking them? Do you have any idea the kind of reaction that would elicit? They may have been on the edge of extinction once, but they're stronger than ever now."

"I hear you. But the character of the victims and their families is not relevant to our job. If the KKK is the connecting link, they need to know that, and we need to protect them. And we can only do that by informing them. For all we know, they've already figured it out and may be preparing a vigilante campaign of their own. If so, we need to stop that, too."

"Fine, Chris. Then I suggest you have Captain Broussard introduce you to Henri Tibbets, the Grand Master of the Louisiana Ku Klux Klan. I'll skip the meeting, since I'm likely to shoot that bastard on sight."

CHAPTER THIRTY-FIVE

Henri Tibbets was a white supremacist through and through. At age fifty-five, he'd been the public face of the KKK in Louisiana for two decades. Most Klansmen kept their identities secret, fearing recrimination and disgust from those not in the Klan and unsympathetic to its principles. But Tibbets didn't harbor those fears. Unapologetic about his prejudice and racism, he veiled his comments under the cloak of the First Amendment and was always careful never to suggest violence among his followers. Instead, he played on the fears of his fellow white sycophants that it was the Black man who was violent and who threatened their safety and freedom. When pressed, he expanded his voice of hatred to Asians, Hispanics, Native Americans and any person of color. Nor did he exclude Jews from his odium.

"My, my, Captain Bro, what could possibly bring you to my offices?" sneered Tibbets. He remained seated at his desk as Broussard and DiMeglio stood. He didn't offer them a seat, and they opted to remain standing anyway. Both hoped the meeting would be brief.

Tibbets's front for the KKK operations was a construction company his family had owned for three generations. Although the company was prosperous, his role in it was only for show. He didn't do any work. That was left to those who worked for him. He never got his hands dirty, preferring to run both the Klan and his legitimate enterprise like a Mafia don. His office looked like a museum of Civil War memorabilia and historical Confederate flags. His white robe and hood hung proudly on a coat rack to the side of his desk.

"Regrettably, Tibbets, it's not to arrest you," responded Broussard.

Broussard and Tibbets had a long and stormy relationship that was a favorite with the press. The KKK vs. a Black captain. Tibbets never lost an opportunity to spew his hatred of Broussard through diatribes against him whenever the New Orleans police force tripped. The press ate it up, fanning the disdain each of them had for the other. "You can't have a Black man policing the Blacks," Tibbets would say. Or he'd spout to the press, "Captain Bro is the reason we have so much crime. He's soft on his own community, where the New Orleans criminals fester." He was always a sure source for a bigoted comment, and the press loved it.

At first Broussard would respond to the press himself by describing Tibbets as a hooded racist who would be better off staying out of the business of the New Orleans Police Department. But that only fueled the stories and pushed the press to reach out to Tibbets for more. So Broussard eventually stopped making any comments on rants by Tibbets. The provocative remarks still made the press, but they didn't last long in the minds of readers because Broussard assiduously avoided engaging in any public dialog.

"And who is your companion, Captain Bro?" continued Tibbets. "He doesn't look like he's from around here." He reached out his hand, half rising from his chair. "Who might you be, son?"

DiMeglio had taken an immediate dislike to Tibbets. He recoiled at being called "son" and being offered a hand to shake.

Tibbets reminded him of the bullies he met while growing up on Arthur Avenue. It was a tough neighborhood dominated by Italians, Irish, and Blacks. Most were people DiMeglio got along with, but among each of the groups were small gangs of misfits that got their way with others by bullying them. DiMeglio had seen his fair share of it, but little was directed at him. He never put up with it, and after a few fights with a couple of Irish tough guys and a few Italian punks, everyone left him alone. He never did have a run-in with any Blacks. Remembering all of that, the thing DiMeglio really wanted to do was take Tibbets's hand and show him how FBI agents can break a man's arm with one twist.

"Mr. Tibbets, I'm Special Agent Christopher DiMeglio with the FBI." He ignored the outstretched hand.

Tibbets sat back again and put on an exaggerated expression of being impressed. "Oh, so you're the hotshot from Washington I heard about that Guidry brought to town to fix Captain Bro's blunders," responded Tibbets.

DiMeglio clenched his jaw to avoid saying something he'd regret, reminding himself of the job he had to do.

"No, Mr. Tibbets," he responded, "I'm not here to fix anything, since nothing is broken. I'm here to help in the investigation as a specialist in tracking down serial killers. I suspect you know a lot about serial killers yourself." He couldn't resist throwing an insult his way.

Tibbets's expression barely changed. DiMeglio assumed Tibbets was used to being insulted. Or like most bullies, didn't care. Tibbets simply continued to stare at DiMeglio with an expression that clearly conveyed he had no intention of respecting him. So DiMeglio decided to get to the point and spend as little time as possible with this asshole. He understood why Simone wanted nothing to do with the meeting.

"I'm here to help save lives, Mr. Tibbets, and to ask you to help us do so as well," DiMeglio said, although he didn't really care much whether Tibbets's life was saved or not.

That got Tibbets's attention. "Help save lives, Agent? Why would you need my help to do that? Unless, of course, you and Bro can't do it yourselves."

"Don't worry, Tibbets, we can do just fine," interjected Broussard. "But your members have an ear to the street. They may have heard something. Or seen something."

"Or done something, Captain Bro?" Tibbets added with a smirk as he turned back to DiMeglio. "Do you think, Agent DiMeglio, like Captain Bro and others, that my members are simply violent? Or perhaps one of them might fit the profile for your killer? And you want my cooperation to help you catch him? Is that what you're really saying, Agent?"

"We'd just like to know if you or your members have heard anything," interjected Broussard.

"I wasn't talking to you, Captain Bro," Tibbets said sarcastically.

Turning back to DiMeglio, Tibbets continued, "If that's all you came here for today, to ask for my help in doing your job, I'd appreciate it if you'd leave. I can be of no use to you. And you are certainly of no use to me."

DiMeglio had enough. "We have reason to believe the Bayou Slasher is targeting KKK members."

Tibbets' expression immediately changed. His reaction confirmed that he had no idea of the suspicion. DiMeglio liked that. It meant Tibbets didn't have vigilantes roaming the streets. More important, DiMeglio had Tibbets's attention. Out of the corner of his eye, he could see that Broussard was not happy with what DiMeglio just said. His frown and stare made that clear.

"And why do you believe that, Agent?" Tibbets asked, staring intently at DiMeglio.

"Because every victim had a connection with the KKK," responded DiMeglio.

Tibbets looked confused. "But I know the names of those who were murdered, Agent. And only one of them is a member of my brotherhood."

"Who was the member?" asked Broussard.

"None of your damn business, Broussard," Tibbets snapped, again turning back to DiMeglio.

DiMeglio continued. "As far as I'm concerned, Mr. Tibbets, I don't give a damn if all or none of them are or were members of the Klan. What I do know is that their parents or grandparents were. So that's a common thread that ties the victims together. Common threads are what we look for in tracking down a serial killer."

"You have to be kidding me," Tibbets responded, leaning back in his chair. "So you're telling me that some Voodoo-practicing Black bastard is out there killing the children of Klan members?"

DiMeglio began to understand the mistake he made in confiding anything to Tibbets.

"No, Mr. Tibbets, I'm telling you there is a killer out there who may be targeting people connected to the KKK. I have no idea what color he is or what religion he might practice. And I don't care."

"Jesus, Agent, I didn't think anyone could be as stupid as Broussard and his band of Keystone Kops. Are you honestly suggesting anyone other than a Black man would want to kill Klan members?"

How could I come to hate someone else so quickly, thought DiMeglio as he stared at Tibbets, determined to keep his cool. "Mr. Tibbets," DiMeglio replied as calmly as he could, "as I said, I don't make assumptions. And there are plenty of people of every race and color who think the world would be a better place without the KKK and its racist views."

Tibbets smiled again and responded harshly, as if to menace Broussard and DiMeglio. "None of them who are intelligent, Agent."

At that point, DiMeglio was unable to hide his growing disdain for what Tibbets represented. Broussard sensed that further dialog would produce nothing and might turn even uglier. His biggest worry now was whether Tibbets would take this to the press.

"All right, gentlemen," interrupted Broussard. "Before this gets out of control, let's get to why we're here, because God knows I'd rather be just about anywhere else."

"Sorry, Captain," DiMeglio responded. "You're right." He was thankful Broussard intervened.

Tibbets said nothing.

Broussard continued, "What we'd like you to do, Tibbets, is tell us whether you or any of your members have noticed anything suspicious. Do any of them have a sense they're being watched or stalked? Have any of them been threatened?"

Tibbets responded, "No, I'm not aware of any of that. Nor do I feel I am in danger. I am not being followed and have not received any threats."

"And your members? Have any said anything to you?" asked DiMeglio.

"No. But I'll be sure to ask," responded Tibbets.

"You should tell them to stay indoors for a while and away from the Quarter," offered Broussard.

Tibbets did not turn his head away from DiMeglio. "I can't tell them what to do, Agent. But you can rest assured that they know how to protect themselves," as if it was DiMeglio, not Broussard, who made the suggestion.

That didn't stop Broussard. "Just don't tell them to take this up on their own, Henri," warned Broussard. "We don't need any vigilantes on the street."

Tibbets turned to Broussard, scorn in his eyes. "Like I said, we can take care of ourselves, Captain Bro," he snarled. "We don't need any orders from you or any other Black man trying to protect his brothers." Looking back at DiMeglio, he added, "Or any Wop."

DiMeglio handed Tibbets his card. "If you do have anything to add, Mr. Tibbets, please call me. Your help is appreciated."

Tibbets didn't get up. "You can show yourselves out," he concluded with a dismissive wave of his hand toward the door.

As they approached the door, Tibbets spoke again, "You know, Agent, you don't have to look too far to find folks 'round here who don't like whites. You can start with your buddy, Captain Bro. You ought to ask him about Billy Jones. Or Simon Dowling. Those are two names he'll remember. And check what your buddies at the FBI said about it when they came down on the NOPD back in 2010 or so."

Neither Broussard nor DiMeglio turned around to respond.

Once the two left, Tibbets called his second in command. “We have some hunting to do,” he told him.

CHAPTER THIRTY-SIX

"Becca warned you about Tibbets," said Broussard as they walked to the car.

"Jesus, what an asshole," responded DiMeglio. "But we need to follow every lead."

They climbed into the car and Broussard pulled away from the curb. "Listen Chris, you need to consider who you're talking to. This is New Orleans, not Washington. You never should have told him you suspected a KKK connection. There's no question that Tibbets is on the phone right now calling out his troops."

"How can you even stand to be in the same room with him? I've never met such an outright bigot in my life. I'm not naïve. I know there are plenty out there, but meeting one so outrageously outspoken is unnerving."

"Tell me about it. I've put up with his bullshit for nearly two decades from when he was a punk to the Grand Wizard."

"How has he lasted so long? Why hasn't someone shot him or run him out of town? There's got to be some folks who really hate him and what he stands for."

"There are a lot of people around here who think just like he does. The only difference is they hide. And I'd be lying if I told you I hadn't thought about finding a way to secretly end his hatred 'with prejudice' as the saying goes, but can't bring myself to sinking to his level. If I did, some other asshole would just take his place. I've just learned to put up with him."

"The devil you know?"

"Exactly. It makes it easier to watch him. Now he'll have his boys all over the Quarter tonight and for weeks until we catch the Slasher, or they get bored and grow tired of paying too much for drinks."

"Sorry. I made the mistake of trying to be honest with him. He just got under my skin. If I were the Slasher, he'd be my first victim."

"And that's why your theory might be wrong, Chris. If the Slasher has a hard-on for the KKK, why start with a bunch of young people who aren't even active in the Klan? Like Becca told you, KKK connections in the South are as common as grits."

"Maybe, but it's all we have right now, and we have to pursue it," DiMeglio continued. "Raleigh, you need to make sure your beat cops are on alert for anyone they suspect is in the Klan. Do you have a list of its members?"

"Most of them, but not all. Problem is, it's possible some of them are also cops."

"You don't screen who you hire?" DiMeglio asked.

"Screen for what, Chris? Prejudice? Bigotry? Racism? Those are questions we can't ask. And background checks are mostly worthless. We just try to make sure our recruits have no criminal record and are clean when they arrive. As for what happened before that and, more often than not, what happens after that, there's nothing we can do."

"So how are you supposed to solve the problem of racist cops, Raleigh? Just ignore the bigots?"

Broussard turned on Dauphine toward Bourbon as DiMeglio admired the unique New Orleans architecture while his confusion with Broussard continued. It was bullshit that background checks couldn't find more. The FBI did it to every agent. Broussard and the NOPD, as far as DiMeglio was concerned, were just too lazy to do so.

"Look, Chris, our cops are good people who care about New Orleans. But they've got an uphill fight with people like Tibbets spreading hatred. And the anti-cop movement only makes it worse. If some bad apples are among the city hires, there's not much else we can do. With fewer people wanting to be cops today, the job of recruiting qualified people is made even harder."

DiMeglio sighed.

"How soon before the press gets wind of our theory, Raleigh? I suspect I tripped on that one too by telling Tibbets what we suspect."

"Telling Tibbets was not your best move, Chris," responded Broussard. "But the paper probably already knows. I'm sure he's called them. No secret is kept long in New Orleans."

"Being from Washington, I should know that, I suppose," observed DiMeglio.

The two rode silently for a few minutes when DiMeglio decided to address the elephant in the room.

"Raleigh, I have to ask. Who are Billy Jones and Simon Dowling?"

As DiMeglio looked at Broussard, the expression on Broussard's face changed and seemed to reflect his thoughts before answering.

"Two perps I arrested way back. Both white. Tibbets complained I used excessive force. There were hearings at Internal Affairs and the charges were dropped."

"What kind of excessive force?"

Broussard's eyes were glued to the road ahead. "Look, Chris, you know as well as I do that police work can get messy. These two guys were caught after a burglary and Jones tried to resist arrest. So, I subdued him."

"How?"

"I shoved him to the ground, cuffed him, and put him in the squad car with his buddy, Dowling. That's all."

"When did this happen?"

"In 2006. I was pretty new to the force," Broussard answered.

"Were you ever charged with excessive force in other arrests?" asked DiMeglio, knowing it was a sensitive question but one he had to ask.

"Chris, don't profile me. I don't need that shit. I told you, the investigation was dropped."

"Sorry, Raleigh. It's an occupational hazard. I ask a lot of questions."

"Well, ask someone else," Broussard said. "It's only three weeks to Fat Tuesday and we've got bigger issues to deal with than your questions about my past."

The two did not speak for the rest of the drive.

CHAPTER THIRTY-SEVEN

"I'm not here because I wanna be," began Manning.

"I understand," replied DiMeglio. He asked Manning to join him in a conference room in the courthouse where he thought Manning would be comfortable.

"My lawyer told me I should cooperate now that all the charges are dropped. So, I'm here."

"But you don't want to be. Why?"

"Because I was set up and got screwed by the police. No matter what happens now, I'm stuck with a label that I was the Bayou Slasher. So, cooperatin' more with the police who started it isn't what I care to do."

"Then why did you agree to see me?"

"Because my lawyer told me to and because you're FBI. I still think the FBI knows what it's doing and doesn't ramrod people. I've had enough of that in my life."

"Like in the Marines?"

"The Corps didn't screw me. I left when I was done. I just didn't have anywhere to go."

"I understand," replied DiMeglio. "So tell me about that night, Wallis. Take it from the beginning. I'm particularly interested in what you heard and saw. What you felt. All of it will help me get a better picture of the killer."

"Like I told the cops, I got a text on my phone."

"But your phone has no text on it."

"Someone erased it."

"OK, let's assume you're right. Who do you think did that?"

"C'mon, Agent. That's obvious. The cops. My best guess is that asshole Bundy did it. He processed the arrest and took everything from me. He's a real hothead."

"But why would he do that?"

"How do I know? Maybe he didn't want me to have an alibi."

"That's not necessarily an alibi, but I understand your point," DiMeglio responded. "Tell me what happened, start to finish. And please be as specific as you can. Start with what you were wearing the night you went into the alley."

"What difference does what I was wearin' make?"

"You'd be surprised, Wallis. I can learn a lot. The more I know, the better. Just trust me. And as you remember things, however unimportant they may seem to be to you, it may trigger other important things to come to you."

"Whatever," responded Manning in a dismissive manner. "I was wearin' jeans, a beat-up shirt and a cap."

"And shoes and socks?" asked DiMeglio.

"Sneakers. No socks. You wanna know if I had on underwear? Jeez!"

"No, that will do."

"I was a couple of blocks away, so it took me just a few minutes to get there," continued Manning. "It was dark and hard to see what was down the alley. I got a little nervous whether I was bein' tricked, so I called out. No answer."

"But you kept going into the alley?"

"Yeah, my curiosity got the better of me. I needed some cash and thought I might as well see what was there."

"OK, then what?"

"It was pretty simple. I came up to the bodies. They were dead."

"Why do you say they were dead?"

"I shot a lot of people in Iraq, pal. I know what someone looks like when they're dead. They were both dead."

"Go on."

"So I looked around and not seein' nobody, knelt down and went through their pockets."

"How careful were you?"

"Careful?"

"Yeah, did you rush and pull apart the clothes to find the wallets, or were you careful?"

"I was respectful. You can call it careful if you like. Why?"

"Because if I accept your and your lawyer's theory that you were set up, the hair samples found on the bodies would have been there. But they could have easily come from your cap after you were taken into custody. Why didn't whoever you think set you up put hair samples or DNA on the knife or crosses?"

"Your guess is as good as mine. Maybe they're just careless. Or my hair didn't fall out in the cap. Shit, if they wanted to, they could have gotten my DNA from all over my apartment and rubbed in on the knife and crosses. But they didn't."

"Or maybe someone had gotten your hair and planted it."

"Sure. And it might have been the fuckin' Easter Bunny, too," responded Manning, obviously aggravated.

"What else, Wallis? What happened after you took the wallets?"

"I got up and walked away, same way I went in."

"And you saw no one? Not even a shadow?"

"There's shadows everywhere in New Orleans. If I saw one in that alley, it wouldn't have mattered to me."

"But it's important to me, Wallis. Because I think the killer was there, watching you, and making sure you were robbing the bodies. Making sure you got set up right."

"I don't remember."

"OK. Think hard. Is there anyone you know that could be the killer? Because somehow, he knew to call you. That doesn't happen randomly."

"I don't have no friends who'd do that. And I don't know killers. I mind my own business and keep out of the way."

"OK, Wallis, I understand. But as you think more about it and if something comes to mind, just jot it down and send me your notes. It will jog your memory. Then we can talk about it more. It will all help."

"Sure," Manning replied. "Nothing like homework. If I

remember things, I'll send you love notes. Will that make you feel better?"

"No need to be sarcastic, Wallis. I'm just doing my job. We're almost done. Just a few more questions, OK?" DiMeglio asked. He didn't want to push Manning too far and lose any chance of cooperation.

"Yeah, sure," Manning replied flatly.

"You've been arrested more than a few times for petty crap. Right?"

"Yeah. So?"

"So, let's take your theory a little further, Wallis. If you believe you were set up and that someone at the police station erased your text, what does that tell you, Wallis?"

"That the cops are in on it," replied Manning.

"In on a rush to find a suspect they can charge? Which is just what they did. Is that what you mean, Wallis? Because that's not much of a help."

"No. Because maybe, Agent DiMeglio, the Bayou Slasher is a fuckin' cop."

CHAPTER THIRTY-EIGHT

That evening, back in his hotel room, DiMeglio thought more about his interview with Manning, and his talk with Broussard. Something about the captain's curt responses about Jones and Dowling arrests bothered him. Why was Broussard so sensitive? Cops get accused of using excessive force all the time. Charges are rarely brought, and most investigations end quickly.

DiMeglio wrote down a list of personality traits that might provide clues. Controlling. Short-tempered and impulsive. Quick to anger. Unforgiving. Unwilling to take blame. Narcissistic. Paranoid. Loner.

Does Broussard fit such a profile? DiMeglio asked himself.

He certainly controlled his domain but didn't seem impulsive or quick to anger. Yet he did seem to have some anger with the system. But what cop doesn't? With all the respect Broussard had from his officers, DiMeglio could not imagine that Broussard was unforgiving. DiMeglio pushed the pad away and concluded that Broussard fell short of the profile of a serial killer. Broussard didn't check enough boxes. But DiMeglio also reminded himself that not every serial killer neatly fits into a stereotype.

He turned on his laptop and logged onto the FBI server

to enter notes on the interview with Manning. The last report entry he filed was on the meeting with Tibbets. It concluded with Tibbets's comment about looking at what the FBI thought about of the Jones and Dowling arrests.

Just as he was shutting down the computer, he changed his mind with another thought. He switched to the records files and searched for Raleigh Broussard.

CHAPTER THIRTY-NINE

DiMeglio's non-dates with Simone became more regular as the investigation continued. Usually about two or three times a week. He was being careful not to let others know. It was entirely unprofessional, but increasingly, he just didn't care.

In truth, their trysts were not as confidential as he thought. But no one wanted to interfere. Simone seemed happy, and that's what her colleagues cared about.

As the two walked Sully in Woldenberg Park, a dog-friendly area on the Mississippi riverfront, they talked shop.

"I'd like to run another theory past you on the Slasher case," Chris said as Sully pulled him toward a nearby bush.

Walking Sully was an experience. Wherever Sully wanted to go, Sully went. DiMeglio wondered what he'd do if Sully ever caught whatever he was looking for in the bushes.

"Now what? You've already stretched it to the point where we're protecting bigots."

"The Slasher may be a cop."

Simone stopped and looked at DiMeglio, her mouth open in surprise. "Well, now you're really going off the deep end, Chris. Where did you get that idea?"

"At the end of my interview with Manning, he suggested it, and the more I thought about it, the more it hit me as a logical conclusion. It just sort of fell into place. So, I looked at the idea and the more I did, the more I believed it to be true. It just makes sense."

"How?"

"Let's look at the facts, Becca. This serial killer is smart. He knows how to cover up evidence at a crime scene. That's a lot harder than meets the eye. Simply rubbing off fingerprints never works."

"Chris, that's hardly a secret that only cops know."

"This killer not only knew how to clean a scene but also to be certain there were no witnesses and no DNA. There was no sign of struggle. So, every victim needed to know the killer or be comfortable with him when they went into the alleys or parking lots."

"OK, but none of that necessarily supports your theory. So far, you've said nothing that leads to the conclusion that the killer is a cop."

"There's more," continued DiMeglio, pulling Sully away from some garbage on the ground. "The killer was strong. Very strong. Strong enough to subdue a grown man—or two. And he knew exactly where to cut their throats. Then he carefully staged the scene with the crosses and Xs on the foreheads."

He could see that Becca, shaking her head, wasn't convinced.

"Great, Chris. So maybe it was a former pro wrestler turned surgeon."

DiMeglio ignored the remark and continued. "While I

agree that all of this could mean the killer is anyone, the double murder and the frame-up of Manning is the final clue. He keeps sending me notes to follow the evidence that someone either stole or changed. He's obsessed with the phone."

"No one on the force screwed with the evidence. And as for accusing a cop, there's plenty of them who might carry a racial grudge and have the strength you say they needed, but you have no evidence to support your belief it's a cop."

"Every crime scene except the double murder was clean," DiMeglio continued. "When I first looked at the Walsh-Landes killing, I was initially convinced it was unrelated or a copycat. Our serial killer would never make those mistakes. Or, as I now think, there is another explanation. Manning was put there by the killer for a reason. The killer sent him the text that 'opportunity knocks.' It was all to lead us on a wild goose chase. To take the heat off the killer while he decided where to strike next. He played us for fools."

"You weren't on the case then, Chris. So, I guess you mean he played me, Bundy, and Broussard for fools."

"I'm not being critical, Becca. I would have probably come to the same conclusion," DiMeglio lied. He knew that good police work required a lot more forensic evidence than the NOPD recovered at the scene.

"And that leads you to the conclusion that a cop killed them and all the others?" Simone asked incredulously.

"Exactly."

"I hope you realize what this would mean if you're right. The last time we had a serial killer on the force was in '95. Victor Gant."

"I know, Becca. He allegedly murdered twenty-seven women, mostly prostitutes, and dumped their bodies in nearby swamps. But he was never formally charged, and the press speculated that the police were covering up for him."

"Yes, and the murders remain unsolved to this day. They've been a black eye on the department ever since. Every year it seems that someone tries to resurrect the case and describe us as inept or, worse, corrupt. But that doesn't mean we have another serial killer cop, Chris."

"Becca, Gant was all before your time and it's not as if cops can't be serial killers. Gant was not the first and he won't be the last. Joseph DeAngelo with the Auburn Police Department in California, and Gerald Schaefer with the Martin County, Florida, Sheriff's Department are two examples. Combined, it's alleged they murdered over one hundred people. Cops can go bad, Becca."

Simone, shaking her head, asked, "So you think it's someone on the force? If your theory is right, it could be a cop from anywhere. Why the NOPD?"

"Or a former cop," responded DiMeglio, not answering Simone's question.

"Why not military? We've got plenty of them around here," added Simone.

"The killer is not likely military. They're not that cunning.

And I'm pretty convinced he's a current member of the NOPD. How else can we explain the deletion of the text that got Manning to the scene?"

"Because chances are that text never existed. Manning may simply be lying. He's certainly done enough of that," replied Simone.

"Maybe, Becca. But the killer also had to know the patrol schedules to avoid capture on the last murder."

As they approached a bench, Simone sat down as if exhausted. DiMeglio joined her on the bench. Sully lay down in the grass beside them.

"So now what?" Simone asked.

"I have to tell Broussard. But first I need to review some more files," he said.

"What files?"

"Broussard's files. I need to be comfortable that he's not a suspect himself. I have some stuff I need to dig into a little deeper. I need to eliminate some red herrings."

"You're looking at Broussard's personnel files to decide whether he's a serial killer?"

"No, Becca. FBI files. I don't have access to the New Orleans PD files. Yet. But the Department of Justice investigated the NOPD in 2010 and after an eleven-month review, hundreds of interviews, and reading thousands of pages of files, issued a report finding that the department was rife with bad procedures and behavior. The city entered into a consent decree in 2012 that mandated changes."

"We all know about that, Chris," responded Simone. "Broussard makes us sit through monthly training on procedures because of that damn decree. It's a huge waste of time. And worse, it makes us think twice before we do our job."

"One of the incident reports in the FBI files is about Broussard's and Dickenson's arrests of Billy Jones and Simon Dowling. It was one of many cited incidents, including some others involving Broussard."

"Broussard was involved in others?" asked Simone.

"Yes," DiMeglio said. "He's cited in four incident reports."

"Then why wasn't he let go if the FBI thought he was a bad cop?"

"Discipline was up to the local force. Some officers were fired. Broussard was not one of them. Nor was Dickenson, his partner at the time."

"Dickenson?" Simone asked. "What the hell's he got to do with it?"

"He was with Broussard at all of the questionable arrests. And Dickenson now runs the work assignments. He knows the schedules," Chris answered.

Sully stood and looked beseechingly at the couple. They rose and continued their walk.

"I don't know enough about Dickenson," DiMeglio continued, Sully pulling on his leash, leading the way. "We need to keep an eye on him. But my gut tells me Broussard's not a killer. He does not fit the personality. He's a team player and genuinely cares for his officers. He stands up to authority when it's right to do so. I see no psychosis in his behavior."

"Then why look at his file, Chris?"

"Because one thing that keeps troubling me," DiMeglio responded. "Broussard was charged with using excessive force at least four times. Two of those arrests were mentioned by Tibbets as we were leaving."

"Jesus, you're going to trust something said by a psychopath like Tibbets? Do you have any clue what would happen in this town if the Slasher is a Black police officer who kills KKK members?"

"I have to go where the evidence leads me."

"When are you going to confront Captain Broussard, then? Whether this is true or not, the mere allegation could cost him his job. And he's a good man."

"I know, I know, Becca. It's not something I want to see. But he's a professional and he will handle it. I'll do everything I can to protect him." DiMeglio paused. "Assuming he's innocent."

CHAPTER FORTY

DiMeglio picked up his phone and punched in Manning's number. "I got your note that you wanted to see me again, Wallis."

"Yeah, I wanted to talk to you about how you figure this shit out as a profiler. 'Cause it seems to me you got this all wrong."

"Wallis, I'm in the middle of chasing down a lot of leads and don't have time for idle thoughts or discussions about profiling. And I don't need you telling me how to do my job."

"OK, but it seems to me that the answer is staring you in the face and you just don't see it. Or don't want to see it."

"Really, Wallis?" DiMeglio responded impatiently. "Why don't you tell me what's so obvious? You can certainly do that on the phone."

"Well, it seems to me that it's pretty simple."

"How so?"

"You've got a bunch of dead white people in New Orleans with their throats slit. In a town where the KKK is big and strong. Where Blacks are suppressed and denied their rights every day. Where Voodoo reigns among them. Looked at any Voodoo congregation lately, Agent DiMeglio? See any whites among them? What does that tell you, Agent DiMeglio?"

“Wallis, I don’t have time for this. What’s your point?”

“That you’ve got some Black man obsessed with Voodoo taking his revenge on white folk. Isn’t that what’s obvious, Agent DiMeglio? And if it is, then why not look at who takes out his shit on whites? Black bastards do.”

“That’s too simple, Wallis.”

“Really? So you think it’s some white guy who just likes to kill people? Shit, Agent DiMeglio, that could be you or even me. Put that in your profile box.”

DiMeglio heard all he wanted to hear. “Wallis, you were a sniper who never once killed a man hand to hand. You shot them from a comfortable distance. You wouldn’t know a knife from a fork. And honestly, you’re not smart enough to be a serial killer. At least not the Bayou Slasher.”

“I may be smarter than you think, and I know what I see.”

“Unless you have something meaningful for me, please keep your speculation to yourself. It doesn’t help.” DiMeglio hung up the phone.

CHAPTER FORTY-ONE

Broussard was dumbfounded when DiMeglio suggested the killer was a cop. "You can't be serious," he said, putting down his cigar and leaning back in his chair as if in shock.

"I am," responded DiMeglio. "Everything leads to that conclusion."

"I'm not sure I agree, Chris, but take me through it again."

For forty-five minutes, DiMeglio took Broussard through the facts just as he had with Simone. Broussard's reaction was no better than hers.

"C'mon, Chris," Broussard picked up his cigar again, and looked hard at the agent. "Now you're telling me that we might have a cop on our hands obsessed with killing members of the Klan? I hate to tell you, but cops hating the Klan means it could be anyone, including me."

"Yes, I've ruled you out," DiMeglio said matter-of-factly. "You don't fit the profile. You had a good childhood, did well in school, and your history shows none of the psychopathic tendencies we see in serial killers."

"Gee, I find that so reassuring, Chris. As a Black man, I just love being profiled."

DiMeglio chose to ignore the sarcasm and continued. "What did trouble me were the four charges of using excessive force against you around the time of the consent decree."

"They were all dropped," Broussard responded. "Are you're telling me that you've been investigating me?" Broussard stood up and leaned over his desk.

"They were dismissed," responded DiMeglio. "But you can understand that they raised questions."

"No, Agent DiMeglio, I do not understand that," Broussard snarled. "Police work was different back then. We were trained differently. Sure, I was tough. Too tough at times. But I never used my service weapon on anyone, and beating on a few folks went with the territory."

DiMeglio decided to press a bit. "Then why is it that a Black man never filed charges against you, Raleigh? Why were they all white?"

Broussard smiled. "Agent DiMeglio, you can be so naïve at times. I was rough with Black men, too. But they don't talk. At least not back then. I can assure you, I beat on anyone who resisted me, regardless of their color."

DiMeglio felt foolish. Of course there was an unstated code among Blacks not to cooperate with police or file complaints, fearful of worse repercussions. Fears that were too often validated.

"Sorry, Raleigh, but I had to eliminate you. I'm sorry if it upsets you" Broussard sat back down.

"And I suppose that's a compliment?" Broussard asked, still glaring at the agent. "And you know that because you investigated *me*?" he added.

"It's my job to investigate everyone."

"So what about Bundy, Simone, Evans and the rest of my officers? Did you investigate them, too?" replied Broussard, his facing turning red in anger. His reaction was to protect his turf, triggering his paternal instincts for his brood.

"Not yet," responded DiMeglio. "I did tell Becca. But before I told you, I needed to be sure you were clean."

"Clean?" objected Broussard. "I suppose I should thank you, but for some reason don't feel like doing so. Don't screw with my people without my knowing. We've got a killer out there. And if your new theory that he's a cop is true, it's my job, not yours, to find him. You got that, Agent DiMeglio?"

"Captain Broussard, you can fire me at any time. But until then, we need to work together, and you need to let me do my job too, even if it bothers you."

Broussard picked up the half-done cigar, relit it, and looked at DiMeglio, pondering his next words. "OK, Chris, so now what?"

"Now I have to go through all the personnel and disciplinary files over the past ten years for all the former and current officers."

"Chris, that's dozens of people. How are you going to do that?"

"I'll get help from Washington. But it has to be confidential. No one else can know, or it will compromise the investigation."

"And how am I supposed to let some outsider from the FBI look at personnel and disciplinary files without word leaking out? These are not digital files that can simply be downloaded. We're not that modern, Chris. Doing this without a leak will be impossible."

"Hopefully, by the time it leaks, we'll have the killer."

"We're less than a week from Mardi Gras. My officers will be swamped with patrols in addition to all the surveillance you ordered in the Quarter. If they find out they're being investigated by you, you can kiss their cooperation good-bye."

"I know. But that can't be avoided."

"Shit, Chris. This is not going to be easy. But if you want to do this, you're doing it by the book."

"Agreed."

"That means the first thing you need is a search warrant for the files. Then we'll see where it leads. But I have to tell you, I'm still not convinced, and I hope you're wrong."

"I hope I'm wrong, too, Raleigh. But I seriously doubt I am."

CHAPTER FORTY-TWO

Enfield's reaction to DiMeglio's request for a search warrant was blunt.

"You're asking for a lot here, Agent DiMeglio," the judge said. "Your theories sound more like speculation than sound thinking. I'm not sure you have enough here to support a warrant into sensitive files, particularly the disciplinary files that are under seal. And as much as I appreciate that cops can go rogue, it's a very serious allegation."

DiMeglio expected Enfield to be tough despite his suspicion of the New Orleans police department. Although he supported the police and gave them a lot of leeway, he came down very hard when they made mistakes and didn't approve of wild goose chases. But DiMeglio knew Enfield staunchly believed that a strong, honest police force was the only way to keep New Orleans safe even though its crime rate was consistently among the highest in the nation. He was counting on that to get the subpoena he needed.

"Your Honor, I appreciate you seeing me on this," DiMeglio answered. "And I appreciate Attorney Gaudet supporting my application. But I am very serious."

"I supported you coming to see Judge Enfield, Agent DiMeglio," interjected Gaudet. "I did not say I agree with your suspicions." The last thing she needed was to leave an impression with Enfield or the police department that she believed the New Orleans police force was corrupt or, worse, included a serial killer.

DiMeglio frowned at the interruption, but continued. “My apologies, Ms. Gaudet. I did not mean to imply that you agreed with anything.”

“OK, Agent DiMeglio, you have my attention,” interrupted Enfield. “Don’t waste it.”

“You Honor, I’ve personally investigated over twenty-five serial killers and helped bring more than a dozen to justice. I’ve advised on countless more. That experience has taught me that the facts that lead to apprehension are often obvious but overlooked.”

“I’ve certainly seen enough of that in my court,” replied Enfield. “But what you’re asking for is highly sensitive, and even if an officer is your killer, I’d be letting you look at an awful lot of sensitive and confidential information that is irrelevant. And worse, information that the officers involved have been led to believe is sealed.”

“Except where it is needed in a legitimate investigation,” Gaudet pointed out. She thought the request was without foundation, but she did not want Enfield to lose sight of his right to grant the request if he felt there were adequate grounds. She was committed to her sworn duty as an attorney and officer of the court to do what was right.

“I understand that, Ms. Gaudet. I certainly don’t need you to educate me on my powers as a judge.” Gaudet regretted trying to help and decided she'd remain silent from that point on. Everyone knew that once you got on the wrong side of Enfield he held a grudge you'd be haunted by whenever you appeared before him.

Turning to DiMeglio, Enfield asked, "Agent DiMeglio, with all the files you need to review, you've asked permission to have other agents assist. Is that correct?"

"Yes, Your Honor, I want to get through them as quickly as possible."

"Because you fear there will be another murder if you don't?"

"To a degree, sir, yes. The sooner we solve the case, the more likely we'll prevent another killing. But it's impossible to know when or if the killer will strike again."

"But he's a serial killer, Agent DiMeglio. So, isn't it certain he'll strike again?"

"Actually, no. Many serial killers go on hiatus, particularly when they feel they may be close to getting caught. Some even stop entirely. The percentage of those who keep killing once a full public investigation is under way is relatively small. It's that small group who like to challenge those chasing them. 'Try to catch me' becomes their mantra."

Despite her reservations, Gaudet could not stay quiet and added, "And if we don't look under every rock, Your Honor, what do we tell the family of someone who is unlucky enough to be a target of that small percentage?"

DiMeglio nodded in agreement.

Surprisingly, Enfield was sympathetic. Turning to DiMeglio, Enfield asked, “Yes, Agent DiMeglio, what would you say to that family?”

“The same thing I say to every victim’s family. That I’m sorry for their loss, with an assurance that we’re doing all we can do,” DiMeglio replied. “That is why, Judge Enfield, I’d like to take a look and prevent that kind of conversation from ever having to occur again. I want to be able to say that we truly did everything we could.”

Enfield stared at DiMeglio for what seemed an eternity. The agent shifted slightly in his seat, waiting for the verdict. He was annoyed that the judge had the power to doubt his experience and wisdom when it came to serial killers. But, such was the setup of the judicial system. He took a breath, and stared at the judge.

Finally, Enfield spoke, like a god delivering a decree. “OK, Agent DiMeglio, you may look at the files. But only you. So don’t expect to get any sleep any time soon.”

“Thank you, Your Honor,” responded DiMeglio. It was the break he wanted, however impossible the task ahead of him might be.

On the way out of the courthouse, Gaudet asked DiMeglio, “So how are you going to pull this one off, Chris? It will take you forever to go through the files, let alone the time to put them together.”

“Are you volunteering to help, Harper?”

“Sorry, Chris, the judge’s order said that task was all

yours." DiMeglio suspected that Gaudet wanted to stay as far away from looking at those files as possible. If she participated and the police officers found out, even if the serial killer was among them, she'd never have their cooperation again.

CHAPTER FORTY-THREE

DiMeglio quickly found that the task he'd insisted on doing was going to be overwhelming. Even if he had the time, he'd need months to go through the personnel files of the New Orleans Police Department. And all for what might be a wild goose chase. Maybe Simone was right.

He also needed to be on the streets, working with the task force tracking down real leads to the killer. Otherwise, the police would be suspicious. So he was forced to work on the files at night. Enfield's warning that DiMeglio shouldn't expect to be getting much sleep proved to be painfully true. Worse for DiMeglio, it was taking him away from his evenings with Simone. He could see she was getting suspicious, and she even asked him straight out what he was hiding. "We agreed you would tell me everything, remember?" she reminded him.

He wished he could be honest with her, but Enfield's order mandated complete confidentiality. And that meant he could not tell Simone. This was the first time he lied to her about what he was doing, but he felt it was unavoidable.

"Unfortunately," he told her, "the FBI believes I can work more than one case at a time. They've dragged me into an investigation in California. I have to look through files and the only time I can do so and still keep on track with our investigation here is from midnight to eight. My hotel room is too cramped. So, sleep is not an option and finding time to be with you is pretty much impossible."

"Is there anything I can do to help?"

"I wish you could, Becca," DiMeglio said. In that case, he wasn't lying.

"Well, you can certainly take an hour off now and then, no? I miss you."

"I miss you, too. But for now, my hands are tied. I expect to be done with this soon." Another lie.

"Wow," replied Simone. "Will that put you past Mardi Gras?"

"Probably. And with all the prep for the coverage we have to have on the parade routes, I don't expect any sleep any time soon."

"Well, after it's over, let's find some time for a little trip to relax. You've earned it."

"Together? Is that going to cause a problem?"

"Slow down, big boy. It's not like I'm asking you to move in with me," responded Simone. "But you don't know New Orleans, Chris. If you think our relationship is a secret, I want what you're smoking. What's nice here is that no one judges. It's our business. So yes, together. On a trip. No problem."

"I'd like that," he said. "And anyway, I doubt Sully would approve of a new roommate." In truth, he'd fallen for her. He knew it was wrong to mix up work with a love affair, but there was so much about her that DiMeglio desired. He resolved to let the romance develop on its own timetable and that once the case was solved, he'd try to take it to the next level.

CHAPTER FORTY-FOUR

The seventh victim was found just two days before Fat Tuesday, next to a dumpster in another alley, this time off Dauphine. Throat slashed. Three Xs. Cross in hand. Clean crime scene.

At the scene, Broussard took DiMeglio and Simone aside. "If the Slasher is a cop," observed Broussard, "he's rubbing our noses in it."

"That's predictable," responded DiMeglio. "As serial killers keep getting away with killing, they sometimes begin to think they're invincible and take more risks."

"Like Jack the Ripper," observed Simone.

"Yeah, Jack the Ripper. But he's only one example. You can add at least a dozen more who dared the police to capture them."

"And those are the ones who got caught. How many never were?" asked Broussard.

"Too many, Raleigh. You have to remember that at their core, serial killers are psychopaths. They have a God image of themselves. That helps them justify what they do. So 'catch me if you can' is typical."

"Hey, Becca," yelled Bundy. "Help me out over here. I can't do this alone."

"It's OK, Becca," said Broussard. "Go help your protégé."

Broussard turned back to DiMeglio, frowning. "What can we expect at the parades? How bold will the Slasher get? If he really wants to stick our nose in it, will he try to kill someone one of those nights? The parades go on for hours. It's a madhouse."

"That's my fear. That he will strike then. With what he knows now about our investigation, it may be too tempting for him. And if he's really bold, it will be the last night, on Fat Tuesday. It makes sense. With a crowd like that and all the confusion, we need to anticipate it. We need to plan for it."

"But why would he hit when it will be so hard not to get caught?" asked Broussard. "It's not as if no one will see someone going into an alley."

"That's not necessarily true," DiMeglio countered. "The more confusing the moment and the bigger the crowd, the easier it is to conceal the obvious. With so much going on, people don't see the specifics. They're just a mob moving in unison. When someone drops out—say to go into an alley—the rest of the mob just keeps moving on. Unless they know someone personally, mob members will never notice who left."

DiMeglio got back to the task at hand and returned his attention to the crime scene and the officers attending.

"OK, Smitty, see what you can find on victim number seven," he asked.

"I already did," responded Evans.

"What? Not possible. We've only been here half an hour."

"I do have a cellphone, sir. So I can easily access Google. While you and Broussard were talking, I was searching to find more about the victim."

DiMeglio smiled. He suspected Evans did more than just Google, something anyone knew how to use. Evans clearly had his own collection of apps and tricks in using search engines. DiMeglio made a mental note to learn more about that later.

"So what do you have, Smitty?" asked Broussard.

"His name is Cyrus 'Bubba' Lang," Evans responded.

"Shit," said Broussard. "Lang is a full-fledged member of the Klan. One of Tibbets's right-hand men. He was being groomed by Tibbets as an heir apparent. He's only in his twenties, but as deep down a racist as they come. And he doesn't hide it. There's going to be hell to pay for this one."

"Maybe the Slasher wants to send a clear message to Tibbets that no one in the KKK is protected," suggested DiMeglio. "What about his family, Smitty?"

"Just what we saw in the others, sir. His daddy and granddad were both members. His father spent fifteen in Pollock."

"Let me guess, Smitty," interjected Broussard. "I bet he spent those years on the farm."

"Yep," replied Evans. "He was one of the lucky ones."

"Or connected," added Broussard.

"What's the farm?" DiMeglio asked.

"Pollock is named after the Louisiana town where it's located," Broussard explained. "It's a high-security federal prison housing over 1,200 inmates. It includes a minimum-security facility for those inmates lucky enough—or connected enough—to avoid the animals in the high-security facility and confinement with them. It's known as the farm, and by prison standards it's a Ritz-Carlton.

"This one's too close to home, Chris. A card-carrying member. That's in your face."

"Any way to tamp it down in the papers, Raleigh?" asked DiMeglio. "We're going to have enough on our hands Tuesday night."

"I can try, but any story with a racial angle is hard to keep out of the press. They love this shit. And this story has the spin of Blacks killing whites. The press will eat that up."

"We don't know if the killer is Black, Raleigh," noted DiMeglio.

"Tell that to Tibbets," concluded Broussard.

CHAPTER FORTY-FIVE

Victor Richards, owner of the *New Orleans Gazette*, a local tabloid, inherited the paper from his father. Unlike most publishers, Richards loved getting his hands dirty and didn't let facts necessarily get in the way of his editorial slant. Richards was a muckraker, through and through, and had his run-ins with Broussard. He also believed Guidry was corrupt. But Louisiana politics kept him from effectively exposing Guidry or making points against Broussard.

"How long have you known the Klan connection, Raleigh?" asked Richards, his gray hair neatly combed off of his tanned, well-lined face.

"We developed the theory about a month ago."

"And you say you met with Tibbets about it?"

"We did."

"How did that go?"

"Not well."

"Yeah. I know. He called me. Told me the two of you visited him." Turning to DiMeglio, he added, "And he said you didn't impress him much for an FBI agent."

"I consider that a compliment," responded DiMeglio.

"You probably should, coming from the likes of Tibbets. I thought the idea was total bullshit. But after the killing of Lang, I wonder if you're right."

"We think the theory is sound," responded DiMeglio.

"And now you're asking me to keep it off my pages until Wednesday?"

"Yes," responded Broussard. "We're going to have enough on our hands on Tuesday, Victor. We don't need amateur vigilantes trying to find a killer."

"But Tibbets is going to send his thugs into the crowd, Raleigh, whether we publish something about it or not."

"We know that, but we can identify most of them. And he's only got about ten or fifteen in his crew who are stupid enough to go. So, they're somewhat manageable. And if they so much as look the wrong way, we'll take them into custody for the night."

"To hell with due process, huh?" Richards sarcastically observed.

"No more than in the past, Victor," Broussard replied.

"And the other papers have agreed?" asked Richards.

"We're asking," responded Broussard, "but we wanted to start with you."

"Precisely. So, there's no assurance that some other paper or digital blogger will report it anyway whether we do or not. In today's world, Raleigh, it's impossible to bury a story."

"But it is possible to refrain from adding gas to a fire," replied Broussard. "I'm only asking you for restraint to help us control a very bad situation."

"So you're asking me to not tell my readers of a danger

that might exist on the biggest night of Mardi Gras? You want me to let them go in harm's way without warning?"

"Come on, Victor," Broussard snapped. "Your readers are going to party in the Quarter and go to the parades no matter what you tell them. In fact, if you do report on this case, I bet even more of them will go just to be in the center of the storm."

"Are you insulting my readers?"

"I meant no disrespect."

"That's OK, Raleigh. They are stupid. A rag sheet like the *Gazette* doesn't attract Mensa members."

Broussard agreed, but chose not to say so. "I'm just trying to keep a lid on this until we can be less strained in manpower and better able to control the situation."

"OK, I'll wait forty-eight hours unless another paper or blogger reports it. If someone does or I even smell that they will, all bets are off and we'll fully cover it."

After they left, DiMeglio asked, "Can we can trust him?"

"Not likely. But he knows we can be a source for him in other situations, so he'll hold off at least until Wednesday morning. We'll have to wait to see if that changes depending upon what others do."

CHAPTER FORTY-SIX

"OK, you all have your assignments," Dickenson stated on the morning of Fat Tuesday. "Keep your eyes open. If you see anyone suspicious, confront them. If they don't have answers you like, take them into custody. We'll have detention vans every four blocks. It's Mardi Gras time, folks, so let's stay on top of it."

More than three hundred officers were assigned to monitor the weeklong festival. Although Mardi Gras celebration had been around since the 1780s, its popularity never waned. Originally held secretly to avoid church condemnation, it has ballooned over the centuries into what New Orleanians call "the greatest free show on earth!"

The state police assisted the local police department in watching the revelers closely. Hundreds of arrests were routinely made every year, although few were for serious crimes. FBI monitors were also assigned. The bureau had learned the importance of monitoring public events after their surveillance efforts helped find Dzhokhar and Tamerlan Tsarnaev, the brothers responsible for the 2013 Boston Marathon bombings.

But it was Fat Tuesday, the day of the biggest parades, most outlandish costumes, and largest celebrations, that most concerned Broussard. It's the night New Orleans doubles down on amorality with the arrival of countless partygoers.

Dickenson continued with his morning briefing. "The main parades along St. Charles Avenue will attract the largest crowds. They can go on for miles. That's our biggest nightmare." The officers all nodded their heads knowingly. They went through this every year. In addition to the sheer size of the crowds and the inability to control them, the carnival masks allowed anyone with ill intent to roam unrecognized. Drinking is always rampant and unrestrained. Violence is inevitable. And with all of the police concentrating on the Quarter, the outskirts of the city go pretty much unpoliced. It's a perfect environment for burglary and theft.

Broussard and DiMeglio decided everyone would work in pairs. If the killer was among them, they wanted him with a babysitter that night. Evans was assigned with Bundy. Simone with Dickenson. Broussard and DiMeglio would make up an additional pairing. Thirty more pairings were assigned. Everyone would report to Broussard and DiMeglio with anything suspicious they saw. The state police and FBI agents sent to New Orleans to help had their assignments as well, ultimately reporting to Broussard. When Broussard asked if Guidry wanted to join the surveillance, he got the reply he expected. Gaudet assured them that both she and Guidry were on call if needed, knowing Guidry would respond only if it served his interests.

CHAPTER FORTY-SEVEN

Early in the afternoon on Fat Tuesday, DiMeglio had finished what personnel files he could and saw no reason to keep digging. He hadn't found anything and resigned himself to giving it up. There just wasn't enough time.

Back at Simone's condo, the two enjoyed some time in bed, relaxing before what would be a long night once the final Mardi Gras festivities began. They fell fast asleep.

As evening approached, DiMeglio was awakened by Sully's wet tongue. Simone was still asleep and the dog seemed to know DiMeglio wouldn't ignore his pleas for a walk. *I'm a sucker,* DiMeglio thought, petting Sully's big head.

He dressed quietly while Sully wagged and pranced at the door. His walks with Sully had become a pleasant routine and a time for DiMeglio to reflect.

As they walked along Iberville toward the river, DiMeglio was racking his brain over what was missing from the investigation. It was only a few hours before the chaos would begin. At this point, he had more than enough clues and should have had a better picture of the killer. He knew that the Bayou Slasher was targeting the KKK, and he was convinced that the killer was a cop. DiMeglio was increasingly convinced that the killer had no loyalty to Voodoo principles. But what message was the killer trying to send with the Voodoo symbolism? Was it some sort of ruse, and could he be misunderstanding the killer's motivation? Could it be the killer liked Voodoo's evil as represented in movies and on television? Or was the message something else he didn't see? Was there any religious symbolism at all? Maybe the three Xs were nothing more than a sadistic branding of the victims.

The walk was longer and more leisurely than usual. The weather was perfect, with the air fresh after earlier thunderstorms. The storms helped wash away the grime left on the streets in the Quarter from the parties the night before. They were now ready for the mess they'd become again as late-night revelers marched and caroused. DiMeglio remained deep in thought and oblivious of time as he and Sully walked along the river, lined with old wharves and warehouses all the way to the French Market. The two turned up Ursulines and down Decatur, where he decided to stop at a café for a coffee and beignet. It was a new indulgence for him so late in the day, but he'd become addicted to beignets no matter what time it was.

As he sipped his coffee, he looked out at the still-quiet street and wondered, for the thousandth time, what he was missing. *Connect the dots*, he thought to himself.

A waiter put down a bowl of water in front of him and Sully started lapping it up thirstily. DiMeglio realized he'd been so lost in his thoughts that he had just about forgotten Sully was there. The massive dog was dutifully lying on the pavement in front of his table, blocking most of the sidewalk. No one had complained, respecting Sully's size.

DiMeglio and Sully left the café and continued on Decatur to Toulouse and then down Rampart back to Iberville. By the time he got back, it had been over two hours, and the sun would set soon. It was time to get to the Quarter. He had only a half hour before he was supposed to meet Broussard outside the Royal Sonesta. He realized he'd left his cell phone at Simone's apartment, and there was no way anyone could have reached him.

Simone had left a note on the counter with his cell phone on top.

> Chris—Not sure if you and Sully decided to leave me since I couldn't call you! Here's your phone. Loved our earlier oysters! I'm off to the Quarter to meet Dickenson. Let's catch up later tonight. Love, Becca.

Picking up the phone, he saw that there were five missed calls, four from Simone and one from Broussard.

Sully was pushing on his leg. He wanted his usual treat after a walk. Giving him a dog biscuit after a walk was a routine Sully never let anyone forget. He did his part; now you had to do yours.

DiMeglio grabbed the box of dog biscuits from the cabinet, but it was empty. *Why the fuck would someone put back an empty box?* he thought. And then he realized since he wasn't the one, Becca must have done it. He felt guilty at being so critical so fast, remembering that he often put empty or near empty things away. It was not as if he was perfect either. He was determined to do right and find Sully a biscuit. He glanced at his watch. He still had some time, and Sully was now whining and nudging his leg. "OK, OK, Sully. Let me see what I can find. There must be another box here somewhere. Becca would never forget your biscuits."

He started in the cupboard and came up empty. Then he tried a few kitchen drawers. Nothing. DiMeglio checked out the refrigerator, thinking of giving Sully something else and pretending it was his usual treat. But there was nothing a dog could eat unless he was a vegetarian who loved salads. Sully was definitely not a vegetarian.

"OK, Sully, let's think. Where would Becca put extra groceries?" DiMeglio went into the spare room. Simone used the room to store everything, so it was possible she used it like a pantry. It was his last hope.

Drawer after drawer, no luck. Moving to the closet, he found nothing except a couple of wigs. For a fleeting moment, he wondered why he'd never seen Simone in a wig. Sully began poking his nose under the bed. *Of course!* DiMeglio thought. *The perfect hiding place for biscuits. Sully could never get under there.*

He looked under the bed, but all that was there was a plain box with a rubber band around it. He shook the shoebox and it sounded like it had loose items in it that could well be biscuits. *Eureka!* he thought.

"OK, Sully, we might have hit pay dirt, buddy. Let's see what we've got for you here," DiMeglio said as he opened the box.

What he saw stopped him cold.

CHAPTER FORTY-EIGHT

DiMeglio stared unbelievingly at the contents of the box in his hands. Wooden crosses. A sharpening stone. And a few prepaid cell phones from Walmart still in their packages. *How can this be?* But then he ran through his checklist: the crosses, the stone, cell phone calls, her job, her broken family upbringing, her lone wolf attitude, her arrogance. It all began to add up. *Why didn't I see it? Where's the fucking knife*?

Outside, the crowds in the Quarter were jamming the sidewalks and streets as they partied and waited for the parades to begin. He tried calling Simone, but when she didn't pick up, he called the desk sergeant.

"Where are Simone and Dickenson?" DiMeglio asked.

"I don't know. I assume they're out on patrol in the Quarter."

DiMeglio felt his heart pounding. With shaking hands, he called Broussard.

"Where are you?" he nearly screamed into the phone.

"What's wrong, Chris? Is there a problem? You know where the hell I am. I'm in the Quarter. Right where you should have been ten minutes ago!"

"Becca may be the Slasher," DiMeglio blurted out, feeling his voice waver. "We need to find her. Now!"

"What are you talking about? That's preposterous. Hold on," said Broussard. DiMeglio could hear him on his walkie-talkie.

"Detective Simone, please report."

No answer.

"Lieutenant Dickenson, please report."

No answer.

"Fuck!" shouted Broussard.

DiMeglio heard Broussard continue on his walkie-talkie. "All officers, this is Broussard. If any of you have seen Detective Simone or Lieutenant Dickenson, reply immediately."

A few seconds passed. No response. Then a few reports came in that no one had seen them.

Back on the phone, Broussard continued with DiMeglio, who was now on foot to meet him. "Dammit, Chris, what the fuck is going on? Meet me at Bourbon and St. Louis instead of the hotel. We'll organize a search from there."

DiMeglio was already only a block away.

Broussard again tried to raise Simone on the walkie-talkie. Still no response. And no response from Dickenson. Realizing everyone could hear him, Broussard needed to find a way to get in touch with his officers on the street without tipping off Simone to what DiMeglio had told him. If DiMeglio was right, Simone would be suspicious about what Broussard was asking. She might vanish. Crowd control was virtually non-existent, so finding her would be nearly impossible if she decided to go into hiding.

DiMeglio and Broussard arrived at Bourbon and St. Louis at the same time. Each had recruited assigned pairs of uniformed officers along the way. The street was crowded with revelers in costumes, and music blared. Many of the partiers were already drunk, and it was still early in the night.

"Come with me," yelled Broussard as he went down Bourbon and led DiMeglio and the officers into an alley across from the Hideout Bar to get away from the crowd.

"OK, start patrolling the streets looking for Detective Simone," Broussard ordered. "If you find her, try me on your walkie-talkie. If you can't raise me on it, use your cell phone. You all have my number. And set your phones to vibrate so you know a call is coming in or if I need to get to you. You'll never hear the ring over all the noise."

"Why are we looking for Becca, Captain? Can't you just call her?"

"I did. She didn't respond."

"Is she OK?" asked another officer. Simone was very popular among the young cops, always going out of her way to give them tips.

"Raleigh, she's not likely to be on Bourbon," added DiMeglio. "She'll most likely be in an alley or a parking lot. We all need to start looking there."

"Alleys?" asked an officer. "Why would she be in an alley?"

"Because that's where the killer has been murdering

his victims, you dumbass, and she intends to go where the action is and catch the fuckin' bastard," said another officer.

Broussard didn't need to hear any more. "Just concentrate on what I told you to do. No questions. Go in pairs. Find Simone! And find Lieutenant Dickenson, too," Broussard ordered as the men began dispersing down the street.

CHAPTER FORTY-NINE

"Mike, let's get off the street," Simone suggested. "Patrolling through this half-drunk crowd can be exhausting."

"Works for me," Dickenson said, as he pushed through a rowdy group blocking the sidewalk. "I'm not used to being out in the streets. Been at a damn desk for ten years."

"Don't worry, Mike. I'll take care of you."

Dickenson smiled. "Thanks. I know I'm in good hands. Just keep close. I can't hear a damn thing with all the noise."

He followed Simone into an unlit parking lot off the Quarter.

CHAPTER FIFTY

DiMeglio and Broussard stayed together as the officers on the street started to comb the alleys and parking lots. DiMeglio assumed Simone would know she was under suspicion by now. She had ignored calls to report. It wouldn't take a rocket scientist to figure it out.

"At least we can be sure she won't kill someone else tonight if she knows we're looking for her," Broussard said.

"I'm not so sure of that. She was very bold in her last kill. She may get a rush out of it, particularly if she thinks she's about to be caught. It might be that nothing would please her more than to see us fail again in stopping her."

Please just let me catch her alive. I want to understand why she killed these people and why I missed the signs. And how the hell I fell for her.

The festivities in the streets were growing wilder as the night continued. DiMeglio wondered who in the crowd might be tonight's victim and how Simone would pull it off with so much police presence focused on the alleys. Only luck would keep another person from dying. *Where the hell is Dickenson*? he wondered.

Alley after alley, lot after lot, they came up empty. They found some drunks passed out in the gutters, but all were alive.

In police work, luck is often the difference between apprehending a suspect and losing track of them. That luck usually turns out to be bad, and the guilty remain free. DiMeglio prayed they'd have better luck that night and not lose another killer in the wind.

He believed they'd eventually catch her. He needed to believe that no one can hide forever. But he also knew she was smart enough to outwit most of those pursuing her. Despite well over three hundred police at the scene, state and local, together with some FBI agents, escape was still possible. So waiting until the night was over to try to find her was not an option. She'd be long gone by then. They had to assume she was on the run and would use the crowded streets to find the opportunity she needed.

They also knew that her target would not be random. She had a purpose in her killing spree. They just needed to be patient and diligent in the search.

"Captain, we may have something," reported an officer in a parking lot off Royal, just two blocks from where Broussard and DiMeglio were standing. Pushing aggressively through the crowds, it took them less than five minutes to arrive at the scene.

They knew immediately they were too late. Dickenson lay next to a dumpster, throat slit ear to ear. Three Xs carved into his forehead. A cross in his hand. This time, however, there was a bloodied note on his chest, held in place by an eight-inch butcher's knife, just like the ones in the butcher block on the counter in Simone's condo. Broussard's anger overcoming him, he grabbed the note, ignoring proper evidence preservation procedures and read aloud.

> Chris—So now you know your killer. You and all your experts couldn't stop me this one last time. How many hints did you need? I guess there weren't enough. But don't worry, I'm done here. You will find me at my condo with Sully. Come and fetch me.

Broussard looked at DiMeglio, giving him the note, his hand shaking, his voice cracking. "Fuck, she's rubbing it in our face. 'Done here'?" he repeated.

DiMeglio took the note and read it. "It's over, Raleigh. She sent the message she wanted. So all that's left is to pick her up."

"Over?" angrily replied Broussard. "That bitch just murdered someone who has been at my side my entire career. What did he do wrong to deserve this? What am I supposed to tell his wife and kids? I want her dead."

"Raleigh, it was my suggestion he be paired with Simone, so this is my fault," replied DiMeglio.

"And why did you do that, Chris?" asked Broussard, his suspicion rising. "Did you think he was a suspect too? Just like you thought I might be? Well, it sure looks like you did a damn good job eliminating him."

DiMeglio thought it better not to respond. He did think Dickenson was a suspect. And when he asked Broussard to team Dickenson up with Simone for the night, he was the reason Dickenson became Simone's last victim. He hung his head, not able to look Broussard in the eye.

"And you believe a New Orleans police officer about to face the death penalty will not put up resistance? Bullshit. It's a trap," Broussard raged.

"I doubt it. And I doubt she'll resist, either," DiMeglio replied, trying to calm the emotions with procedure. "She may want to face a bullet rather than an execution, but she's not going to kill anyone else she works with. That's not in her plans. She knows she's caught. Just keep your guns down and don't take the bait if she's looking to be executed by a cop."

"I'm not putting any of my men at risk, Chris. If she so much as looks at them the wrong way, their orders will be to shoot."

"OK. Then let me be the first in the apartment. She won't shoot me."

"Why not?" asked Broussard.

"Because she wants to tell me why she's done what she's done. A serial killer wants the world to understand, particularly after they're caught. It's their way of atoning. They almost always expect one day to be caught. That's why so many write a manifesto of their crimes. I wouldn't be surprised if she's writing hers right now."

"Well, she's dead one way or the other," concluded Broussard. "I just hope she makes a wrong move. Nothing would please me more than to put a bullet through her fucking head."

CHAPTER FIFTY-ONE

As they approached the door, they could hear Sully behind it, growling.

"Chris, if that dog so much as moves, I'm shooting it," said Broussard.

"That won't be necessary, Raleigh. He'll recognize me and back off."

"Why do you know her dog?" asked Broussard.

"It's a long story, Raleigh, and not one of my most shining moments."

"Yeah," added one of the officers. "She won't shoot her boyfriend." Broussard looked confused, but was silent.

DiMeglio knocked.

"Come in. It's unlocked," Simone calmly responded. Sully was still growling.

"I swear, Chris, I'll shoot the fucking dog and then her," warned Broussard.

"Relax. The dog will not be a problem," DiMeglio repeated, as he slowly opened the door.

Sully recognized DiMeglio and backed off.

"Down, Sully," ordered DiMeglio. Sully obeyed and lay down beside Simone, who was sitting at the kitchen counter, facing the door. Her service revolver sat in front of her. DiMeglio entered first, holding his arms away from his body, no weapon in his hands.

"Becca, I don't want to see you die here," he began.

She said nothing, moving her hand closer to her revolver.

"If you keep moving your hand, Becca, someone behind me will shoot you," continued DiMeglio. "If you shoot, you're likely to hit me before you do any of the others. And you know you don't want to kill me, Becca."

"I don't, Chris," responded Simone. "But I will if I have to."

DiMeglio kept approaching her. As instructed, Broussard and the three officers flanking him kept their weapons at their sides, barrels pointing to the floor. DiMeglio prayed they'd follow his orders and only raise their hands if Simone went for her gun—and that they'd stay behind him so he stayed in the line of fire.

He could hear his heart beating in his chest. This was either a brave move on his part, or a stupid one. Only time would tell. Precious little time.

He kept slowly approaching her, staring into her eyes to keep her attention. He could see the tears begin and her hand tremble. When facing death, the nerve of even the most committed psychopath falters. They may have no compunction in killing, but being killed was an entirely different matter. Most serial killers think they are invincible. When faced with the reality that they are not, they tend to cower, not fight. DiMeglio was counting on that.

Simone kept her eyes on DiMeglio. They seemed to be

pleading to let her go for her gun. His eyes told her no.

She pulled her hand away from the revolver, and by the time DiMeglio got to the counter she had dropped her hands to her side, softly crying as she lowered her head, as if in shame. Sully was at her side, not understanding what was going on. A confused dog of that size was a factor DiMeglio needed to consider. If anyone grabbed Simone, even him, Sully might react aggressively. That would result in chaos.

"Sully," DiMeglio ordered. "Come here."

The dog looked up at Simone. Simone nodded. "Go," she said. Sully shuffled over to DiMeglio.

"Sit, Sully."

He obeyed.

As he approached Simone, he added, "Stay, Sully." To his relief, the dog sat still.

He took the revolver and placed it outside of Simone's reach. Coming to her, he placed his hand on her shoulder "Get up, Becca. Slowly. The two of us are going to calmly walk out together."

Without looking back to Broussard and the officers with him, DiMeglio ordered, "Captain, please take your men and wait for us in the hallway."

He sensed no movement behind him.

"Now!" he ordered. "If you don't do as I say, someone will die here. And I don't want it to be me."

He could hear the footsteps behind him, leaving the room.

Simone rose, and DiMeglio put his arms around her in what would be their last embrace. She offered no resistance as he led her out of the room. Sully started to move.

"Stay, Sully," DiMeglio ordered. The dog obeyed as DiMeglio closed the door behind him, still holding Simone's arm to prevent her from trying to flee.

Then things happened fast. Broussard took Simone by the arm and turned her around briskly, twisting both her hands behind her back. She let out a quiet yelp in pain but otherwise did not resist. It took Broussard only a few seconds to place the handcuffs on her.

DiMeglio let out a silent sigh of relief at being spared, but he felt a deep sadness. He never knew any of the killers he'd caught in the past. This time, he not only knew the killer, but had fallen in love with her. *How could I have been so blind?* he'd ask himself for years to come.

CHAPTER FIFTY-TWO

In an ironic twist, Simone now found herself in the same interrogation room where she questioned Manning. This time, she was on the other side of the table, with the shackles restraining her wrists and ankles. She had already signed a confession and was now in the room waiting for whatever was going to happen next, sitting across the table from DiMeglio and Broussard.

"Why, Becca?" Broussard asked.

She said nothing.

"Do you want us to get you a lawyer?"

Silence.

"Help us here, Becca," pleaded Broussard. He was devastated that his most respected detective was a serial killer and that she'd killed his best friend. It just didn't make sense. He wanted her dead. And yet he was pained to see her now as such a despicable person.

Evans arrived with a folder and handed it to Broussard. He took a glance at Simone, but she avoided his eye contact.

"Thanks, Smitty. You can go," said Broussard.

He opened the file, read the single page and passed it over to DiMeglio.

The revelations only served to put more nails in Simone's coffin, not that they were needed given the overwhelming evidence in the note she pinned to her last victim and her confession. They also knew that this time, there would be DNA at the crime scene. As he read the file, DiMeglio highlighted certain passages by underlining them:

> Father: Nathan Simone Jr. Cotton farmer. Member of the Grace Baptist Church and the Ku Klux Klan.

DiMeglio thought it bizarre that membership in the KKK and a church were listed as though they were equivalent. He made a mental note to talk to Evans about it.

> Mother: Diedra Simone, nee Jones. Housewife. Grandfather: Nathan Simone Sr., Grand Wizard of the Ku Klux Klan; charged with murder in lynching a Black teenager in 1955. Acquitted.

How did I miss looking into this? thought DiMeglio.

"I don't get it, Becca," continued Broussard. "You kill Klan members and yet your father and grandfather were members."

Simone fidgeted in her chair but did not say a word.

"Is it about being guilty and seeking revenge for others?" pressed Broussard.

Simone took a deep breath, finally talking as she looked at Broussard. "I've said everything I have to say to you."

"But you didn't tell us why, Becca," he continued. "And we want to understand why."

"I'll only talk to Chris," she responded, looking at DiMeglio.

"That's not going to happen, Becca," responded Broussard. "If you're going to talk to anyone, you're going to talk to me. I don't care if Chris is here or not. But it's talk to me or to your lawyer. We're happy to get you one if you'd like."

"I don't want a lawyer and if it makes your record any easier, I waive my Miranda rights."

"Then talk to me, Becca," pleaded Broussard.

Staring at Broussard with contempt in her eyes, she responded, "Captain, like I said, I've said all I intend to ever say to you. I'll talk to Chris and Chris only."

A long silence followed. Realizing he was going to get nowhere with Simone, Broussard rose. "OK, Becca. Have it your way. But you know all of this is being recorded." He left the room, leaving DiMeglio alone with Simone.

DiMeglio was unsure where to begin and remained silent.

Simone finally spoke, smiling. "So, Chris, are you in the mood for oysters?"

"That's not funny, Becca," responded DiMeglio sternly. "Tell me why you killed all those people."

"You wouldn't understand, Chris."

"Try me. I really want to understand."

"Why, so you can profile me?"

"In a word, yes. I want to stop people like you, Becca. The more I understand why you killed innocent people, the better I can do my job."

"They weren't innocent, Chris."

"What? None of them had a single thing on their record indicating that they'd done anything with the Klan except Beckett and Lang. And Landes was just a tourist who got in your way. What was he guilty of doing?"

"I regret Landes. He was a nice enough guy but at the wrong place at the wrong time. Collateral damage. He should have just gone to his hotel. The others were guilty."

DiMeglio did not understand what he was hearing coming from a woman he had deep personal feelings for, a woman he might have been able to spend the rest of his life with. How did he miss the monster she was? Or did he want to miss it?

"Guilty of what, Becca? What did Jackson Walker, Maria Benson, William Hitchcock, Richard Walsh, or any of your victims do wrong?"

"Sometimes fate puts you in the wrong place." Simone smiled ruefully.

"I don't understand. Please explain."

"I grew up the daughter of a Klansman," she said. "He was an animal. Abused my mother and me. He put hate into my mind every day. He made me listen to him and his fellow Klansmen rage against Blacks. Against Jews. Against anyone they didn't like."

"I'm sorry for your childhood, Becca, but that's not a reason to murder."

"When I was fourteen," she continued, "he took me to my first lynching. I went to four before I ran away to college. He forced me to watch four Black boys hanged. And he got away with every one of them."

"Why didn't you call the police?" asked DiMeglio in shock.

"The police? They were *at* the lynchings."

"Jesus, Becca. I'm sorry you had to see that." DiMeglio could not imagine what psychological damage that would do to someone at such a young age. Four lynchings. And with the police part of it.

"Don't be sorry, Chris. Be happy it didn't turn me into one of those murderers."

"But it did, Becca. You murdered seven people."

"That you know of."

A chill went down his spine.

"That I know of? What are you saying? There were more you killed?"

"I'm not going to answer that question."

DiMeglio was having trouble hiding his emotions. "Becca,

this is sick. It makes no sense. You need to explain it to me."

Simone took a sip of water and looked at DiMeglio.

"Chris, if we ultimately destroy every seed of prejudice and bigotry, we will rid ourselves of it forever. That's the answer to the problem. I killed those seeds."

"And that means you kill anyone who was in a family that included a KKK member? Is that what you're saying, Becca?"

"Yes. Opportunity knocks, Chris."

"Then why not kill yourself, Becca? Aren't you part of the problem?"

"Yes, I am part of the problem, Chris, and I don't ask to be forgiven. I'm pretty sure the state will take care of me for my Daddy's crimes."

"You know, Becca, a large part of me wants to walk away and let you face an executioner as quickly as the system allows it."

"I'm so glad you care."

"But I need to understand where your psychotic motivation came from and if there are others dead somewhere."

"My motivation is pure, Chris. I already explained that to you. Weren't you listening?"

"So, the sins of the fathers fall on their children?"

"That's as good a way as any to look at it," Simone coldly replied.

DiMeglio paused, looking down at the table. When he looked up into her eyes again, he felt the anger surging. "I need you to tell me everything. And the first thing I want to know is how you found your victims and killed them without any evidence of resistance."

"OK, Chris," Simone replied. "But you'll want to check the video to make sure it's working. I'll only tell you once."

Over the next two hours, Simone took DiMeglio through each of the murders, as Broussard, Guidry, Bundy, and a few others watched and listened intently on the computer monitor outside the interrogation room.

"Walker, the bartender, was the easiest," Simone began. "After sitting at the bar at Arnaud's for a few nights, he started talking to me, giving me free drinks. I asked him to walk me home. That started quite the romance for a while."

"You slept with him?"

She ignored the question.

"Then one night, I waited until he closed the bar. We walked down Bourbon, holding hands. I squeezed his hand, brought him to me and kissed him. Deeply." She paused.

DiMeglio could see she enjoyed telling the story, almost as if she got sexual gratification from it. Another trait of a serial killer—sexual gratification in a kill. He forced himself to suppress any visual reaction.

Seeing no particular response from DiMeglio, Simone continued. "He responded by moving his hand down my back. We were just outside the alley. I pulled him into it. Once we were in the alley, he started groping. He offered no resistance when I turned him around. Slitting his throat was simple. He fell to his knees, staring at me as I watched him die. I carved the Xs in his forehead and put the cross in his hand."

"Then why didn't we find your DNA?"

"Because I always wore lace gloves. They helped me look sexy. And I wiped everything clean. You'd be surprised what a Lysol wipe can do to DNA on a dead man's lips."

"How did you find him?"

"It's simple to find them. I start with social media, looking at people's history of where they lived before coming to New Orleans. Finding names of KKK members was the easy part. Finding their children was a little bit harder. But people post all sorts of information, including the most intimate stuff. And the pictures! They're a gold mine."

"So you found your victims on Facebook? Is that what you're telling me?"

"Not just Facebook. They're just as easy to find on LinkedIn, Twitter, and Instagram. And TikTok and Clubhouse? They're gold mines too. I'm surprised you don't use them to find your killers, Chris."

"I'll make a note of that. Thanks."

"But you want to know the best way?" Simone asked coyly.

"Don't toy with me, Becca."

"C'mon, Chris, I've got to make you earn it. Go along with me. Consider it the last request of a condemned woman."

"Fine, Becca, what is the best way to find an innocent

victim so that someone as sick as you can kill them?"

Smiling, Simone replied, "Ancestry.com."

Figures, he thought. The FBI has been using that to track down killers for a long time.

Simone continued, "If you think it's easy to find out about people on social media, you haven't seen anything like the ancestry sites. You can ask all sorts of questions among the curious who wonder where their ancestors came from. You just log on to the Ancestry.com or 23andMe and ask that your DNA be shared. If anyone else asked the same, there's lots of ways to connect. Get the name of a KKK member and start the search. It's amazing what turns up."

Simone could see the concern in his expression. "What's the matter, Chris? You think the FBI has some sort of monopoly on finding people? You just tell them you might be a distant relative or know of someone who is. It's that easy." Simone's words turned DiMeglio's stomach. *Typical sociopathic thinking of a narcissist*, he thought.

"And Maria Benson? How did you lure her?"

"She was the hardest. Women are so damned emotional. They need you to really like them before they'll go to bed with you. So, she took me the longest. Dinners, drinks, long walks. But she eventually came around. After her, though, I decided to go back to men."

DiMeglio began to understand the sexual prowess Simone used to lure her victims. New Orleans was a city where sex was part of its ethos. Like most cities where partying and drinking were steeped in its culture, anything goes. New Orleans. Key West. Las Vegas. Cities where behavior that would be reprehensible in any civilized city were promoted as an attraction to tourists. What happens in Vegas, stays in Vegas. And so it was with New Orleans.

Simone continued, “I’m surprised you didn’t follow up on the lesbian angle.”

DiMeglio refused to respond to another insult. He asked Simone how she met Benson.

“I met her through Ancestry.com, telling her I knew someone who might be a relative. I could tell she liked women from everything she posted online. She was married, but every sign was there.”

Simone took another sip of water. The glass was almost empty. Usually, DiMeglio would ask a prisoner if they’d like more. He had no intention of doing so with Simone. His growing disgust made him ignore standard protocol to keep the prisoner comfortable. The last thing he wanted Simone to be was comfortable.

“You know I’m a SoBou regular. Didn’t that make you wonder when we ate there how the waiter knew me, but I said I never saw Maria, another regular?”

“I guess I missed another clue, Becca. Were you intentionally trying to give them to me?”

“I don’t know. I just got a kick out of taking you to the place where I picked up a victim. It was fun.”

He was reminded of the scene from *Silence of the Lambs*

and imagined her now describing a fine meal of Chianti and fava beans.

"So, after a few dates and wining and dining, I brought her back to my apartment, where things got hot. I enjoyed it. Maybe I'm a lesbian, too," she grinned.

DiMeglio realized that she was trying to get under his skin. He kept his expression blank and ignored her.

"Pretty soon, Maria and I started going for walks after sex," Simone continued. "Helped her relax. It was easy to get her into an alley. The rest is history."

"So why didn't we find some DNA with the ones you had sex with before you killed them?"

"C'mon, Chris. You think I'm that careless? We always took a nice long hot shower afterward. I washed them well. Everywhere. They liked it."

Christ, DiMeglio thought. She bathed her victims before killing them. In the same shower the two of them shared. Sick.

"Maria was the funniest. She wanted to make sure her husband didn't smell me on her when she went home," Simone said, grinning at DiMeglio.

Each description gave him more of the profile of a serial killer. It was his job to find those common traits, but Simone was unlike any killer he'd encountered before. DiMeglio was feeling exhausted. He rubbed his eyes and sat back in his chair.

"Chris, do you want to take a break?" Simone asked as

if to suggest he was weakening. "You need to be sharp here. Besides, I have to pee. And it's not as if I'm going anywhere."

"Actually, Becca, I could use a break. I'm kind of hungry, so I think I'll grab a bite to eat, too. And you're right. You're going nowhere. I'll be back within an hour or so. The guards will take you to a cell and give you some food."

The door immediately opened. Two uniformed officers arrived, cuffed Simone, and took her to her holding cell.

CHAPTER FIFTY-THREE

DiMeglio left the room and joined the team. At first, no one spoke a word. It was obvious to them that DiMeglio was in no mood for advice.

"You OK?" asked Broussard, breaking the silence.

"Yeah, I'm fine," he responded. "I just need something to eat."

"We can go across the street to the café. Good food," suggested Broussard.

With that, he and DiMeglio left. The others stayed behind, no doubt, DiMeglio thought, gossiping about Rebecca Simone's sexual exploits and her liaisons with DiMeglio.

After the two ordered sandwiches and coffee, Broussard started the conversation, "Chris, you're not OK. You're getting too emotional in there. And now I know why," Broussard said. "Why don't you let me sit in with you on the next session?"

DiMeglio snapped back, "That's not going to happen, Raleigh. While you can overrule me and step in, I can assure you that will end the conversation. Becca will shut down. She will only speak to me. Alone."

"Why? What makes you so important?"

"Because in her eyes, I'm a victim. She didn't kill me but she used her tricks to rope me in like all the others. Now she wants to humiliate me as you watch the show on the computer screen. That's her way of killing me. Like every serial killer, they need to feel they dominate their victims. That's why she's baiting me more and more as I question her. As long as I keep letting her do so, the more she'll talk."

Broussard's surprise was obvious. "So you're not being emotional in there? It's all an act?"

"I don't know, Raleigh. That's how it started and that's what I'm trying to maintain. But I have to be honest. She is getting under my skin."

"So let me sit in. Let's just see if she objects. She's already opened up, so maybe it won't matter. I can promise you she won't get under my skin," responded Broussard.

"No. I won't change my mind on this," DiMeglio answered. "One more session and I'll have all I need. I'll write up a report and then she's all yours. Try to your heart's content to get more out of her."

"I have to ask. Assuming you include it in the report, what will the bureau do to you when you admit you slept with her? I can't imagine they look kindly on such things. Let me in there with you, Chris. It will give you cover."

"I'm doing this alone," DiMeglio replied. "I'll no doubt be disciplined. Could get a pay cut or short suspension. But I won't be thrown out. There are very few profilers in the bureau, and none of them are more successful than me. While we're all expendable, I should survive."

"But maybe you want me in there with you so no one

can say you were influenced in your questioning by the personal feelings you have for Simone. That might only add to your problems."

"It's too late to give a shit about my problems. You want to get in the room with Becca. I get that. But it's not going to happen. Overrule me if you like. But that will mean none of us will get another thing out of her. And there's a lot we still need to learn. We need to keep her talking to me as long as we can."

Broussard, sighing, continued. "Well, if you need a good word from me, I'm happy to do so. You've done an amazing job. You were right from the outset. We did have the wrong man and wasted a lot of time. Lost more innocent lives."

"I may take you up on the endorsement. But as for doing an amazing job, I don't see that. Three people died while the killer was right under our noses. I can't measure success when there are bodies in the streets."

"Well, Chris, in this city that *is* success. New Orleans has a long trail of bodies. Any time we can make it shorter, the better. And if sleeping with Becca made that happen, then sleep with as many serial killers as you like. Becca Simone's killing spree is over thanks to you. That's a success no matter how I cut it."

The two finished their meals in silence. Broussard sensed DiMeglio wanted to be left alone, so he said nothing else.

CHAPTER FIFTY-FOUR

Simone was brought back to the interrogation room and shackled to the table. She looked calm and comfortable. The guard brought her a cup of water.

"OK, Becca, let's continue. I'll dispense with repeating that this is being recorded and the rest. Is that OK?" began DiMeglio.

"Yes, Chris, that will be fine," Simone calmly replied.

"OK, so tell me about William Hitchcock, Becca, the councilman's son."

"First tell me more about your meal with the captain, Chris. What did you have?"

"How do you know I ate with Broussard?"

"The walls here have ears. You can't get away with anything. And besides, I have some good friends here, too. Friends who think I did the right thing. Who want to help me." Simone's confidence was another trait of a serial killer, DiMeglio noted. He decided to keep the conversation going to see if she'd volunteer information rather than making him pose one question after another.

"So tell me more about your friends who are helping you," DiMeglio continued.

"That's not in the cards, Chris. If I told you more about

them then you might figure out who they are. Let's just leave it that they're closer than you think."

DiMeglio wanted to pursue it further but knew he'd get nothing. He decided she was simply trying to bait him. He refused to fall into that trap.

"Hitchcock, Becca. Let's get back to Hitchcock."

"He was an interesting one, Chris. A real ne'er-do-well. Didn't think his shit smelled, coming from New Orleans royalty. Bragged about how his father gave him whatever he wanted. Spoiled brat."

"But he had no known hangouts, Becca. How did you meet him?"

"Easy. On Tinder."

DiMeglio leaned back in his chair. *Tinder!* he thought. More social media. He made a mental note never to use social media again, including Tinder, an app he'd have to confess using. Usually without success. But at least he never murdered anyone he hooked up with on it.

Smiling, Simone continued. "I guess you could say he swiped right one too many times."

Whatever glimmer of feelings DiMeglio had for Simone had faded over the hours since Dickenson's murder. At this point, she was as much taunting him as telling him what he wanted to hear. He intended to keep it professional.

"No problem getting him into the alley, too, I suppose?" asked DiMeglio.

"Not at all. Men will do just about anything to get laid. Isn't that true, Chris?"

Blushing, DiMeglio now felt used. *Was all the affection faked? Was she that narcissistic?*

"Let me help you here," Simone went on, reading his mind. "Yes, Chris, for me you were part of the game. There I was getting fucked every other night by the man trying to find me. It was exciting. And you were so easy. Much easier than any of the others. For such a smart guy, I was surprised how easy it was to set you up that first night."

All DiMeglio could do was stare, thinking more and more about what the spectators outside were thinking.

"And Chris, why didn't you wonder why a dog as big and dangerous as Sully so quickly liked a stranger in the condo? It's because he was used to strangers, Chris. That's another clue you missed."

DiMeglio asked, "So you'd bring these men—and the woman—back to your apartment to lure them into your scheme, and then kill them?" He could not hide his disgust.

"What's the matter, Chris? You upset that the victims fucked me in the same bed you did? Does that bother you?"

She was trying to test him to see if he'd break. And it was beginning to work.

"And I suppose you fucked Walsh, too," concluded DiMeglio. "The guy who you killed when you also killed Landes."

"I remember his name. You don't have to remind me,"

she calmly replied. "And of course I fucked him. Remember the story we learned as kids about the praying mantis? How the female praying mantis kills her male lover after mating? Think of it that way, Chris. It was just nature."

DiMeglio shook his head in disbelief.

"And I loved how he played the saxophone for me. Actually met him for the first time in a club where he was playing."

DiMeglio was intent on learning every detail. He would not let this happen again. "And after a few times in the sack, it was time for the alley, huh, Becca?"

"That's a bit harsh, but about right. He certainly got better treatment than the three men his granddaddy murdered and the woman he raped, too. His granddaddy might have gotten off and died of old age, but that wasn't the fate for poor Richard."

"And I don't suppose you ever feel that killing an innocent child of a guilty man like Beckett was wrong, Becca?"

"Samuel Beckett, Chris?"

"You know who I mean, Becca. Don't play with me."

"Like father, like son, Chris. He was as guilty as the rest."

Struggling to keep his cool, DiMeglio continued, "And what about Bubba Lang? Now he's clearly a guilty one by your standards. He was a bona fide member of the KKK. One of Tibbets's right-hand men. Was he your most satisfying target, Becca? A bad seed that sowed the hatred you so fervently want me to believe you could stop? When exactly did you fuck him, Becca? We were together then. When did you find the time? Or place? Or did I miss something else?"

"He's one I didn't fuck, Chris. Not that I didn't want to, mind you. I found it pleasurable to lure them in with sex and then do away with them, as their ancestors did with so many innocent people."

DiMeglio needed to keep her on his agenda and not let her continue to try to shock him. Getting back to Lang, he asked, "So what was your game with him?"

"Like the others, he was easy too. All you men are. There's one thing you can be certain of with men, particularly ones who think they're better than anyone else," she said. "Like all men, old Bubba only thought with his dick."

"That's a cheap cliché," retorted DiMeglio.

"No, Chris, it's not. At least it wasn't for Bubba. All I needed to do with him was pick him up at a bar and let him imagine he was going to get lucky. He was more anxious to get into the alley with me than I was. I still love the surprise in his eyes when I cut his throat."

"All right, Becca," continued DiMeglio. "What about Mike Dickenson? He had nothing to do with the Klan. No connections in his family. Why him?"

"That was your fault, Chris. You put us together and it got me thinking, particularly when you told me about the 2009 charges against Broussard. Mike was the captain's partner back then."

"Another person in the wrong place at the wrong time?"

"Not at all. While I had someone else in mind for that

night, Dickenson was in the way. You're not the only one who can look into files. Turns out, he was a real head banger and bigot. Check it out when you have a chance. Why Broussard put up with that is beyond me. After the FBI investigation, they wanted him fired. But Broussard intervened and worked out a compromise for him. I'm surprised you didn't see that in your FBI files. Broussard made a deal that Dickenson would get a desk job and not be on the street."

"And how did you do it, Becca?"

"He was mostly improvised. I realized time was probably running out. We went into the parking lot and I told him I thought I found something and asked him to take a look. I was on one knee looking down at nothing. Like a dutiful dog, he knelt down beside me. I made sure I was close enough to the wall that he had to kneel on my left. That made it easy to turn and use the knife. All I had to do was get up quickly and make sure the knife slit across his throat. Honestly, I don't think he saw it coming."

"Jesus, Becca, you say it so nonchalantly. Doesn't any of this bother you?"

"The only thing that bothers me, Chris, is that I won't be able to finish the job. There are others I wanted to take care of."

DiMeglio slid another folder on the table, asking, "I'm curious who you had planned to kill. Care to tell me?"

"Not really," Simone coldly replied.

DiMeglio opened the folder and slid a single piece of paper across with a name and family history on it.

"Any chance this was your target?"

She smiled back as if to say yes. DiMeglio didn't expect to get any more than that.

Simone then volunteered, "I couldn't keep up with you much longer before you became a problem that I'd have to deal with, too. You weren't getting all that close, but you were taking up too much of my time."

"Deal with, Becca? As in kill me?"

"Of course not, Chris. You're innocent. No family history," Simone responded coldly.

"I'm not buying that. You never asked me to leave. You never told me to go. So it's a bit too convenient for you to tell me that I was someone you didn't want to deal with anymore. Or that I interfered with your killing spree."

"Oh, don't be naïve. You're so typical. Don't take it personally. You were just a tool."

"Bullshit, Becca. It was more than that and you know it. Stop with the crap."

He could see in Simone's eyes that she was getting emotional, a trait not common in serial killers. DiMeglio decided to push and find out if her emotions were real or feigned.

"Do you kill people you love, too, Simone? I fell in love with a police officer I met one night in New Orleans." He paused. "I'm sorry, a detective. We enjoyed oysters."

Simone's eyes were beginning to water.

"C'mon, Simone, talk to me. Tell me the truth," DiMeglio pushed.

Now with tears flowing down her cheeks, she responded, "Yes, Chris, I was falling in love with you. You're all I thought about. But when it made me think I might stop doing what I had to do, I knew it wouldn't work. I had to end it. I had to end all of it."

"So you decided to get caught after one last hurrah?" DiMeglio didn't expect an answer.

"Who says I thought I'd get caught, Chris?"

"Well, you did get caught. All because you ran out of fucking dog biscuits. If I hadn't had to search the apartment looking for them, you might have gotten away with it."

Simone wiped the tears from her cheeks and regained her composure, responding, "Leave it to Sully."

"I could have helped you, if you'd told me the truth. It would have saved lives, maybe yours. But why choose Mardi Gras as the next site for your murder?"

"I planned to end it with you after Mardi Gras. At first, I had every intention to play it through and wait to kill someone else." DiMeglio could see her disposition change as her eyes filled more with contempt than compassion. That sort of schizophrenic reaction was yet another trait. "Think about it: your dick might have saved lives if you'd gotten any closer. Too bad for them it didn't happen. So that night I saw an opportunity that seemed too juicy to pass up. To take care of Dickenson right under your nose. So I decided to kill him in the parking lot."

"But you had to know you'd get caught this time," DiMeglio said.

"I knew you'd figure it out sooner or later. Particularly when I didn't report in and you couldn't find Dickenson. But I never thought Sully would rat me out," Simone responded, smiling.

"You got careless, Becca. That's usually how we catch killers like you. Your ego gets in the way and you make mistakes. Not having something as simple as a biscuit for your fucking dog was how you tripped."

"I guess that's better than you figuring it out on your own, Chris," Simone sarcastically responded.

"I'm happy whenever I catch a killer. I don't care how it happens."

"Well, when you started asking everyone where I was," Simone continued, "I knew something was wrong. Did you forget that my radio could pick up all the chatter? Remember that next time, Chris. So, it was just a matter of time. Precious time I could use. It was over and I wanted to go out with a bang. To make sure I'd be remembered. It was worth it before I was caught."

"OK," responded DiMeglio, shaking his head. "Let's move on. Two more things, and we're done."

"Just two, Chris?" Simone asked coyly. "Don't you want to talk more about you and me?"

"No, Becca, I don't. As far as I'm concerned, I'd like to forget all of that."

"That's so cold," replied Simone.

"No worse than being a cold-blooded murderer like you, Becca," he replied.

She smiled. "Suit yourself. But I bet you want to know more about what kind of man you are. What kind of man you are in bed. No?" she pressed.

He ignored the bait. "Tell me about Manning. Where did he fit into this?"

"Ah, yes, Wallis Manning."

"Why set him up other than for the obvious reason of sending us on a wild goose chase?"

"Don't you remember Jack the Ripper, Chris?"

The letter! thought DiMeglio. The letter Jack the Ripper sent to a reporter telling him how inept the police were in their attempts to capture him.

"So you wanted to rub incompetency in our face?"

"It wasn't hard. You, Broussard, Bundy, Guidry. All of you. Took it hook, line and sinker," Simone responded with a satisfied gleam in her eye.

"I never thought he was the killer, Becca."

"Good for you."

DiMeglio asked her if she wanted more water or coffee. She declined.

He gathered some of the files and stood. "I'll be right back. I want to get a cup of coffee. Sit tight."

Simone smiled and replied, "It's not like I'm going anywhere."

CHAPTER FIFTY-FIVE

Once out of the room, DiMeglio joined Broussard and Bundy by the coffee machine.

"She is such a bitch," observed Bundy.

"She may be a bitch, Joe, but she's a smart bitch. She fooled us all, including you."

"What's that supposed to mean?" Bundy asked angrily.

"Explain to me how you can have a partner with you every day and not suspect anything," DiMeglio replied.

Bundy's reaction was swift. "You're not pinning this thing on me, Chris. I did my job. So did she. I never had any reason to think she was bad. Never." He paused. "And at least I wasn't fucking her!"

"That's enough, Joe," ordered Broussard.

"I'm not trying to pin anything on you, Joe," continued DiMeglio. "Just curious what you saw. You might have missed something, just like I did. Just like everyone did. Did she ever talk about her personal life with you? What she did off-duty? Her family? Racism in New Orleans? The KKK?"

Bundy calmed down. "Sorry I flew off the handle. But I never saw a thing. And she almost never socialized with any of us. God knows we tried. Even I almost had to practically beg her to have a drink with me, and I was her damn partner. For her, when we were together, it was all work. She kept her secrets. Obviously."

"Indeed she did. But I had a hunch, Joe, based on some information I'd gotten from Smitty. Let me read you the note I wrote that I handed Becca when I asked her who she intended to kill that night before Dickenson found himself in the wrong place at the wrong time."

> Joseph Bundy. Born in Columbia, South Carolina. Mother died when he was five or six years old. Social Services took him from the father for alleged abuse and shipped him off to father's sister in New Orleans. Father still believed to be living in South Carolina, whereabouts unknown. Grandfather deceased. Both known members of the Klan although neither served any jail time

Bundy stood frozen.

"Joe," DiMeglio said, "when we first met, you told me you were born and bred in New Orleans. A real Cajun boy. Even with an accent. Why the lie?"

"Yeah, Joe," added Broussard. "And tell me why you lied on your application to become a cop. Since I first met you, you've been saying you lived in New Orleans your entire life. That's grounds for me to dismiss you right here and now. I don't need a racist on my police force."

Bundy responded contritely, "Captain Broussard, Chris, I'm not proud of my father and what he did to me and to others. My Mom died from his beatings, and not a damn thing was ever done to him. I wish I knew where he was 'cause I'd fucking kill him myself. My aunt was a saint and brought me up to hate people like him. I wanted nothing to do with him, and with help from my aunt, I made up the story of my childhood. I swear, Captain, I am not a racist. I'm the furthest thing from one."

"We'll talk about this after we've transferred custody of Becca to the state authorities," responded Broussard.

Bundy stood silently, staring at the paper. "How the hell did she even find out about me? How did you find out?"

"Really, Joe? She found it the same way Smitty got the information typed on that page. A place called Google. And Facebook. And who knows where else," DiMeglio answered. "I had Smitty look at everyone in the department. When he gave me the information on you, I just played a hunch and assumed Becca had to know. A pretty simple trick."

"Shit," Bundy replied. "But why did she wait so long? She had plenty of opportunities to kill me."

"I suspect she either thought it would increase the odds she'd get caught or she got off on being your partner, knowing she'd eventually kill you. She's a psychopath, Joe. That's how she thinks."

"Damn," replied Bundy. "She's one scary bitch."

"Yeah," responded DiMeglio, turning to the door. "Let me get this over with."

CHAPTER FIFTY-SIX

DiMeglio sat down opposite Simone with his cup of coffee and continued.

"So I just spoke to Joe Bundy, Becca. He was pretty shocked that you intended to kill him that night."

Simone smiled. "He would have been one of the juiciest."

"But when did you intend to have sex with him, Becca? In an alley that night? Behind a dumpster in a parking lot?"

"C'mon, Chris," she snapped. "Joe was my partner. It would have been sick to fuck him."

"You have one screwed-up perception of what is sick. Where did that come from? What is there about your childhood that you haven't told me?"

He could see that the question made her uncomfortable. He pressed on. "Were you sexually abused by your father, Becca?"

Simone's eyes began to water up, but she did not reply. DiMeglio knew he'd hit a raw nerve and decided to let that line of questioning go. He had his answer. He mentally cursed himself for not questioning Simone when she told him about leaving home and never going back. He should have asked about that dark past. He should have assumed the abuse.

DiMeglio let some time pass while Simone composed

herself. “OK, let’s move on. Talk to me about the Voodoo connection. What made you conjure that one up?”

She relaxed in her chair and responded, “For such a famous profiler and finder of killers, Chris, you really miss ’em, don’t you?”

“Just tell me, Becca. I don’t need the theatrics,” he replied. “Why Voodoo?”

“It wasn’t Voodoo, Chris. Never was. That idea came out of the press. They jumped on it, so I simply went along.”

“I’m not following you.”

She smiled, “OK, even though you’ve been told already, let me help you. Do you still have the pictures of the victims with you?”

“Yes, you know I do. They’re in the folder,” replied DiMeglio as he put his hand on one of the folders on the table.

“Take out the picture of Walker.”

DiMeglio placed it on the table.

“Now take out a picture of any of the other victims. You choose.”

DiMeglio took out a picture of Maria Benson and placed it on the table.

Simone looked at each and turned them around 180 degrees so that DiMeglio could view them with the right side up, the faces of the dead bodies staring at him.

She waited.

DiMeglio remained confused. “What? What am I supposed to see?”

"Geez, Chris, you really aren't all that good, are you?" DiMeglio tensed at that, but didn't take the bait. She wanted him mad. She wanted to control him. He refused to let that happen.

"Look at the Xs on Walker and on Benson. What difference do you see?" she asked, as if she were a teacher talking to a third grader.

Now that he'd been told what to look at, it became obvious. DiMeglio pulled out the photos of the other victims and lined them up on the table.

The lines of the Xs on Walker's forehead, Simone's first victim, were perpendicular—horizontal and vertical, like a plus sign or a cross. On all the others, the lines were diagonal, like the letter X. Simone went from making crosses to Xs once the media picked up on a Voodoo angle.

"Walker's Xs are crosses," DiMeglio said under his breath, adding, "Christian crosses."

He was loud enough for Simone to hear. "Wrong again, Chris. Not Christian as in Calvary."

DiMeglio was growing frustrated with Simone's game. "Then what are they, Becca? Please don't hold me in suspense any longer."

"The crosses on Walker? They're symbols of the Klan. It's not the wooden cross on which Jesus was crucified. It's the wooden cross the Klan loves to burn. It never was Voodoo, Chris. But when the press assumed it was, it seemed like a good game to play. The truth is I just got a little sloppy after

Walker, and once the press jumped on the Voodoo bandwagon, I went with it. A nice diversion."

"Damn it, I missed that too," DiMeglio said aloud to himself. In spite of comparing the photos countless times, no one noticed the slight differences with the Xs and never bothered to rethink their first assumption. Another failure in basic police work.

"Maybe you're not as good as you think you are," Simone prodded. "They were all staring you right in the face every fucking morning we had to sit in the conference room listening to you pontificate about looking for connections. Not a single person saw it."

DiMeglio sat quietly for a few seconds. "That may be true, Becca. But I get to go home tonight and you eventually go to death row. So who is the one who isn't so good?"

Simone suddenly looked spent. "Are we done now, Chris? I'm getting tired. Can we pick it up again tomorrow?"

"One last question, Becca. Then we won't have to meet again for a long time, if ever."

Looking disappointed, she replied, "And what question is that?"

"Did you ever tell any of your victims why? Serial killers generally do. So I'd like to know if you told them, and what you said."

"I told them all," she said. "I whispered in their ears the last words they ever heard, that this was for all the innocent men and women your daddy murdered. Except for Landes. For him, I just said I was sorry."

The two remained silent for a few moments.

"I don't know what to say to you, Becca. You killed innocent people. Perhaps more than we know of. Even if you thought what you did was justified, just how did you think you were going to put even a dent into a population of people you admit are all over the South? That thinking is beyond me."

"I'm sorry, Chris."

"No you're not, Becca. You're a serial killer. A psychopath. You're not sorry."

Simone nodded. "Please take care of Sully for me."

"I don't need a fuckin' dog. Particularly one that reminds me of you."

"But Sully needs you."

"All I'll promise you is that I'll find him a good shelter," DiMeglio said as he rose and left the room.

CHAPTER FIFTY-SEVEN

This was not a press conference Mayor Pratt looked forward to, even though it put the investigation to an end. It was embarrassing enough that the city got it wrong with the arrest of Manning and awaited an expensive lawsuit from him for false arrest and defamation in the premature celebration of his arrest. But now that they knew the killer was a cop, the department's failure was even worse.

Once again on the steps of the city hall, but without the fanfare of the previous news conference, Pratt stood before a media presence even larger than when she announced the arrest of Wallis Manning. Every network was covering it live. The day was cloudy and chilly, fitting the mood. Pratt hoped it might rain and thin out the crowd as they looked for shelter. No such luck.

"My name is Alicia Pratt, mayor of New Orleans. We're here today with both relief and regret. We're relieved that we've apprehended the Bayou Slasher and received a full confession. But we are saddened that the killer is one of our own.

"Through the joint efforts of the FBI and our police department, we were able to identify the true killer and deeply regret our incorrect accusation against Wallis Manning," continued Pratt. Harper Gaudet asked her to be sure to apologize and begin the process of dealing with that mistake.

Twelve blocks away from the press conference, Broussard and DiMeglio were moving Simone from the 8th Police District Lockup on Royal Street to the New Orleans Central Lockup on Perdido Street. Security protocols required that Simone be transported by van for the two-and-a-half-mile ride.

"Simone, we're taking you to Central Lockup until we decide how best to detain you," began Broussard. "You'll be safer there. You'll be arraigned tomorrow morning."

"What makes you think I'm not safe here?" asked Simone.

"You're a cop, Becca. And you've pissed off a lot of good officers. Security is loose at this station. There's just too much going on here to ensure we can keep you safe."

"Safe for what, Captain? A needle in my arm?"

"Becca, I hope someday to understand why you did what you did," responded Broussard, "but until you're convicted and sentenced, my job is to keep you safe no matter how I feel. But I promise you this. On the day you're executed I'll be there in my Sunday finest. In the meantime, I'm going to do my job."

"Shortly after Mr. Manning was arrested," the mayor continued, "we were contacted by Agent Christopher

DiMeglio, a member of the FBI's Behavioral Science Unit. The BSU specializes in serial killer investigations and assists local police departments in profiling killers and identifying suspects. It is largely through his efforts that we apprehended Ms. Simone. We'd like to thank Agent DiMeglio and the FBI for their help."

Simone stood silently as an officer shackled her ankles and cuffed her hands in front of her waist with a chain attaching them to the ankle shackles. He made no attempt to be gentle. She didn't bother to object, knowing it would make no difference.

"So Chris, I suppose you can put another notch on your belt," Simone said as they began the walk to the door.

"I take no pleasure in this," responded DiMeglio.

"You sure took pleasure in other ways."

"You murdered innocent people, Becca," replied DiMeglio. "I can't stop the justice you'll face. If that's a lethal injection, so be it. As sorry as I am to see that, I can have no pity for you."

"I did the job no one else wanted to do," she said.

"OK, let's get a move on," announced Broussard. He wanted to get Simone out of the station as quickly as possible. Taking her arm, he led Simone down the corridor. DiMeglio and Bundy, together with two additional officers, followed. Outside, a van was parked with reporters anxiously awaiting the "perp walk," so they could get a view of Simone and shout out questions that would never be answered. It was all part of the spectacle so beloved by viewers and readers.

Continuing on her apology tour, Pratt added, "We'd also like to apologize to Maîtresse LeBlanc, New Orleans Voodoo Priestess, for any harm done to her and practitioners of Voodoo. As former Detective Simone confessed, Voodoo had nothing to do with the murders. It was just a ruse she used to confuse the investigation. Here in New Orleans, we cherish our relationship with Voodoo."

Any disappointment the reporters may have had in losing the Voodoo angle dissipated quickly. They had something even better. A killer cop.

"It is also with regret and appreciation that I accept the resignation of Horace Guidry, our Superintendent of Police."

Pratt paused, wanting what she said to soak in. Getting rid of Guidry was the silver lining on an otherwise sad day for New Orleans. "While he had no role in the investigation nor fault in the manner in which it was conducted, he has accepted responsibility and I accept his resignation with an acknowledgment of his many years of service to the city." That was as close to a compliment as she could muster.

Pratt also had a letter of resignation from Broussard. It was her intent to appoint him interim superintendent despite the concerns of others that he had botched his role in the investigation and that leapfrogging him over Chief Gersh would create problems. She trusted Broussard and respected his integrity, something Guidry lacked. She needed to convince Broussard not to resign. That was first on her agenda once the press conference was over.

This wasn't Simone's first perp walk, but this time she was the perp. The van was waiting at the curb in front of the building.

As the doors of the police station opened, the crowd of reporters and onlookers pushed forward to get a closer look. Police officers held them back. No doubt some of them would have liked to let them through and watch the reporters trample Simone. Cameras were clicking and popping everywhere, recording the chaos. It seemed as though everyone was shouting a question.

"Why did you do it, Simone?"

"Are you Voodoo?"

"How did you pick your victims?"

"Are you ready to die?"

Unlike a typical perp, Simone did not lower her head to avoid the pictures. Instead, she held it high, proudly. Let everyone see her face. And remember it. She took her time walking.

"Let us all also be thankful that this nightmare is over," continued Pratt. "We must now heal as a city and remember our blessings. We need to mourn the lost lives and what it's done to the families of the innocent victims."

“This is not a sideshow. Let’s get you in the van,” DiMeglio said as Broussard pulled on Simone’s arm. Suddenly, she went limp as her chest exploded, blood, bone, and tissue flying everywhere.

A second shot hit Bundy, missing the center of his chest, blowing off his right shoulder and the side of his neck. He fell to the street screaming.

No one heard the shots until a second after they hit. When a hollow point bullet travels supersonically, it’s already exploded by the time you hear it.

Everyone ran as DiMeglio knelt to the ground cradling Simone in his arms, looking up to see if he could find the killer. He was covered in her blood and tissue.

“Manning!” yelled DiMeglio, with no idea where Manning might be. He gently closed the lids on Simone’s eyes. Broussard was at Bundy’s body, shielding him from reporters straining to get a good picture while the captain desperately tried to stop the bleeding, screaming for help. Blood was everywhere. Bundy died within minutes. Police officers were pushing the crowds back as their radios squawked for backup.

The shots could not have been easier for Manning from his position atop a building on Royal two blocks from the Royal Sonesta and just three blocks from the scene. He’d killed targets from fifty times that distance dozens of times. With the suppressor on the barrel, there was virtually no sound.

He watched in his sight as the .375 caliber hollow point blew open Simone's chest. In a split second after he killed Simone, he took his shot at Bundy, intending to seal his fate the same way. But he was a fraction off and shattered Bundy's shoulder instead. That made him angry. A professional sniper should be able to get two chest shots off with ease. *Maybe I'm getting a little too old for this*, he thought.

He'd planned it all from the moment Simone was arrested. The fact that Bundy and his search team never found the rifle in Manning's apartment didn't surprise him. It was well hidden under floorboards that were carefully polished to completely blend in. Their search had been superficial, and once they found what they were looking for, it was over. Their mistake was to think he would be careless with the one thing he valued most, and the only connection he had with his past.

Manning had known they'd eventually have to move Simone, either to a new cell or to a court appearance. He just had to be patient. It took him no time at all to set up on the hotel roof and simply wait for the transfer. He couldn't believe his luck—the first time they moved her gave him the opportunity he needed. But if that failed, he'd find another way to kill her while she was at Central Lockup. Or on her way to court. Or in prison. No matter what, the avenging angel was a dead woman walking.

Amidst the chaos that followed and the inability of anyone to know where the shots came from, Manning made an easy escape, blending into the revelers on Bourbon Street, who were oblivious to the bloodshed just a few blocks away.

Pratt ended her briefing without taking questions, only to learn all too soon that a lot more than her press conference was concluded that afternoon.

CHAPTER FIFTY-EIGHT

DiMeglio checked in through security at the FBI headquarters in Washington, as he did every day when he reported to the office. It had been two weeks since Simone's death, and he was trying to get back into his routine and forget her. But getting Simone out of his mind was impossible. The Inspector General's Office had begun the investigation of DiMeglio's affair with her, but it would be months before that was resolved. In the meantime, DiMeglio was at his desk, working as if nothing had happened.

His new routine now included taking Sully for a walk each morning before he went to the office. A dog was the last thing he ever thought he'd want, particularly one that reminded him of a lost love who just happened to also be a serial killer. But Sully and DiMeglio were meant for one another, and when he picked Sully up at Simone's condo after she was booked to take him to a shelter, he'd found a new roommate.

For DiMeglio, the case of the Bayou Slasher was closed. Finding Manning was Broussard's problem, although other units in the FBI would step in to help find him. Manning may have gotten his revenge for what Simone and Bundy did to his life, but he'd never sleep another restful night knowing he was on the FBI's most wanted list.

DiMeglio needed to plow through a pile of paperwork that had accumulated on his desk. He hated paperwork and preferred to be out in the field, solving another case. He just needed to find one.

The runner delivered the mail, and DiMeglio immediately noticed the handwritten envelope from New Orleans. He stared at the handwriting and saw that the postmark was two days after Simone lay dead in his arms. Realizing it could be evidence, he dropped the envelope back on the desk and put on the latex gloves he kept in his desk. While the envelope had undoubtedly already been handled by dozens of people, his training dictated he treat it carefully in case it was needed in an investigation.

When he opened the envelope, he found a handwritten note and some press clippings from newspapers around the country. The note was in excellent penmanship. And it looked familiar to DiMeglio.

> Dear Agent DiMeglio:
>
> By the time you receive this letter, you will think you have solved the New Orleans murders with the death of our sister, Rebecca Simone.
>
> We don't expect any forgiveness for what Rebecca did. The righteous rarely get their due. She took necessary steps to eradicate the seeds of the white supremacists spewing

prejudice and injustice. By ending the next generation of racists, we will end the plague. If you had not discovered Rebecca, she would still be carrying out that mission, letting people like you know that those of us who care can clean up our own house. Yours too. It's a pity she had to be sacrificed. Couldn't have her talking to you anymore. No doubt you had many more questions you'd like to have asked her.

Answering questions is my job now. Maybe you'll start listening.

Don't get me wrong, you did good work. While most people would have left well enough alone, you chose to solve the mystery. And right now, we suspect you are feeling quite proud of identifying the Bayou Slasher and putting an end to her killing spree. For that, we suppose you should feel good.

But understand that you have not brought an end to any of this. Think about it. Think more about all the clues you missed. There are hundreds of unsolved murders in America every year. You can check your own FBI statistics to verify that. In all, there are thousands of cold cases that have long been forgotten. More will be added day after day. Cases that happen all over the country. Do you really think so many of these serial killers who get away with murder every day are unrelated? You're the one who likes to connect dots, Agent DiMeglio. Do you really think that they're all lone sociopaths or sexual deviants? That they're random killers? Or could it be that they're connected through a common goal? Do you really think Sister Simone acted alone? Come on, Agent DiMeglio. From your training, you know better. This isn't about acts by lone wolves. It's about a crusade. A crusade that is long overdue.

Perhaps it's time to let the world know that we're going to end racism through a blood purge, to avenge how the KKK, the skinheads and others wreak havoc through their criminal deeds on innocent Blacks, Jews, and others who defend freedom or just want to be left alone. People from families who have harmed no one. Families like yours.

I know you want to continue your quest. Please feel free to do so. It will be exciting to fence with someone who thinks they're so good at finding the truth. I'll try and send you occasional notes just to keep it interesting. So let's get this game started. For your first hint,

> look into the unsolved murders in Indianapolis and Atlanta from 2018. Look into the cold cases from 2014 in Fresno and, more recently, in Lake Coeur d'Alene. Read the papers I've given you. Solve those, Agent DiMeglio, and you may see a real pattern. A righteous Jihad. One that you cannot stop. We're not individual prophets. We're a network. And we will continue. Connect the dots.
>
> Good luck, Agent DiMeglio. Opportunity knocks.

It was unsigned.

The clippings were from the *Atlanta Journal*, the *Lake Coeur d'Alene Press*, and the *Indianapolis Star*. Clippings that described multiple murders of young white men and women that remained unsolved. Serial killers who were never caught. The clipping from the *Press* reported on a murder of a white male the day before.

He looked again at the note.

> Opportunity knocks.

DiMeglio grabbed his briefcase and pulled out a pile of papers he brought back with him to Washington. One by one he looked at his copies of reports and notes. Then he came to the musings from Manning. Notes Manning sent to him as the case progressed, claiming his fuzzy memory was coming back and giving him more leads.

Damn, it was his way of keeping in touch with what was going on and I fell for it.

Manning had excellent penmanship, just like the penmanship on the note, except the note was far more articulate. It was a manifesto. Not from some drunk in Louisiana, but from someone who knew what he was doing and, in his own sick way, why.

Could Manning have a role in this? Is that why he shot Bundy? Was he finishing the job Simone was supposed to get done? Or was it just revenge? Was Bundy the last name on the list for New Orleans?

He dug deeper through the paperwork and found his notes on Simone with the dates she was in Iraq. He quickly compared them with Manning's dates.

Shit, he said to himself, *they were there the same time. They fucking knew each other! How the hell did I miss that?*

DiMeglio realized Manning was no solo killer. He was part of something much bigger.

DiMeglio called his assistant and booked a flight to Lake Coeur d'Alene for the following day. Manning and others were already there.

AUTHOR'S NOTE

I do not suggest that there is any proof of a network of serial killers with a common motive that unfolds in *Blood on the Bayou*. Perhaps it's just another conspiracy theory that can be dismissed as a figment of pure imagination. After all, does anyone really believe that the CIA engaged in covert mind-altering experiments during the Cold War or that the FBI surveilles innocent Americans believed to be Communists or insurgents, including many civil rights advocates? Both accusations, and many more, were initially dismissed as unfounded and from the imagination of creative minds and conspiracy theorists. Yet many have later been proven true. So before anyone dismisses suggested theories, they are best reminded that sometimes the unthinkable turns out to be undeniable.

My suggestion that social media could be used as a stalking ground by serial killers may also be dismissed by some. Perhaps it is also a figment of my imagination. But no one can deny that today, a majority of people reveal the most intimate things about themselves every day on social media. Who do you think is reading it? Just your friends?

Since 1980, more than 185,000 murders in the United States have gone unsolved. Every year another 6,000 are added. The Murder Accountability Project, a nonprofit that analyzes FBI data, estimates that there are as many as 2,000 serial killers responsible for the cold cases. The United States alone has more serial killers than every other country in the world combined. According to the FBI, there could be as many as fifty active serial killers prowling for victims every day. Most of them will never be caught.

In our society, we continue to make it easier for killers to prey on the innocent. People willingly participate in social media, chat rooms, dating services, and websites that offer personal items for sale or entice the innocent to put themselves in harm's way. Those are all among the paths through which victims are targeted. Finding common links between people is now as simple as a Google search or trolling a Facebook group. Think about that next time you decide to share your inner thoughts and voice an opinion online. You may feel liberated telling the world what you think. Or it may be a death sentence.

ACKNOWLEDGMENTS

As with all my novels, I have many people to thank. First and foremost, my pre-readers, who took the time to read my manuscript and give me guidance. Folks like Mitch Becker, my friend of sixty-plus years.

To Michael Thompson, a sailing mate and fellow author whom I've known for more than thirty years. A novelist himself, Michael's insight is invaluable. Check out his books, particularly his newest, *Clouds Above.* And thanks to the ladies of North Carolina's Compass Pointe Stealth Book Club—Nancy Garland, Gayle Pfeiffer, Cheryl Herland, and Laurie Katz. To my special neighbors, Laurie and Joe Catchings. And to Mike Santangelo, my cigar buddy and a firearms enthusiast who preaches safety above all.

Thanks also go to the experts I consulted to ensure the accuracy of what I wrote, including Fred Ernst, my friend since boyhood and the former chief of the Passaic County, New Jersey, Sheriff's Office, a SWOT team member, and firearms instructor at the Passaic County Police Academy. To Bruce Gilbert, a retired law enforcement agent, and to Roy Landreth, former Assistant Inspector General for Investigations, Office of Labor Racketeering, OIG, US Labor Department (participant in the US DOJ Organized Crime Strike Force) and a former Orlando Police Officer. To my daughter, Meghan, and her husband Brent Jostad, former prosecutors with the Miami-Dade State Attorney's Office. And in particular to Sgt. Jamie Roach and Detective Alicia Pierre of the New Orleans Police Department for their generous time talking to me and taking me through the Royal Street station. My apologies to them and the NOPD for my less than flattering description of the station and that a cop was the Bayou Slasher. Call it creative license. And thanks go to Madame Cinnamon Black, a New Orleans Voodoo priestess who gave me wonderful insight into Voodoo, a fascinating and often misunderstood religion.

To my son, Joshua, and his entire crew at Ruckus Marketing, including Shannon Wilcox, for their help in promotion and keeping my website and blogs in order.

Of course, thanks go to my publisher, Claire McKinney and Plum Bay Publishing, together with her staff and editors—Sonya Dalton and Elizabeth Bachmann. And to Jeremy Townsend, editor. She's tough but makes my books all the better. To Kate Petrella, copyeditor, for finding the mistakes that everyone misses. Thanks also go to Barbara Aronica-Buck for her wonderful design of the book. To Nancy Schulein, my assistant, for her help in balancing my life between being a lawyer and an author. And grudgingly, to Google for the wealth of information it makes available from any keyboard, despite the unsettling reality of Google's and social media's knowledge of everything we do.

And finally, to my wife, Carol Ann, who encourages me

to write and think of myself as an author with stories to tell.

I hope all my readers enjoy the book and first and foremost find it entertaining and a good read. If it also gives readers things to think about, however uncomfortable they may be, all the better. To all of my readers I say, remember—opportunity knocks. Just be careful opening the door.

DEADLY TIMELINE

VICTIM	DATE MURDERED
Jackson Walker	June 26
Maria Benson	August 14
William Hitchcock, Jr	Labor Day Weekend
George Landes	November 18
Richard Walsh	November 18
Samuel Beckett	January 20
Cyrus "Bubba" Lang	March 10
Mike Dickenson	Fat Tuesday

CAST OF CHARACTERS

LEADING ROLES

NAME	ROLE	FIRST APPEARANCE (BY CHAPTER)
Beckett, Samuel	Victim No. 6	Chapter Twenty-Eight
Benson, Maria	Victim No. 2	Chapter Four
Broussard, Raleigh	Captain, 8th District, New Orleans Police Department	Chapter One
Bundy, Joseph	Officer, New Orleans Police Department	Chapter Three
Castagna, Donna	Assistant to Raleigh Broussard	Chapter Three
Dickenson, Michael	Lt., New Orleans Police Department; Victim No. 8	Chapter Two
DiMeglio, Christopher	Agent, Federal Bureau of Investigation	Chapter Twelve
Enfield, Bertrand	Judge	Chapter Seventeen
Evans, Smitty	Officer, New Orleans Police Department	Chapter Eight
Garland, Nancy	Executive Assistant to Horace Guidry	Chapter Twelve
Gaudet, Harper	Orleans Parish District Attorney	Chapter Nine
Guidry, Horace	New Orleans Superintendent of Police	Chapter One
Harvey, Patricia	New Orleans Assistant Medical Examiner	Chapter Seven

Hitchcock, William Jr.	Victim No. 3	Chapter Four
Landes, George	Victim No. 5	Chapter Six
Lang, Cyrus "Bubba"	Victim No. 7	Chapter Forty-Four
LeBlanc, Maîtresse	Voodoo Priestess of New Orleans	Chapter Four
Manning, Wallis	Sniper; suspect in Walsh and Landes killings	Chapter Eight
Percy, Armand	Public Defender	Chapter Thirteen
Pratt, Alicia	Mayor of New Orleans	Chapter Eleven
Simone, Rebecca	Detective, New Orleans Police Department	Chapter Three
Sully	65-pound Catahoula Leopard dog	Chapter Three
Tibbets, Henri	Grand Master of the Louisiana KKK	Chapter Thirty-Four
Walker, Jackson	Victim No. 1	Chapter Four
Walsh, Richard	Victim No. 4	Chapter Seven

EXTRAS

NAME	ROLE	FIRST APPEARANCE (BY CHAPTER)
Applewhite, Marshall	Psychopath	Chapter Twenty-Two
Beckett, Robert	Grand Wizard in the South Carolina KKK	Chapter Thirty-Three
Berkowitz, David, Son of Sam	Serial Killer	Chapter Nineteen
Bond, James	Spy, MI6	Chapter Five
Bondye	Voodoo Deity	Chapter Twenty-Four
Brady, Tom	Football Player	Chapter Six
Brennan, Owen	Restaurateur	Chapter Twenty-Seven
Bundy, Ted	Serial Killer	Chapter Nineteen
Cannizzaro, Leon Jr.	Former New Orleans District Attorney	Chapter Thirteen
Catchings, Joe	Reporter, New Orleans Gazette	Chapter Eleven
Chamani, Oswan and Miriam	Founders of the New Orleans Voodoo Temple	Chapter Five
Cheshire Cat	Literary Character	Chapter Twenty-Nine
Cruise, Tom	Actor	Chapter Six
Dahmer, Jeffrey	Serial Killer	Chapter Nineteen
Dalma, Tia	Actor, role of Voodoo goddess Calypso	Chapter Five

DeAngelo, Joseph	Serial Killer	Chapter Thirty-Nine
Domino, Fats	Musician	Chapter Twenty-Two
Dowling, Simon	NOPD Detainee	Chapter Thirty-Five
Easter Bunny	Egg Hider	Chapter Thirty-Seven
Edison, Thomas A.	Inventor	Chapter Thirty
Fountain, Pete	Musician	Chapter Twenty-Two
Friday, Joe	Sgt., Los Angeles Police Department (Dragnet)	Chapter Seven
Gant, Victor	Serial Killer	Chapter Thirty-Nine
Gersh, Lewis	New Orleans Chief of Police	Chapter One
Grant, Ulysses S.	18th President of the United States	Chapter Thirty-Three
Grisham, John	Author	Chapter Six
Gump, Forrest	Dreamer	Chapter Twenty
Hirt, Al	Musician	Chapter Twenty-Two
Hitchcock, Fredric	KKK Member	Chapter Thirty-Three
Hitchcock, William Sr.	KKK Member	Chapter Thirty-Three
Holmes, Sherlock	Private Investigator	Chapter Fourteen
Iwas	Voodoo Deity	Chapter Twenty-Four

Jack the Ripper	Serial Killer	Chapter Nineteen
Jeff	Bartender	Chapter Six
Jesus	Son of God	Chapter Five
Jones, Billy	NOPD Detainee	Chapter Thirty-Five
Jones, Jim	Psychopath	Chapter Twenty-Two
Jordan, Michael	Basketball Player	Chapter Twenty-One
Kotto, Yaphet	Actor	Chapter Five
Laveau, Marie Catherine	Voodoo Priestess	Chapter Five
Manson, Charles	Serial Killer	Chapter Nineteen
McConaughey, Matthew	Actor	Chapter Fifteen
Miller, Stephen	Plaintiff's Lawyer	Chapter Twenty-Nine
Nobel, Alfred	Inventor and Philanthropist	Chapter Thirty-Two
Orwell, George	Author, Visionary	Chapter Twenty-One
Panzram, Carl	Serial Killer	Page v
Phillip	Waiter	Chapter Twenty-Seven
Phillips, Alice	Reporter, Bayoobuzz.com	Chapter Eleven
Rada	Voodoo Deity	Chapter Twenty-Four

Richards, Victor	Publisher, The New Orleans Gazette	Chapter Eleven
Schaefer, Gerald	Serial Killer	Chapter Thirty-Nine
Shannon, Robert	NOPD Officer	Chapter Twenty-Three
Simone, Diedra nee Jones	Wife of Nathan Simone Jr.	Chapter Fifty-Two
Simone, Nathan Jr.	KKK Member	Chapter Fifty-Two
Simone, Nathan Sr.	Grand Wizard of the KKK	Chapter Fifty-Two
Simpson, OJ	Accused Murderer	Chapter Eighteen
Sullenberger, Chesley	Pilot	Chapter Twenty-Six
Tooth Fairy	Gift Giver	Chapter Twenty
Tsarnaev, Dzhokhar	Boston Marathon Bomber	Chapter Forty-Six
Tsarnaev, Tamerlan	Boston Marathon Bomber	Chapter Forty-Six
Walker, Earl	Grand Wizard, KKK	Chapter Thirty-Three
Wizard of Oz	Wizard	Chapter Seventeen

CPSIA information can be obtained
at www.ICGtesting.com
Printed in the USA
LVHW091752220322
714112LV00014B/262/J